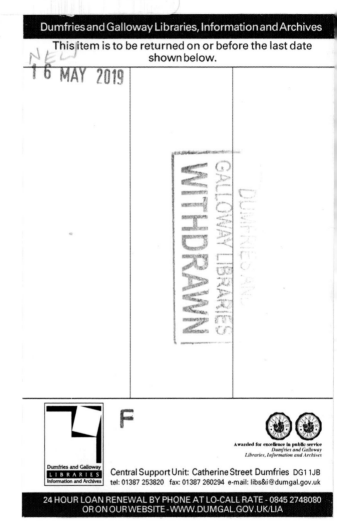

SALLY HINCHCLIFFE

OUT OF A CLEAR SKY

PAN BOOKS

To Paul

First published 2008 by Macmillan

This paperback edition first published 2009 by Pan Books
an imprint of Pan Macmillan Ltd
Pan Macmillan, 20 New Wharf Road, London N1 9RR
Basingstoke and Oxford
Associated companies throughout the world
www.panmacmillan.com

ISBN 978-0-330-45321-9

1 3 5 7 9 8 6 4 2

A CIP catalogue record for this book is available from
the British Library.

Typeset by Intype Libra Ltd
Printed and bound in the UK by
CPI Mackays, Chatham ME5 8TD

Visit **www.panmacmillan.com** to read more about all our books
and to buy them. You will also find features, author interviews and
news of any author events, and you can sign up for e-newsletters
so that you're always first to hear about our new releases.

Acknowledgements

My thanks to Julia Bell, without whose encouragement this book would never have got started. Thanks also to all at Birkbeck, and particularly the full-timers: Sue Tyley, Amanda Schiff, Lamya Al Khraisha, Rachel Wright, Cathy Sibirzeff and Alex Sartore, without whom it might never have been finished.

Special thanks to Jake Smith-Bosanquet at Conville & Walsh for not finding a reason to reject it, and to Maria Rejt at Pan Macmillan for her insightful editing. Both of them have helped to turn my ugly duckling into a swan.

Lastly I must thank my family – particularly my parents – and Paul for giving me the space to let my imagination take flight, and for never asking to read it until it was finished.

My apologies to the town and people of Maidenhead for placing an entirely fictional university on its outskirts. Although Maidenhead is undeniably real, many of the places and all of the people depicted in this book are not. Only the birds are drawn from life.

OUT OF A CLEAR SKY

'An intelligent novel about a woman in a man's world, in which Manda's desire to belong blinds her to the danger lurking behind a shared obsession'   *Sunday Times*

'Anyone who has seen the competitive passion of twitchers in full cry will find this sophisticated first novel both entertaining and credible . . . Highly recommended'
Literary Review

'Crime fiction gains a new voice in Sally Hinchcliffe with her psychological thriller *Out of a Clear Sky*'
Publishing News – the new names to watch

'There is much to enjoy in this first novel by Sally Hinchcliffe . . . fine writing skills, her language is lush and engaging, [and] her detailed descriptions of birds elegantly written'   *Bookbag*

OUT OF A
CLEAR SKY

Sally Hinchcliffe is in her thirties and, having graduated from Oxford with a First in PPE, has spent the last ten years working at the Royal Botanic Gardens in Kew. She completed the MA in creative writing at Birkbeck in 2004, and has also had various short stories published. *Out of a Clear Sky* is her first novel.

PART ONE

RAVENS

Corvus corax, family 'Corvidae'

A pair of them. They pair for life, ravens, like swans. They are generally identified by their size – much bigger than the other British corvids – but size can be tricky. Held in the circle of the binoculars, a bird's size is difficult to judge accurately except by reference to something else: a tree, another bird, a human figure.

These two were displaying their huge wingspan – well over a metre – as they spread and hopped awkwardly around the prone body on the ledge. Easily bigger than a rook or crow. I couldn't see from my vantage point at the top of the corrie whether they had taken out the eyes yet with their heavy beaks. Probably. Those, and the soft belly, are where the carrion eaters attack first, if they are left a find like this by the predators. Fleece and Gore-Tex had protected the belly in this case but the eyes – the eyes are another matter. Fleece and Gore-Tex would probably long outlast the rest of the body, but what else would eat it there, caught on the ledge, if the ravens didn't?

Another pair came in and circled uncertainly as the first two flew up to challenge them with loud hoarse croaking calls. I watched the display fascinated and repelled, unable to tear myself away until several more birds flew in to join

3

them and they finally settled together around the body to share the feast. That was when I withdrew behind the bothy and threw up, heaving yellow bile from an empty stomach, the convulsions continuing until even that was gone and I was retching only air.

I leaned my head against the cool stones of the wall, thinking hard. This was one bird sighting I wouldn't be writing down. I knew now that I must erase all traces of my presence here. I kicked dirt over the spot where I'd thrown up, smoothing the loose earth over and over until no sign remained. I went back into the bothy and surveyed his scattered belongings. It looked as though he had stayed a couple of nights before my arrival, making himself at home. I had a sudden vision of policemen crawling over the hut and his belongings, picking them clean of evidence. I took the sleeping bag out of the hut and held it open into the whipping highland wind and hoped it would scour all signs of me from it. Feeling slightly foolish, I put on my gloves to examine the contents of his backpack. A few oddments of anonymous clothing – white T-shirts and shorts, thick walking socks, a shirt worn and faded with washing. It seemed very little, spread out on the sleeping bag, a sorry assemblage of things to leave behind you. A few empty food cans – a couple of days' worth – had been rinsed and stacked neatly in a corner but there was no more food in the bag apart from a couple of snack bars and a water canteen. I was surprised to find no binoculars or scope, no tripod, no camera. I looked around for another pack but found nothing. He must have been wearing the bins when he fell, I thought. I tried to remember but I could form no clear mental picture and I didn't feel like peering down to have another look at his body. After some thought I took his bar of Kendal mint cake but left his canteen, map and, more reluctantly, his compass. Useful as it would be, it would be the sort of thing that was expected. He had to have died a lonely death. Anything else would just be complicated.

I was about to leave when a familiar shape caught my eye. Tucked into a gap in the stones beside the door was a little field notebook, its black cover held shut by an elastic band. Curiosity made me pick it up and flip it open, unsure of what to expect. The first page I opened was headed 'Manda' in the fine-nibbed map-making pen a lot of birders seemed to use, double underlined. My name. Just the sight of it lifted the hairs of my scalp in a primitive ripple of horror, animal in its intensity. There was a photograph of me too, taken some time ago, a fragment, creased and faded, torn from something bigger. I was smiling uneasily, at some occasion I didn't recall. A group shot from which the rest of the group had been excised, leaving me smiling on, alone.

As I went reluctantly through its pages I saw just how little I had managed to evade him, how futile had been my attempts at escape. Almost every step of my journey up to these mountains had been observed and meticulously noted down, page by page, day after day, well before I'd even guessed I was being followed. There were sketch maps and map references, dates, times, almost a parody of a real field notebook, except that the quarry was different. The quarry was me.

I tore out each sheet as I went with clumsy gloved fingers, hands shaking as I fumbled with the thin paper. My name soon blurred into meaningless scribbles with the repetition and I soon stopped reading the words and just worked back until I had emptied the book completely. I burnt the whole pile of papers right there in the bothy and crumbled their remains into dust. Charred scraps rose feather-like into the air and flew off in the biting wind, taking my name with them, the whole sorry history of the past. The photograph was the last to go and the hardest to destroy. One after another the matches broke in my fingers until finally I tore my gloves off to get a better grip. Even then my shaking hands made it hard to scratch a flame from the worn end of the box. My face – its foolish awkward smile – blackened and curled but wouldn't catch until I blew on it, watching it warp in the flame. I dropped the last flickering corner as the heat threatened my fingers and kicked at the smoking remains, erasing the traces of fire. Then I packed everything back into his bag. I paused at the doorway to check my work. Everything seemed to be left as I had remembered it. As though I had never been there at all.

I stepped once more out of the hut, squinting at the brightness after the gloom inside. Behind me something shifted and coughed and I whipped round to see a sheep backing slowly away from me before it turned and ran, foolishly bleating. Up on the cracked slates of the roof another raven perched and looked at me, unfazed, before taking off with heavy strokes of the wings and dropping suddenly down over the edge of the cliff. Below, the rest of them were still hopping and circling, unsure of how to unwrap their prize. Ravens have very little fear of humans, especially in these remote places. I shouted and waved but that barely shifted them from the prone figure. A volley of stones was more effective, driving them off for a short while. But they're intelligent, and big and bold. Food was food. A prize like this, out of reach of other scavengers, was too good to miss. I gave up when the birds returned for the second time, and started to prepare instead for the long walk out.

I wondered if it was the drop that had killed him or the exposure. Summer or no summer, the night had been a cold one up here but I had heard nothing: no cries, no pleas, nothing after that first inhuman scream when he hit the ledge to suggest he'd survived at all. I had spent the first half of the night huddled quietly in the bothy, staring at the darkening wall until at some point I was forced by the chill to crawl into his sleeping bag and curl up in its warmth. I'd never killed anyone before.

Midsummer's night, it had been; the shortest night of the year, just a brief interval of darkness at these latitudes. Short and endless. Even after I had got into the sleeping bag I lay there with my eyes open against the dark and played out a hundred alternatives that didn't end with his still and broken body lying at the foot of a cliff. I saw myself managing to slip his grasp and outrun him, barring the door to the bothy. I watched us grappling round so that it was me with my back to the cliff, not him, me falling, horribly silent, through the air to hit with that terrible cry. By the time dawn came I must finally have slipped into a doze and these fantasies had merged into repeated brief and futile dreams, treading over the same worn ground. I had woken stiff and cold to the realization that dreaming them had changed nothing.

There's a certain cool clear light that comes when the day dawns overcast. A stealthy light. I have always woken early, from years of starts in the oh-god-hundred hours, getting up while it's still dark, fumbling for last night's clothes and pulling a woolly hat over last night's hair. Leaving silently along the sodium-lit streets to await the first paling of the sky, the first tentative calls of the blackbirds. Those overcast dawns are the best, the truest light. There's no false colour, no shadows or glare. People talk about the cold, hard light of day. There's no escaping what you can see by it. There can be no confusing, in that early morning light, the truth with the wished-for reality of dreams. The body was still there. He was still dead.

With the bothy cleared, and my few possessions packed up, all I could do was get myself out unseen. I started off slowly along the hillside, keeping the sharp drop of the corrie to my right, wishing I had more food, a working phone, a GPS. Ahead of me the drop was gentler, ridge after ridge of heather and scree patches, empty even of sheep. Behind me more ravens were circling over the abandoned shelter, ragged black shapes against the grey sky.

I had walked for no more than a few minutes when the whipping wind brought in cloud that rolled down the slopes of the mountain and engulfed me in fog. One minute I was standing on the ridge looking down towards the burn that I knew would lead me back to safety, the next the world had been wiped out and I was standing in a circle no more than a few yards in diameter surrounded by whiteness. Darker shapes seemed to form and disperse in the cloud around me, disorienting me. What little I could see of the surrounding moor was uniform in all directions, as blankly uninformative as the mist. I knew I hadn't moved from where I had stood and surveyed my route but in my mind I felt as though I had spun round to face the drop. I couldn't shake the conviction that a few blind steps would send me stumbling downwards over the cliff edge. And all around me the ravens rose. Birds are visual navigators, and will generally avoid flying blind, but these ones were everywhere, calling, mocking, their cries surrounding me. In the fog their shapes were nightmarish shadows, advancing, retreating, enormous.

The ravens called amongst themselves, their voices almost human, but speaking in a language I couldn't understand. They are the dark birds of mythology, creatures of ill omen, feared and honoured, messengers of the gods, creators of the world. They circled around me, and as they turned I turned with them, keeping them always before me. We circled together, alone in a world of swirling mist. I had lost all sense of where the drop was. I turned, uncaring.

And then as the birds rose it was as if the clouds rose with them, and I was back in the clear air. The ravens had abandoned me, vanished as though they had never been there, and the world around me was silent and still. For a moment I didn't recognize where I was, the empty upland, the high surrounding hills. I was a child again, lost in an endless sea of savannah grass, afraid to move, afraid I'd never be found, afraid that nobody would come and look for me. My father always said, 'Keep still, stay where you are,' and that's how he'd find me, rooted to the spot, hardly daring to breathe until he came.

The illusion lasted only a moment before it passed. Then I was back on a Scottish mountainside, alone, the solid weight of my pack anchoring me to the earth, the yawning drop no closer than before. I breathed again. I felt the pull of the empty moorland calling, away from the path I'd taken the day before, away from people, from roads, from civilization. I was no longer waiting to be found. So I turned and walked away.

KINGFISHER

Alcedo atthis, family 'Alcedinidae'

The year had started with a very different dawn. Seven a.m. on New Year's Day with the rest of the world asleep. It was still dark as I drove in on the Selsey road but when I stopped the car the sky was just beginning to lighten. I sat in the car park outside Church Norton feeling the deadening effects of the night before. I thought I'd managed to negotiate the fine line between drinking enough to make the evening bearable and keeping sober enough to be able to make the dawn start, but there was still a black ache of hangover behind my eyes. My head was full of the flat buzz of tiredness, and shaking it did little to clear it. I got out and fumbled with the car lock, my scope awkwardly dangling from one shoulder, hands stiffening in the raw cold. There was a brief moment of longing for a warm bed and a lie in, but then the long mournful hooting of an owl recalled me to my senses.

I stepped into the little thicket that leads down to the main hide and the harbour, scanning the trees. I was instantly alert, ears open, eyes straining against the gloom. A second call pulled me further in, off the path. It was darker under the trees, and the ground was covered in twigs and leaf litter. I paused between each step, placing my feet

11

carefully, hardly daring to breathe. Another call, then nothing. As I stood and listened I could hear the bare murmur of the sea and the soft hiss of tyres on the nearby road as a car drove past. My own breathing. And then a different sound: dried leaf pressing against dried leaf as if under the weight of a foot. I held my breath and listened some more, turning my head slowly back towards the way I'd come. Around me, as I turned my head, the wood seemed peopled by shifting shadows. The trees coalesced in the gloom into a single shape, which then vanished. Another sharp rustle, another shadow forming between the trees. I could hear now only the pounding footsteps of the blood in my own veins. My ears pushed against the silence. There was a final sharp movement and I was galvanized.

'Who's there?'

I was answered only by the ringing alarm call of a fleeing blackbird. My heart rate settled back to normal and I returned to the path, and headed to the bay.

With the cool grey of a January dawn, details emerged slowly out of the murk. I was crouched on the shingle bank watching a group of waders follow the ebbing tide, probing with their beaks through the mud for invertebrates. Among the smaller waders a bigger bird, a godwit, was working its way through the mud channels. I had just set up the scope and was trying to get the bird in it to check the colour of the tail and the streaking on the back. Most of the birds were oblivious to my presence, moving busily back and forth on the important business of feeding, but the godwit seemed to be aware it was being watched, and every time I had it nicely in the centre of my lens it would duck behind a hummock of seaweed or into a deeper channel, where it would disappear for a few seconds and then reappear at the worst possible angle. Finally, it hopped up onto a clump and stood showing nicely as I fumbled with stiffened fingers to get it into focus. The slanting sun broke through the cloud and for a few seconds each feather was sharply picked out in its light. The bird was preening and I could see the busy movements of its beak through the plumage, the inward-turned concentration of its eye. We were joined together, just for a moment, in the curious one-sided intimacy of the telescope. But then something spooked the whole flock of them, and first the godwit and then every other bird in the harbour rose with a cacophony of alarm calls. Most of them circled once, calling, and settled, but the godwit was gone.

I turned to look at the source of the disturbance, hoping it was someone just passing through, a dog walker, someone I could ignore. But this was another birder, grinning as though he knew me, dressed in a bright turquoise anorak and a fleece bobble hat that seemed to have been designed to be seen from a helicopter in a blizzard. He was armed with a set of new-looking binoculars, Leicas, 8 x 42s, and had a Swarovski scope slung over his shoulder. My heart sank. I was in no mood to be sociable.

'Anything interesting?' he asked.

'There might have been.' I tried to keep the irritation out of my voice.

'What?'

'Godwit.'

'Bar-tailed,' he said confidently.

'No, black. I could see the tail as you flushed it up.'

He ignored my sarcasm. 'The hide book's got an entry for a bar-tailed.'

I suppressed the urge to point out that hide books weren't infallible, and besides, birds had a tendency to move around. Instead I looked blankly at him and hoped he would go away. No such luck.

'Where is it?' He raised his binoculars, started scanning the horizon.

'It flew away.'

This time I hadn't quite managed to keep the edge out of my voice. He looked at me, feigning hurt.

'Ooh er. Bit hung-over, are we?'

I didn't respond immediately. There was something familiar about him that had been nagging at me through-out our exchange, and now I had managed to place him. He'd shown up on a guided visit the bird group had taken to a sewage works the summer before. He can't have had the scope then because he'd kept borrowing mine, but I remembered the way he'd shown off the brand-new Leicas, hovering anxiously behind them as they were passed from hand to hand. 'Eight hundred quid,' he had said, when they had been returned, and he hefted them in one hand as he spoke, as though their quality was something that could be weighed. I remembered too the smirks behind his back because everything he did and said betrayed his ignorance, and the expensive binoculars didn't prevent him from looking half the time at the wrong bird, misidentifying everything, and finally almost losing his footing and having to be hauled back from the brink of a settling pond. He'd latched on to me in the end, when the teasing from the others became too audible to be ignored, and I had tolerated him then, encouraged him even. Irritating as he was, his chatter masked the fact that Gareth and I weren't really speaking, and hadn't been for weeks. It only served to deepen Gareth's mood, but I didn't care. Someone – anyone – to talk to, someone to pay me a bit of attention, was better than the lengthening silence between us. And maybe I'd thought it might pique Gareth's interest a bit. So I had taken the time to show this guy where to look for the rarer gulls, how to tell them apart, let him use my scope. But Gareth ignored me anyway, walked on without speaking, shutting me out.

I softened. He was probably right, I was hung-over. Any other year, I would have been tucked up in bed early on a New Year's Eve, ready for an early start. Our big celebration for New Year was the day itself and the chance to kick off the year list together with as many birds as we could, making every bird suddenly fresh and new, something exciting. But that was then, when there was an 'us'. Now Gareth would be birding somewhere else, with someone else – if he could drag Essex Girl out with him. And my sister, guilty at abandoning me over Christmas, had insisted I spend the night with her friends. I had worn a social mask all evening, uncomfortable with the effort. Zannah had treated me with the careful handling you'd give to recently mended china. Her friends had been polite, friendly, ultimately remote. I had left as soon as I decently could, walking through the damp alien London streets, but the late night had taken its toll on my mood. I had had my fill of semi-strangers.

Still, there was no need to be rude. I had been a new birder once, and probably just as annoying. I mustered the closest I could manage to a smile. 'Maybe a bit hung-over, yes,' I offered, and he grinned.

While we had been talking a few more waders had flown in and the rest were feeding again as though they had never been disturbed. Out of the corner of my eye I could see the constant bustle of the birds as they probed for food side-by-side in companionable silence, like so many little sewing machines stitching through the mud. I was itching to get back to watching them. In peace and on my own.

'Anything else?'

'Cattle egret over on the big shingle bank,' I lied.

'Cool!' He trotted off, and I was alone at last.

By eight-thirty, a couple more birders had set up on the shingle and every ten minutes or so another would arrive. There were nods of recognition at half-remembered faces, rueful acknowledgements of one too many the night before, a sense of a community building up on the barren shore. Seeking a more solitary pursuit, I packed up and drove down to Selsey Bill to do a bit of quiet sea watching. Red-throated divers would have been nice, even a common scoter or two, but actually what I really wanted was just an hour or two of quiet concentrated watching.

I found a sheltered spot and hunched down and let my eyes scan the sea for birds. I was looking for some little anomaly in the movement of the water, something bobbing, or flying, or diving. Crouching down further, I caught it: almost nothing, just a disturbance in the pattern of the wind-blown waves. This was what I had come for: the moment when I get the binoculars onto something and a shape resolves itself – what is no more than a speck against a sparkling sea instantly categorized into duck or gull or diver. The moment when there was nothing in the world but me and the bird. My mind filled with the particulars – the diagnostics that make that one bird uniquely itself and nothing else, my whole concentration focused through the narrow circle of the lens. I was as still as a hunter, projecting my gaze towards the tiny distant speck. And then, nailed, the bird was named, labelled, pinned down. Just a cormorant this time, floating low in the water as though holed and sinking. I watched it for a minute or two until it slipped back down under the waves, and then I began scanning again, for the next flash of movement, the next prize.

It was absorbing stuff. When I checked my watch it was gone eleven; I had been watching for about two hours. My left leg was completely dead, and my fingers were blue. I'd spent the last few minutes just watching a young lesser black-backed gull as it tried to smash shells by dropping them onto the shingle below. It would fly up and drop the shell, spend a few minutes hunting around for it on the beach, retrieve the unbroken shell, fly up and drop it again. Eventually, it had a bright idea and flew round to drop it instead on the road that ran along the seafront. It was immediately robbed of its prize by a couple of black-headed gulls half its size, who then got into a huge fight over it and flew off, still squabbling. The lesser gave up and sat on a groyne instead, ruffling its feathers. It was hard not to imagine it was sulking.

As I stood on the seafront, still stamping the blood back into my leg, I realized that not once in the past two hours had I thought of Gareth. The black mood of the morning had gone, and I no longer had that wretched loop of memory playing in my head of the last time I had seen him, driven off in Essex Girl's car, his notebooks clutched in his lap, and that last triumphant wave of hers as her car had dwindled down the road and vanished round the bend. The hours had simply disappeared. And the birds I'd seen in them were purely mine. I straightened and stretched the kinks out of my neck and spine and even my scalp seemed to lift and lighten. For the first time in four weeks I began to feel that I had been somehow liberated.

Selsey that morning had the shut-up air of all seaside towns in winter. There was only one open cafe, a tiny place with a window that was so steamed up I couldn't see in, but I didn't care. I just wanted a hot breakfast and somewhere to make some notes, list what I'd seen. A whole morning's worth of birds clamoured and jostled in my head; diagnostics and calls and primary feathers and bill lengths confused together until they were funnelled down into neat rows on the paper. Gareth's best friend, Tom, always used to scold him about his obsession with keeping score. 'It's not about the numbers,' Tom would always say, and he was right. Well, half right. It's not *just* about the numbers. But when your boyfriend – partner, live-in lover – of ten years leaves you three weeks before Christmas, and when he's always been the one who has seen the most birds, and when he's going to be in the pub in a few days' time with the rest of them to see who got off to the best start for the year, then, you know, it is about the numbers. I added up my total for the morning and allowed myself to feel just a little bit pleased.

I went on to make some more detailed notes; some reminders on the godwit colouring so I could check it later. I'd been a little more confident with Neon Bobble Hat Boy than I'd really felt, and I wasn't about to get my field guide out of my pocket in public. I made a note about the gull and its abortive attempts to open shells and was just putting the notebook into my pocket when someone sat down heavily opposite me.

My fragile good mood ebbed away. I didn't need to look up. My peripheral vision had clocked the bright turquoise jacket as soon as he entered the cafe. He had, at least, taken off the hat.

'Thanks for that cattle egret,' he said. 'Superb. My first for the UK.'

Slowly, reluctantly, I moved my belongings to make space for him. The cafe was crowded now, and there were no free tables. I was trapped.

'There's been a fair few sightings round here these days,' I said, masking the irritation as best I could. I was annoyed though. Even he couldn't mistake an egret, so there must have been one after all. That would have got me off to a good start.

'You're Manda, aren't you? Gareth's girlfriend? Where's Gazza then?'

No putting a brave face on that one. 'His girlfriend no longer.'

'Oh God,' he said. 'I'm sorry.' I shrugged, trying to convey that it didn't matter, that I didn't care. I was grateful for the distraction of the waitress, the bustle of taking his order. The tea I was drinking had gone cold and nasty, but I buried my face in my cup anyway. By the time the waitress had gone, I had managed to regain my composure.

'I'm David, by the way,' he said. 'We met a few months ago, that trip to the sewage works. So sorry about you and Gareth. But I'm glad I bumped into you here, I've been hoping to meet you again. You do remember, don't you, that time we met last summer?' His eyes sought mine anxiously and I nodded again.

'Of course,' I said. He grinned again, a strange too-eager grin. I looked away, embarrassed by his eagerness, wishing I were elsewhere, wishing I'd thought to get the bill when I had the chance so I could get away.

'You were a real inspiration to me, you know, that day. I just remember how kind you were, putting up with me, my bumbling, my stupidity.'

His face, thawing in the heat of the cafe, was as bright now as his coat. He had blue eyes that seemed to bore into me as he spoke, still trying to hold my gaze. His skin was pulled taut and thin over the cheekbones. I'd thought him good looking in the summer, in a flashy way, though not my type. Now I wasn't so sure. I began to look around rather more desperately, seeking a means of escape. The waitress seemed determined not to meet my eye.

'I've remembered everything you told me, you know. About the birds, about finding them, identifying them, watching them.'

'It was nothing.'

'Not to me,' he said. 'Not to me. I was inspired. I rushed out and bought a scope that same day, the same one you had, the same tripod and everything.' He laughed self-deprecatingly, but his manner was flushed and hectic, over-heated.

'They've good optics, Swarovskis,' I said, as neutrally as possible.

The waitress passed almost within touching distance, her face still resolutely averted. Finally, my despairing wave attracted her attention. I gestured for the bill and started gathering my belongings.

'Do you have to go? Are you in a hurry? Can't you stay and chat? I saw that godwit again and you were right. Of course. How could I have doubted you? I'm sorry, I'm talking too much again. I'm driving you away. I do that, sometimes.'

'Look, I'll see you around,' I said as the bill came at last and I could escape. It was something to say, meaningless, a commonplace pleasantry to blunt the brusqueness of my departure. But he smiled again as if I'd said it as though I had meant it, as though it were a gift I'd given him, a promise I'd made. I left the cafe with relief.

*

The cold air hit me as I turned up the street towards my car. All that was waiting for me in London was an afternoon spent rattling round the confines of my sister's flat until I could decently leave and go back to the unwelcome prospect of the empty house. Delaying the moment, I stopped off at the Pagham reserve, checked out the Ferry Pool hide for some of the freshwater ducks and then strolled along the banks of the silted-up harbour. Sitting on a sheltered bench was an old couple who must have been in their seventies. Both had ancient binoculars around their necks and they were dickering gently away about who had misidentified what bird some time back in 1957. They both smiled vaguely at me as I passed, and the man, seeing my binoculars, suddenly said, 'Nice kingfisher up by the cut. Probably still there; fishing, it was,' before he turned and resumed their running argument. I could believe that it was one that had been running, on and off, for the last forty-odd years. There had been a time when I had thought Gareth and I would end up like that, still birding for as long as we could totter.

Leaning over the parapet of the bridge I looked up the cut and lingered there, half hopeful, half just waiting to see if the kingfisher would appear. The river banks were a tangle of dead stems; the only movement came from the weed that flowed in the water, waving in the current. As I waited and watched I became one more still thing in a world of dull greens and greys and browns and the birds which had fled at my approach began to re-emerge. It was a drear winter's day, really, raw and drizzling, but to the birds, acutely tuned to the lengthening of the light, the year had already turned and spring was on its way. I could hear a great tit calling, then a chaffinch, then the persistent territorial chucking of a wren. The only human sound was that of the couple's voices carried to me on the wind in bursts, nothing I could make out – just a tone of voice, equal parts affection and exasperation.

I had almost given up on the kingfisher when a flash passed under the bridge and shot straight to the vegetation on the river side. I saw nothing but a glint of blue and it took another minute of close searching with the binoculars before I found the bird again. It was perched swaying on a dead stick, staring down into the murk of the water. Even in the dull light it glistened, blue and turquoise and coral, incongruous among the drab fretwork of the bare bushes.

A kingfisher was the first bird I can really remember seeing, shown to me by my father. Not the common kingfisher, the one we see in England, but one of the African ones. The English avifauna are pretty impoverished. Apart from ducks and waders, and some of the forest birds like tits and warblers, we tend to have just one of each kind: kingfisher, bittern, heron, each instantly identifiable, whereas in Africa each bird comes qualified with a host of similar relatives. I have never been able to work out exactly which species of kingfisher it was that my father and I watched through the Land Rover window – probably a pygmy or a malachite. I don't recall much else about the day or why we were out driving alone together, with me sitting in the prized front seat. Maybe my mother was ill that day, maybe she was off doing something with Zannah, maybe it was some special treat I'd earned. I would have been about eight, my head filled with animals, not birds. I remember only my father stopping the car abruptly and backing up the dirt road, the engine whining with the effort, until we were level with a small tangled stream, choked with debris.

'Look, Manda, there, on the reed.'

I looked, willing to do anything my father asked of me. Held my breath in silence at his hushed tone, even though the Land Rover's diesel engine ticked and grumbled louder than ever in neutral. When I saw it, everything else faded away. The bird sat, impervious, jewelled in turquoise and blue feathers. It was stilled and attentive, its whole being focused down towards some point in the muddy water beneath it. What fish could be small enough to be caught by this tiny toy? For a minute it hung motionless from the reed, then took off and seemed to hover over that spot in the water before plunging downwards. It returned briefly with a minnow squirming in its beak and then was gone, as though the whole scene had been something my father had conjured up for me and then dispelled. I turned to ask him what we'd seen but he was still staring at the space where the bird had been, as though patient watching could call it back. I let the words die and the spell held us both in silence until we regained home.

I'd rushed to boast about it to Zannah, that I'd seen a bird, that Dad had pointed it out to me, a bird catching a fish. I tried to describe it, couldn't find the words, my arms windmilling in frustration, Zannah disbelieving.

Finally, I appealed to my father. But he was gone, the door to the study shutting behind him with a click.

The English kingfisher I was watching was bigger and less magical than my remembered bird. But it too could hover for a moment of suspended time as it chose its point to strike. It seemed to barely disturb the water and then it was back on its branch, a fish held firmly in its dagger beak. I saw now, as I had been too mesmerized to see then, the tearing cruelty in the way it mastered its struggling prey, surrounded by the flashing drops of water. Fish and bird both glittered for a second against the drab of the bank and then were gone.

On my way back to the car I passed the couple again, gave them the thumbs up.

'See it, did you?' They both smiled, the same smile, grown alike together. I smiled back, feeling very much alone, walked back to the car in the eye-watering wind.

As I turned the corner, the loneliness dissolved into irritation. There David was again, in the car park, leaning against my car. This time he seemed lost in a reverie, gazing into space. I was surprised he could be so still. His hands hung down by his sides as though in readiness for something. Without the vacant grin his face was drawn and wary. Only when he turned and saw me did the animation return.

'We meet again.'

I hadn't the energy to humour him this time, to do

anything but stand and wait for him to move so I could get away.

'Leaving already?' he asked.

'When you stop using my car as a resting place, yes.'

He sprang aside, motioned me in, bowed clownishly as I started to drive away. I dismissed the whole encounter from my mind, thinking of the road ahead, the long drive back to town. But I couldn't quite shake off the lingering image that I had of the capering figure with the grinning face, watching me as I drove away.

RING-NECKED PARAKEETS

Psittacula krameri, family 'Psittacidae'

I had meant to go back home the next day but Zannah, little sister from hell, trapped me, pleading that we never spent enough time together. Naturally, once I had agreed, taken the extra day off work and stayed, she then started moping round the flat not sure what to do with me. The two of us were stuck, alone together. We had exhausted all topics of conversation. It was drizzling again. We were reverting to our childhood selves, prickly, restless.

'Why don't we go to Kew?' I suggested, flicking through an old copy of *Time Out*. I had already spent an hour pacing the limits of the flat: kitchen, sitting room, spare bedroom, back to the kitchen, where Zannah sat, still in her dressing gown, nursing a cooling tea, watching me as I went.

'So expensive,' she sighed.

'It's free entry if you take in your Christmas tree to recycle it.'

'Manda! You're supposed to be the observant one.' I went back to the sitting room and took a closer look. It was a plastic tree, and oddly familiar with its gappy branches. The decorations looked familiar too.

'Is that our old tree?' The moment I looked at it properly

I could see that it was, and suddenly I was nine again, piecing it together with my father, transforming the prickly bundles of plastic. I let my fingers trail across the branches, setting the tinsel into uneasy shimmering motion. 'You hated that tree.'

'I know.' She joined me now in the sitting room, and grimaced at it ruefully. Every Christmas she had whined about having a plastic tree, wanting the sort of Christmas we read about in books: snow, and robins, and chestnuts. It was our mother's fault; she'd filled Zannah's head with stories of her childhood holidays. But even our mother had enough sense not to go out looking for a fir tree in Tanzania and we'd made do with this one. Every December in the sticky heat we would deck it with sledges and snow flakes and apple-cheeked carol singers, and frost it with tinsel. We pulled the heavy curtains against the tropical sun for the moment when we would turn the fairy lights on and watch the tinsel shimmer. Except that the lights, damp-infested and rat-gnawed, would rarely work. That was always the favourite part of Christmas for me, the afternoons Dad and I spent patiently testing each bulb one by one, Dad re-twisting the wires and taping them into place, while I held the tape, the pliers, the spare bulbs, handing them to him as needed. By the time we got the lights working, Zannah and my mother would have drifted off and Dad and I would stand and admire them together. But then he'd retreat back into his study and I'd be left alone to run out into the sunshine where Mattie was waiting, hoping I'd throw him some sticks, his ragged flag of a tail waving in surrender.

Zannah's voice recalled me to the present. 'Juma shipped it over with the rest of Dad's stuff. What Mrs Iqbal didn't nab. I thought I'd put it up for old times' sake.'

'What did she get?'

'The grandfather clock and the zebra-skin rug. And God knows what else, before he died.'

Given what I'd heard of Dad's condition in the last few years of his life I felt Mrs Iqbal had earned her souvenirs, but I was a little sorry about the rug; I had fond memories of it. It used to lie on the cool hall floor in the shadowed centre of the house and I would spend hours sprawled on it, leafing through the *Field Guide to East African Mammals*, its pages worn soft with years of use, telling Mattie stories about how we'd fly on the magic zebra rug over the plains and up and up to Ngoro-Ngoro, where all the animals could talk. Mattie would lie with his eyes shut and his tail hopefully thumping at the rise and fall of my voice, until Juma came and found us and shooed us out. But Mattie was dead now, and Juma ill, old before his time, and the rug would be a sorry threadbare thing, a relic of another age.

'Christmas is over. You should take it down.'

'Not till the sixth.' I'd forgotten Zannah's obsession with correct procedure over all things Christmas, indeed all things traditional. I turned my back on the tree and went to stand at the window and watch the wind buffet the ragged clouds over the tops of the nearby buildings. Somewhere a siren tore the air and then faded into silence. A pigeon, its wings held up in a sharp vee, fought to hold its course against a sudden buffet of air. I felt the old restless longing to be somewhere out there with wide-open skies, not festering indoors watching the weather close us in.

In the end we settled on a walk in Richmond Park. Zannah agreed I could take my binoculars as long as I didn't spend four hours staring into a bush at little boring brown birds, and I agreed as long as she agreed to shut up if I did see something interesting. The day had settled down into a grey flat dampness, not quite raining, but always ready to. Someone, somewhere, was burning leaves, and the unseasonable autumnal smell hung in the air. We stumped along with our hands in our pockets, neither of us being much able to handle the cold, and after a while the walk took on a rhythm of its own and the mutual silence became a restful one. She stopped, uncomplaining, as I checked out a green woodpecker's bounding flight, or searched for a jay I could hear squabbling in the branches of a tree. She even pointed out the still, hunched figure of a heron and as it took off on massive wings and beat away towards the river she watched in silence, a faint smile on her face.

We walked on towards a clump of trees and I saw what I had come looking for. Four or five bright green birds swooping above us, soon joined by two or three more, their long thin silhouettes unmistakable even without the colour, or the screeching calls.

'What are they?'

I handed her the binoculars. 'Ring-necked parakeets.'

'My God, what are they doing here?' I thought she'd hand the binoculars back but she hung on to them, watching, as more birds joined them in the tree.

'No one really knows. There were probably some escaped birds, originally, but they're now established as breeding.' This lot certainly looked to be checking out nesting holes. She handed back the glasses but kept her face tipped upwards, her eyes on the birds. I could see some of the strain of the last few days' festivities ease out of her.

'Fantastic,' she said.

'Yeah, I like them.' It was true, even though I shouldn't, even though they're non-native birds, probably a crop pest, or they would be if they weren't in London; possibly driving out native species from prime nesting sites because they nest earlier, nabbing the best spots. But the sheer joy of seeing their bright green tropical colours against the flat grey of an English sky outweighs all that. One bird hung acrobatically upside-down, balancing with its long slender tail. I felt myself smiling.

'Remind you of home?' Zannah asked. When was it, I wondered, that home, to Zannah, had become Africa? Home, in our family, had always been the England Zannah and I had never seen.

'Hardly. They're from India.'

'You know what I mean. They must be freezing here.'

I refrained from pointing out that they probably hatched right here in Richmond. They certainly didn't seem to be feeling the cold as they scrambled around the branches. Not the way I was, and the way Zannah looked to be as she huddled deeper into her jacket. The afternoon light was already thickening into dusk, and it was barely tea time. We watched the birds a little longer, then admitted defeat and retreated from the cold into the warmth of a cafe.

Once we were seated, Zannah pulled out a photograph from her bag.

'I forgot, I was going to show you this. Juma sent it, with the last of Dad's papers. Remember? The day the uniforms came.'

The photo had the washed-out candy colours of all our childhood pictures, faded over almost twenty years. Two little girls, Zannah and I, standing stiffly under a thorn tree in full school uniform. We are squinting into the sun, but my father, standing beside us, is grinning under the shade of his floppy hat, his face in partial shadow. I could remember putting on our uniform the day it all arrived, though not having the picture taken. I could remember how I couldn't believe that one person would be expected to wear so many clothes all at once. I thought I would be driven through the floor by the weight, and I sweltered under the itchy and unfamiliar wool. In the picture Zannah is smiling but I have a strange, wary look, standing up straight, ready for some unspecified threat.

'I don't know what they were thinking, sending us off at that age.' I slid the picture back towards Zannah, wishing she hadn't shown it to me. The two little blonde girls stared up at me from the table, unaware of their fate. I wanted to put my coffee cup down on them, hide them, blot them out of existence, as though that could save them from their future.

The clothes had come with the six-monthly shipments from England. A shipment day was a red-letter day for us, one that meant strawberry jam, and cornflakes, and dark treacly sugar that stained the powdered milk in the cereal bowl brown. A shipment meant my mother smoothing out the damp newspapers the jars had been packed in as she read the fragments of stories from home. It meant my father hefting the weight of books with dry titles about husbandry and engineering, and disappearing with them into his study before taking them into the college. It meant a sudden rush of plenty, and then the slow dwindling back to normality and tinned plum jam on toast for breakfast.

But the strange scratchy clothes didn't disappear with the strawberry jam and the cornflakes; they hung on in the wardrobe in my parents' room all summer long, shrouded in plastic to protect them from the damp and the insects. Zannah would go and push her face into the wool and smell them, would open up the boxes with their stiff black shoes and smell them too, and I'd hear her talking to herself, telling herself stories. She loved to listen to my mother's tales of her school days, loved to read the Mallory Towers books, talked endlessly of going back to England, our mythical home, the land of plenty.

I leaned down to look again at the little Manda. It seems such a trivial thing, a name. Amanda and Susannah, we'd been christened originally, but soon shortened by a series of African nannies who didn't know that in England there were rules about everything, but above all, it seemed, about how you shortened your name. There was so much about us that would have marked us out as strange to the other girls at school but it was the names they latched on to in those first few weeks when we arrived. My familiar name followed me everywhere, transformed into a dead weight of difference, an instrument of torture. I'd hear it ringing sarcastically across the tarmac of the school playground, hissed contemptuously in the dark of the dormitory, and I'd brace myself for the next round of misery.

Peering closer I could see that my pictured hand is on Zannah's shoulder, a curious gesture at once protective and repelling. One thing I did recall about that day was how young she looked, drowning in wool, the sleeves of her blazer covering her hands. Now, of course, we both look young, absurdly so, in the uniform which was old-fashioned even then. Even my father, who stands somehow detached from us with his hands in his pockets, looks like a young man, carefree.

'Look after her, Manda,' he had urged me as he left us at the airport. 'I'm counting on you.' The trusting way she put her hand in mine left me feeling at once exasperated and protective and I dropped it as soon as my father was gone, pushing her away. I didn't want the responsibility. I didn't want to think we had no one else but ourselves, lost in the echoing noise of the school. Having Zannah to look after only made me feel more alone. And besides, she seemed to thrive there, after the first few weeks had passed, found herself friends, found a niche for herself. It was I who needed looking after. I never understood why these girls were so hostile, what it was about me that repelled them. They turned on me the way a flock can turn on its weakest member, driving me out of their circle. I soon stopped looking for any friendship among them and withdrew to a world of my own. I saw Zannah settling down with her friends, their heads close together, sharing some confidence, and I kept away. My presence could only make things worse.

'Who took the photo, do you think?' I asked, turning it over to look at its blankly uninformative back.

Zannah shrugged. 'Mum?'

'Hardly.'

I'd known, even then, that we weren't going to school in England just to get a decent education, not at ten and eight. The school had had to be begged to take us from so far away so young. I had hovered at the study door and heard my father persuading them down the echoing line, sweating at the cost of the call, enunciating each word as clearly as he could. I'd been drawn to the sound of his voice, wondering why he was shouting when my mother was having one of her lie-downs. Even after he had stood up, still talking, to push the door closed against me, I could still hear the words. *Breakdown. Can't cope. Desperate.* They entered my games half understood and wove themselves into my dreams.

Once I'd caught Juma topping up the gin bottle with the filtered water from the fridge as I stood silently in the kitchen doorway. I knew what to think about that. All the servants steal, the expatriate wives said, as they took tea with my mother and competed as to who employed the most ingenious thief in their house. My mother sat and gazed vacantly into space, clattering her teacup into its saucer, ignoring them; it was I who listened to their tales as I handed round the biscuits in silence, following Juma with the teapot. He always moved unflinchingly about the room while the wives were recounting their tales of lying and cheating and theft, his face blankly indifferent as though he spoke no English.

Juma turned and saw I had caught him at it; red-handed, the wives would say, but he didn't seem to mind. I could see the pale undersides of his fingers refracted through the green glass of the bottle, floating like fish.

'For Madam,' was all he said, and I nodded as though I understood. I never told on him, not to my mother. I didn't want him to become an anecdote. And it was she who drank the gin, anyway. I'd seen her, in the kitchen, while the wives sat impatiently on the veranda, pursing their mouths and thinking up new stories. It was my father who checked the levels in the bottles in the drinks cabinet, against the marks he'd made on the labels. I didn't tell him, either. Little girls shouldn't tell tales. I'd learned that much the hard way.

Instead I took to spending more and more time in the kitchen, badgering Juma for stories, the ones I liked, the ones he told about the animals. He would sigh and sit down with some suitable task, like polishing the silver or gutting a fish, and would work and talk while I listened, entranced. He seemed to have an endless fund of them. I watched his hands moving uninterruptedly about their work even as his voice halted and reached for the right English word to describe the pride of the tortoise, or the slowness of the elephant, or the fierceness of the lion. His children were far away, his wife was living at his village miles upcountry, and maybe he saw their round attentive faces in my own. Or maybe he just humoured the spoilt child of his employers, filling her imagination with stories. My father said we were bored, isolated, needed friends our own age, but this was what I lived for – the long slow afternoons with Mattie, or Juma, lazy in the heat, or loose in the scrubby wilderness of the garden. Being sent away to school felt like a banishment, exile for a crime I hadn't even realized I was committing.

I looked out of the cafe window. The light outside had almost gone and the warmly lit interior competed with the dim outlines of the trees against the sky. Zannah's reflected face, pale and distorted, appeared in the window, floating in mid air. I could still hear, faintly, the screeching of the parakeets, competing with the splattering of a renewed rain against the windows. She was lining up the knives and forks in front of her, squaring them up against the table edge in a neat row. Zannah always liked to have things straight.

'English rain,' I said, and Zannah's face nodded in the window.

'I know what you mean,' she said.

We'd arrived at school in England for the first term in what I thought was the middle of winter. I could not believe that any sky could rain for so long without ever running out of water, that the cold could go on and on, that it could get colder and darker with every day that passed. That every single day could dawn with the same low hanging sky as the last, so low that even the sun barely rose in it.

And then, when the winter really started in earnest, I found myself a retreat of sorts high up in the cloakroom in a niche above the hot-water tank, where I could pretend the warmth that seeped up from the tank was the sun-warmed blast of heat sent up from the African soil. I set myself up a little refuge there, and tried to dream of home. Shielded by the ranks of coats and scarves, I could curl up with the pages of my *Field Guide to East African Mammals*, tracing the familiar pictures with my finger. Each animal in profile, both males and females where they were different, the distinguishing marks labelled with neat lines. I closed my eyes and tried to conjure up the sounds of home.

But it was only a temporary refuge. They always tracked me down in the end, looking for someone to torment, something to pass the time. Their faces were hard and pale and cold, as pinched and grey as the sky. I can still see the ringleader now, a smallish girl, sharp featured, with thick and bloodless skin.

'I heard your mum's a loony,' she said once when they'd cornered me in the playground with no teacher around to intervene. 'Heard they put her in the bin, the loony bin.' The others looked shocked and nervous, and even she seemed frightened at her own daring. Other people's parents were off limits even in the dog-eat-dog world of the school. She stood her ground, but the rest had backed off a little, the playground falling silent, all eyes on the confrontation. She had crossed the line, and she knew it. They waited for my response.

They were expecting words. Girls didn't fight here in England, not like the boys did. They sat in their groups and used words as their weapons, taunting and teasing, leaving no trace. So she didn't sense danger when I unshouldered my satchel, laden with books, and doubled the strap in my hand. She was smiling in triumph when she thought I'd given in, was turning away, not contesting her jibe. The bag swung through the air, heavy and low, winding her, leaving her speechless. I watched her face flatten with shock. Maybe my father was right, I had been allowed to run wild. They left me in peace after that, to count off the slow days until the holidays came and I could return to Africa.

With only a week of term to run, my father showed up at the school boarding house, my mother drifting palely behind him.

'We're having Christmas in England, this year,' he announced. My mother smiled benevolently, at both of us. I hated her.

We weren't to return to Africa for years, it turned out. Holidays became a succession of rented flats, or awkward stays with distant relatives, aware we were wearing out our welcome, not sure where else we would be expected to go. Sometimes my mother stayed with us, drifting through the days or making a brittle approximation of normality. Sometimes my father shuttled between us and the latest clinic or hospital or home that seemed to be offering some hope. There always seemed to be a reason why we couldn't go back as each term ended, some complication, a last-minute change of plan.

Finally, we wore him down, Zannah and I, and made it back for the summer holidays the year I turned fifteen. My mother was in a clinic in the UK that year and we flew out on our own. As soon as we got off the plane we were hit by a wall of humidity and the glare of the unrelenting sunlight. I felt myself expanding in the warmth, memories flooding back to me like a forgotten childhood language. When we got there, the house at first seemed barely changed: smaller, shabbier, but full of the bright light I'd remembered, and the deep contrasting pools of shade. We sat on the seats of the veranda still dazed from the long flight, our ears assaulted by the alien familiarity of the calls of the insects and birds, and the weeks stretched out in front of us like a promise. But when we awoke the next morning, it was to an empty house, a note on the breakfast table from my father saying he would try and be back early. Zannah was on the phone straight away, summoning up friends, but I had no one I cared to get in touch with and ended up drifting alone around the house, touching the old familiar surfaces, trying to bring back the sense of home. Mattie followed me round as I went, treating me with polite indifference, until with a sigh he tired of my wanderings and lay down stiffly on the old worn hide of the rug and slept, twitching in his dreams. My school books breathed the grey damp air of England and I couldn't settle to them. Juma was no help, busy in the kitchen, slamming a knife through a joint of meat as though it had offended him.

'Bwana will be back soon?' I asked, but he only shrugged.

'College is finished,' he said, and he stared at me, some challenge on his face. I was in no mood for riddles and left him to his work, drifting once more out onto the veranda and curling up on my father's chair, nothing to do but wait. I watched as the shadows shortened with the swinging sun, shrinking under the trees, then lengthened back across the grass the other way. At four, the sun began to work its way up my feet and legs, burning my England-pale skin. At six it dropped decisively behind the trees. My father returned as the brief twilight finally faded.

'You'll get bitten to death out here,' he said. He lit a mosquito coil and in the brief flare of the match his face appeared and disappeared, unreadable in the shifting light of the flame. Wordlessly he sat beside me, and we watched the steady glow of the burning coil unwind its spiral. The chemical smell of the smoke threw me back more surely than anything else had done, into the past, into my child-hood. Then without a word he rose again, placed his hand for a second on my shoulder, and was gone, leaving nothing but the quiet click of his study door behind him.

And so the weeks passed. My father barely inhabited the house, coming back at odd and unpredictable hours, some-times seeming startled to find us at the breakfast table, sometimes not appearing at all. I didn't mind the loneliness, the empty passing hours. But I could see he had his own life here, a life we were no part of, and that we, to him, were somehow less present, only dimly perceived, like ghosts or memories in comparison.

We found out eventually, of course. We were bound to. The affair had been an open scandal for years by then, my father and Mrs Iqbal. Some kind soul could stand it no longer, and let it slip to Zannah, avid for her reaction. Zannah didn't disappoint. She went and raged at him, white with fury, accusing him of betrayal, wishing him dead. He stood in his study doorway and took it all, making no excuses, letting her blow out her anger until she subsided in spent tears. I didn't blame him for the affair, I never did. But I had seen the way he stood and watched us and saw how he wished us gone, and that felt like the keenest betrayal of all.

Walking out of the cafe, with the parakeets swirling overhead, Zannah asked, 'What was that bird we used to call the rain bird? With the sad call?'

'The rain bird? Probably a Burchell's coucal.'

'But what was its call supposed to be saying? In Swahili?'

I could remember the legend that Juma told me of the bird who, orphaned, sings in the forest its song of loss and loneliness. The Swahili words came back unbidden just as I'd heard them from Juma. I could hear his voice in the dark syllables and the long dying fall at the end that we had likened to a pouring bottle. And as I recited them Zannah joined in too, nodding with the memory.

> 'Sina mama, sina baba,
> Nakaa peke yangu tu, tu, tu tu . . .'

Then Zannah repeated the words in English, almost to herself. 'I have no mother, I have no father. I live all alone in the forest on my own, own, own . . .'

'What made you think of that?' I asked.

'Oh, I used to sing it to myself at school after lights out, to try to get to sleep at night.'

'Did it help?'

'Beat the hell out of crying myself to sleep.'

'I always thought you were happy there.'

She just shrugged, and smiled, her eyes unreadable, the shades of the little girl I remembered almost vanished from her face. Then she turned and walked on, leaving me hurrying in her wake.

GREAT CRESTED GREBES

Podiceps cristatus, family 'Podicipedidae'

'What do you mean, "Feeding party of long-tailed tits (heard only)"?'

'Just what it says. I heard them feeding in a beech hedge, but before I could track them down, they were gone. Oh come on, Tom, I think I know longies when I hear them.'

Tom looked up and fixed me with his green eyes, clear as glass. I sat back, enjoying the monthly ritual of jousting over what I could and could not keep in my list. At some point, back in the past, Tom had taken it upon himself to keep us all honest. And as he and I were the first ones in the pub, as usual, I was bearing the brunt of it.

'Could have been any mixed tit flock. Or something else imitating them, like a starling.'

'You're obsessed with starling imitations.' He tightened his mouth at this, disallowed my long-tailed tits and moved on.

'I heard there was a nice cattle egret at Selsey. How did you manage to miss that?'

'Ah yes, the egret. Look, Tom, I think that was my fault. I made it up.'

'You made it up?' He looked up again, frowning this

time. Lying about birds was almost as bad as lazily ticking them when you hadn't properly seen them. Worse, in fact.

'I was joking. Well, sort of. Someone was hanging around irritating me, and telling him there was an egret on the other side of the harbour seemed like the best way to get rid of him.'

'Who?'

'I don't know. This guy. David somebody. Anyway, he came back later having actually seen the wretched thing so it turned out I wasn't lying after all.' I stopped, having run out of words, beginning to squirm under Tom's steady gaze. He had a way of just watching as you spoke, not interrupting, letting you dig yourself deeper into the mire.

'Some people just see what they want to see,' he said. Finished with Thursday, Tom turned over to Friday, and my outing with Zannah. 'Ring-necked parakeets? Not a native bird.'

'They're on the breeding list.'

'Could have been escapes.'

'They were in and out of tree holes. They were looking for nesting sites.' I sat back and folded my arms, feeling I'd won that round, waiting for the verdict. He looked at me sideways and smiled his rare smile, there and gone in an instant, transforming his features.

'Seeing as I'm feeling generous . . .' He moved down my list to Saturday. 'Ah, your great crested grebe pair, nice. Bit early for them to be dancing now, I suppose?'

'Yes. And besides, it's a long-established couple. They hardly bother any more. Just a card on Valentine's Day and a bunch of flowers from the garage if she's lucky.'

Tom looked at me and decided I was joking but that it didn't merit more than a blank stare. He turned the last page over, looking for more, not finding it.

'Nothing on Sunday? You didn't go out?'

Sunday had been grey and damp, cold, miserable, a day for sitting at home feeling sorry for yourself. I had meant to go out anyway, drive out and find some clear skies, some thin winter sunshine and lose myself in the busy world of the birds, but I had let my own busyness be my excuse and the short day had faded into darkness before I could leave the house.

'You should have come up to Great Missenden with me, to see the red kites. It was beautiful up there. Four of them, quartering the fields and the road. Two of them definitely juveniles, play fighting, sparring in mid air. Amazing.' He had forgotten my list, forgotten everything but the birds, and he conjured them up with his words so I could see them too, dancing around each other, bright in the winter sky.

'You should have asked.'

He glanced at me uncertainly, as though unsure of how to take my response. He turned back to my list in his hand, frowning.

'And what about today? There's nothing here at all for Monday.'

'Tom, I work in an underground, windowless office in the university. What am I going to see?'

'You need to get out, Manda, get out more, do more, not sit around indoors . . .'

'Feeling sorry for myself?' I finished his sentence for

46

him. He shook his head slowly, not really denying it, looking at me oddly, a frown drawn between his brows, as though we were talking about more than birds for a moment. But this was Tom, I remembered, Tom the obsessive, Tom who ate, drank and slept birds, who thought of nothing else. Of course we were talking about birds. I reclaimed my list from him and looked around for any sign of the others.

I could see Will's round face heading towards us through the after-work crowd. He grinned through the packet of peanuts clenched in his teeth and put three brimming glasses down on the table.

'Alan's on his way,' he said indistinctly, then dropped the peanuts like a well-trained Labrador. 'Ah, year lists,' he added, pulling a scrawled piece of paper out of his back pocket. 'I suppose Tom's is in taxonomic order again.'

I looked at Tom's list, which I held in my hand with my own. Not only was it in taxonomic order, but it was admirably detailed and precise. He listed only birds he had seen and positively identified. He had noted the sex, approximate age, behaviour and location of each bird. I gave it back to Tom.

'I don't see the point of not doing it properly.' He shrugged, picking up Will's list and putting it down again without comment. I picked it up and peered sideways at it, trying to decipher Will's handwriting.

'Coffee, sugar, cornflakes, bread, bog roll,' I read. 'Blimey, Will, some of these are firsts for the county, I think.'

'Ah yes, here we see the rare shy, retiring cornflake, its

habitat destroyed by modern farming practices and an influx of muesli from the continent, creeping through the undergrowth . . .' Will grinned and substituted his shopping list for another, equally scrawled and scrappy piece of paper. 'No wonder I couldn't find what I wanted in the supermarket this afternoon. Spent four hours trawling the aisles for a packet of bitterns – no, don't panic, Tom, I haven't really got a bittern on that list.' And then, because he was Will, and because he couldn't stop himself, 'Once bittern, twice shy.'

Birding with Will was a non-stop succession of weak puns, from 'leave no tern unstoned' to 'look at the pair of tits on that', some of which had over the years wormed themselves so deeply into my brain that I found myself thinking them whether Will was there or not. Gareth's nickname for him was Mostly – short for mostly harmless – but over the last few years I'd noticed Gareth seemed to seek him out more and more in preference to Tom, his childhood best friend. It was Gareth and Will who went on trips together, they, and to a lesser extent Alan, who egged each other on to worse and worse puns in the pub while Tom and I faded into the background, there merely to listen, to be entertained. Tom now favoured Will with a look of blank indifference that cut off whatever remark he was going to make next, and dropped back into brooding silence, looking no further at Will's list.

Alan joined us, slightly breathless, his face as red as his coppery hair. 'Sorry I'm late. Kids playing up. Jenny couldn't make it.' His wife, Jenny, never could make it, and every month we got the same hurried apology. Jenny was a birder too, as keen as Alan in her youth or keener, but the children had clipped her wings the way they hadn't seemed to clip Alan's. He was older than the others, a graduate student when we had been undergraduates, but he didn't seem to have aged at all over the years, as though letting the rest of us catch up. In Alan's world, Jenny was always going to come to the pub, if not this time, then next time, if the kids weren't playing up, of course.

'What's that you got there, Manda? CD-Rom and half the phone book?' Will asked.

'Gareth's list. I split it off the database. I was going to give it to him tonight.'

Alan paused in the act of sitting down, exchanged a quick glance at Will, then settled himself. 'Ah, Manda,' he said. Will shifted uncomfortably, concentrated on opening the packet of peanuts. Tom wasn't listening, distracted by the list, unable to resist the opportunity of going through Gareth's entire life.

'Manda, Gareth rang, about half an hour ago,' Alan continued. Will finally wrenched the peanuts open, spraying half of them across the table. Tom looked up briefly from the printout, caught my eye and looked away again quickly.

'He said he was thinking of bringing, er, Ruth tonight.'

'What? Essex Girl?'

'Well, she's getting a bit into birding, now, starting a list of her own.'

'She's not a birder, she's a bird,' I said. Will snorted, but shut up at a look from Alan.

'It's that kind of thing he wants to avoid. Look, Manda,

we've known you a long time . . .' He didn't finish the sentence, and he didn't need to. *But we've known Gareth longer.*

'You can still be in the main group, use the website.'

'Will, I maintain the fucking website.'

Alan looked uncomfortable. I knew I was making his point for him. I put my hands up, tried a smile. 'I'll be civil, I promise.'

'It's just, these evenings, it's always been about the four of us, since uni, since before then, even.'

Instinctively, I looked to Tom for support, but he avoided my eye. I wondered with a sharp pang if this was even news to him or if he had known, if the four of them had discussed it already, and he had let me sit there this last half hour in my fool's paradise, my happy ignorance, thinking we were friends. And if this, then what else had they all concealed from me, loyal to Gareth as they were? What else had they known and kept hidden behind their blandly friendly faces? How often had they sat and watched me, here in the pub, out in the field, laughing along with me and thinking, poor Manda, if only she knew?

I wasn't about to beg. 'I can finish my drink, I suppose?' Will nodded, but only after checking with Alan, who glanced discreetly at his watch and then started playing with the catch. I felt the three of them watching me as I forced the beer down as quickly as I could.

'Peanut?' Will offered. I shook my head and finished my Guinness in a silence broken only by the clicking of Alan's watch strap: open and closed, open and closed, as though he were trying to break it.

'Give Gareth the list,' I said as I got up to go. 'Tell him

everything is on the disk.' They nodded again. As I made my way away from the table I could hear the conversation start up again slowly, something about a ringing day coming up, a big twitch Will had been on in December. I turned to look. They had closed their chairs up round the table, erasing the place where I had sat.

Outside in the car park the cars and the tarmac gleamed damply, reflecting the bright spill of light from the pub. My own car was sitting right by the entrance, but I postponed the moment of getting into it, of admitting defeat. When I'd arrived the place had been almost empty, just Tom's work Land Rover parked by the skip, towering over everything else. Now the car park was filling up and as I stood irresolutely in the doorway trying to summon the will to leave, I saw Gareth and Ruth threading through the parked cars, their faces lit orange by the street lights.

Without thinking, not wanting to be seen, I slipped back into the shadows behind the sheltering bulk of the Land Rover. There was a sour stink of stale beer and wine from the skip full of empty bottles behind me, but I was safe here, hidden from their approach, watching through the windows of the car. I could hear the harsh grate of her voice and see her, distorted by the glass, clinging to his arm, tottering on too-high heels. It used to be my arm that slipped so familiarly into the crook of his elbow like that, my hair that he kissed as we paused at the door into somewhere, gathering ourselves for an entrance. He said something and she laughed, a whinnying high laugh, and then they were gone, swallowed into the pub, shutting the door so the car park was left to the darkness.

'Annoying, isn't she?' said a voice behind me.

I whirled round, startled, heart hammering with shock. David was standing right behind me. It was too dark to see his face clearly but the high beaked nose caught what there was of the light and his eyes seemed to glitter as he leaned forward.

'Sorry. I didn't mean to creep up on you, but you seemed somewhat absorbed.'

'What, are you following me?'

'No, not exactly. I had just seen you and was on the point of warning you that Gareth was on his way when I realized you had anticipated me. I'm sorry I gave you a fright.'

'It's OK,' I said, and I hoped I had kept myself under control as I watched Gareth and Ruth together, that my face had not betrayed my feelings. 'And thanks. For coming to warn me.'

'Not at all,' he said. 'It was my pleasure. Can I do anything else for you, though? Buy you a drink? A meal? Give you a lift home?'

I shook my head, fumbling for my car keys, wanting now only to be left alone. 'I'm fine. Thanks.'

'Not even a quick cup of coffee?' He followed me across the car park, impossible to shake off. My car bipped in greeting as I pressed the button on the key chain and he leapt to pull open the door for me, waving me in with a flourish. Then, when I'd climbed in, he wouldn't let go of the door, but hung on to it, leaning down, still talking.

'He's not worth it, you know, Manda. You're worth ten of him. Twenty. Thirty.'

I wanted to wrest the car door from his grasp but I knew that would play into his hands, make a joke of it, a game. 'Please,' I said, starting the engine. 'I just need to go home.' And he finally let go, opening his hands in surrender.

'You're a cruel woman, Manda Brooks.' I shook my head. 'And yet you're worth a million of her.'

I brushed off his remark at the time. It was only as I started off through the emptying streets that I started to wonder how he had come to learn my full name, and how he had come to be there, so conveniently, waiting outside the pub.

I drove back slowly to the house, which was now lopsidedly furnished after Gareth's predations over New Year. As we had arranged, he'd come over to pick up 'his' stuff while I was staying with Zannah. An interesting concept, after almost ten years of living together. I wandered through the empty rooms and noted once more the gaps, the lines in the dust, where a book, the stereo, a picture, had been. New absences kept jumping out at me, ones I hadn't noticed when I first returned on Saturday. Only that morning, opening the wardrobe to dress for work, I had heard the chatter of the empty hangers; seen how much space had been taken up over the years by the substantial mass of Gareth's dark suits. Now only my work clothes remained, hanging forlornly at one end. I spread them out along the rail, but that only made it look worse and I shoved them all back and slammed the door, triggering the faint echo of the hangers again, wire against wire.

We had agreed I would keep the car; we still had to decide what to do with the house. In the gaps where familiar objects had stood I could feel her presence, standing beside him, egging him on. The rug we bought in Morocco, together, had become a square of unfaded carpet on the sitting-room floor. The maps, one for each trip, birds and dates marked in Gareth's scrawl. They had filled a whole shelf and now they were all gone – even the ones we hadn't used yet, the trips we'd once planned, with the maps spread out on the rug before us as we sprawled beside the fire. The windows blazed black and empty in the sitting room, the new curtain rail still propped up beside them, curtains draped over the back of the nearest chair. It had been almost our last act as a couple, that purchase; a parody of marriage – the trawl round the DIY store, still exhausted from the recriminations, still moving forward as though on auto-pilot, because we couldn't stop. Three weeks before Christmas, the shop almost unbearable with crowds and cheerful music, but I was clinging to the normality of it. It had seemed to me as though as long as the rail remained there, leaning expectantly against the wall, he would stay. He had promised, after all, that he would put it up. He had owed me that much.

On that last morning I had woken with the grey drugged tiredness of a bad night's sleep. I had spent that night, as I had spent so many nights, picking over the details of his betrayal, the few hard facts I had. I could tell even as I lay there that he was awake beside me, locked in his own cycle of thoughts. There was no point in talking, not any more, not to each other. He had found someone else, and that was the end of it and nothing I could say would change anything. In the early hours he had got up and I had fallen finally into an uneasy sleep. When I dragged myself out of bed to prepare for work, he was already dressed and packed to go. He fiddled with his keys and sat opposite me as I ate my breakfast. I stared at him, exhausted.

'I'm leaving,' he said.

'What about the curtains?' It was all I could think of in reply.

He shook his head and looked at me again. 'I'm leaving, Manda. Ruth is coming to pick me up in an hour. It's over.'

'But you promised,' I said, and heard the childish whine in my voice.

'Manda, I'm leaving. My bags are packed. This is it. It's not about the curtains.'

I suppose some part of me still didn't really believe it was the end. Even after he left, after we'd had our businesslike telephone conversation about picking things up and dropping off keys, I had clung on to that one promise of his. He'd come in over the weekend and he'd put up the rail, as he said he would, and then he'd step back to admire his handiwork and see the life we'd made together still spread out around him, and he'd realize his mistake. It was only when I'd opened up our front door, stepped over his set of keys, sprawled on the mat with their familiar brown leather key ring, put down my weekend bag and walked into the sitting room to see that rail still leaning there against the wall that I realized he'd really gone.

While Tom was out watching the red kites soar, I had spent the weekend unpicking the last of the knots that tied Gareth and myself together. Other couples might have to divide their record collections. Birders have to split their lists. We had almost ten years of listing together, all of them painstakingly databased by me on a system I'd built clandestinely as a student on the university network. I'd taught myself enough Oracle to do it and when the system administrator finally caught up with me he was impressed enough to offer me a job when I graduated. I was still working in the same job; and I was still using the same design for the database, although the software it was written in had moved on. Night after night I had sat in the computer labs and entered every sighting from Gareth's notebooks; spelling his whole life out, bird by bird. His past became mine, in a way, as I worked my way through his lists. Birds I'd never seen, places I'd never gone to becoming as much a part of my memories as of his. I grew used to the quiet hum of the almost empty rooms, the glare from the strip lights in the corridors, the intent and silent stares of the other night owls, their faces lit with the green glow from the screens. It took me three weeks of long nights to work my way through the stack of Gareth's notebooks and then I started with our own, our joint birds.

Appropriately enough, I began with an owl, a barn owl. The first one ever for me, just one of many for Gareth. It was the year that Gareth had bought an ancient motorbike, the proceeds of his first job, and with it the freedom of the country. At last we had the mobility to chase birds as they were reported, not waiting for a train, or a lift, or the weekend. That Friday we had headed off to Suffolk, looking for an Icelandic gull that had been reported hanging around Aldeburgh. It proved frustratingly elusive, that wraith-like bird, always just flown wherever we went. By the Saturday afternoon, tired and cold from the knife-like wind that scoured the shingle beach, I was ready to give up and retired to the seafront to thaw my hands on a cup of tea while Gareth watched on, promising to run and get me the moment he saw anything.

He didn't, so I lingered over my tea, enjoying the tingle of blood returning to my fingers and face, then pushed myself back into the wind. Gareth's face was aglow.

'It came just after you left. You should have seen it, Manda, swooping down over the beach. It was fantastic.'

I was furious. 'You said you were going to come and get me.'

'Yeah, but it was only here a second.' He was looking away, turning to watch a herring gull that was picking over a fish head a few yards away, only meeting my eyes for a brief moment.

'You did see it, didn't you?'

'Manda!'

I narrowed my eyes. They had happened before, these mysteriously appearing birds of Gareth's. 'Couldn't it have just been a light herring gull?'

'No way. The wings were too pale, the bill too short. Come on, let's get some tea, I'm perishing.'

I was torn. I wanted to stay and look for the gull. But I felt that standing there would imply I didn't believe him, that I was doubting his word, his honesty, his identification. Tom berated Gareth all the time about his habit of conjuring up birds from thin air. But Tom could do that. Tom had known Gareth forever.

Gareth had taught me everything I knew about birds. I was still learning, then, still looking in the wrong direction half the time, fumbling with my binoculars, hastily paging through my field guide. It had been half the basis of our relationship, me learning, him showing, sharing his knowledge with me. I followed him up the thick shingle, my feet slipping, turning my head as we left the beach for one last look.

By the Sunday the consensus was that the bird had gone. Gareth's was the last sighting by a long way and I could see the exchanged glances of the other birders when he mentioned it in the pub and the way the conversation was quickly turned to other birds, other sightings. We packed up that afternoon and the short winter day was already over by the time we set off. Later I would learn how to sleep on the back of the motorbike on those long night rides, slumped against the comforting warmth of Gareth, trusting him to keep me safe. But that night I was prickly and cross, sitting upright with my arms braced behind me. Over and over I revolved the little scene on the beach in my head. Why didn't he get me, if it was the bird? If it wasn't the bird, why did he say it was? Either way I was disturbed beyond the simple irritation at dipping on a bird we'd come miles to see; it was the dishonesty, the readiness to boast, those exchanged glances of disbelief from the others. The pitying looks had included me, by association. I found myself for the first time edging away from him, no longer willing to be encompassed in his glow.

I was roused from this futile cycle of thought by the sudden shock of silence and stillness as the engine was switched off. I asked Gareth what the problem was, but he shushed me, motioned me to look over his shoulder. In the circle cast by the bike's headlight I saw what I took to be a cat sat bolt upright in the road. But as we both watched with held breath it rose, ghostlike, on white silent wings, and flew steadily away, held briefly in the beam until it jinked and vanished into the woods.

'Barn owl,' Gareth said, 'guarding its kill.' A rodent lay dead on the roadside before us. I knew that hundreds of young owls died each year, guarding their prey from the roaring metal monsters on the roads. Gareth got off the bike and gently moved the dead mouse to the side of the road where a bird could safely take it. He stood for a moment just waiting, watching the spot where the owl had vanished, the edge of his face caught in the glow from the headlight. I sat quietly, my eyes on his face as he reluctantly turned and came back to the bike. Just before he restarted the ignition we heard a long haunting screech from the trees. Gareth raised one hand as though in salute and I wrapped my arms back around his solid warmth, grateful once more for his presence.

*

The owl was still there, the memory crystallized in the bald facts – place, time, name – of the sighting. Merely viewing the record on screen, as I checked what I'd been doing, was enough to bring it to life and send it once more rising up silently before us and vanishing into the dark woods.

I was pleased that my original design for the system had held good. With a single query it was possible to unzip Gareth's birds from my own, retaining on both sides the ones that we had shared. I ended up with a single file combining all his sightings; twenty years of history. I was going to give him a copy of the database too, but the thought of him and Essex Girl sitting in front of it putting in their birds stopped me. It had always been one of our Sunday night rituals, filling in the weekend's birds – Gareth sitting in the corner, calling out the names and dates and places from his notes, me typing as fast as I could to keep up. Let him write his own database. Let her write him one. If she could.

I finished the weekend's work by putting in my own birds for the last two days – a thin crop, Tom was right. The best were the grebes, a regular pair from our local birding patch, a flooded gravel pit a few hundred yards from the house. When the pit had been exhausted the quarrying firm had done a bit of half-hearted landscaping and planted some trees. Not a great site, in truth, but it was ours, walking distance from our house. Over the years its raw edges had softened as the trees grew up and nature began to reclaim it. The cars roar by on the M4 on the other side of a strip of trees, unaware that yards to their left there are ducks and lapwing and grebes, and one small, solitary birder walking her way around the lake, looking for peace of mind.

When we had bought the house the pit was even rawer, only fully flooded a year or two before. But it was one of the things which had attracted us to this suburban pocket on the outskirts of Maidenhead. Even its rawness had seemed like an advantage to me. It was a chance for us to start something together, to watch as it grew up from nothing. Over the years we had recorded, visit by visit, the colonization of the site, and with it I began to understand the quiet attraction of this country, a place that had up until now felt only alien and cold to me, repellently drab and grey. In Africa this would have been a riot of vegetation within weeks, loud with insects and birds, rampant with new life. Here, the process was more insidious, a gradual softening of the hard edges, almost imperceptible until one spring it just blossomed, a froth of white flowers appearing against the green, and I saw how the whole rough unpromising spot had quietly transformed itself in its subtle beauty.

The birds were subtler, too, not giving up their secrets to the casual eye. Cormorants had quickly colonized the edges of the water and sat in lines along the abandoned machinery, hanging their wings out to dry like ragged laundry, guano streaking everywhere they perched. The two grebes that followed shortly afterwards must have been young to adopt such an unpromising nest site. When they arrived the first year we visited they were slim and pale, silvery grey unspectacular birds that swam low in the water, making barely a ripple. They can dive deep, grebes, flattening their feathers to expel any pockets of air, driving themselves down to the bottom with powerful feet, placed well to the back of their bodies for maximum efficiency. On the surface they seemed a little awkward, bobbing under the water as quickly as they could, as though getting away from an alien world.

And then, early one spring morning when we had returned from a trip away, we found them transformed, the winter moult over, and their bright breeding plumes forming great ruffs, framing their heads. As we watched, the male brought the female weed, and little fish plucked from the depth of this brand-new lake, and they turned and faced each other to dance. In turn they bobbed and tucked their heads, mirroring each other. We sat and watched as they danced across the surface of the water side by side, their bodies held upright out of the water, propelled along by their lobed feet. Awkward, almost comical, to human eyes, but there was a tenderness to it, especially in that mirroring of each other, that almost made me believe the birds dressed up their mating rituals in fine emotions as well as fine feathers. And then, the courtship done and the pair bond formed, the dancing stopped, and they got on with the serious business of rearing a family.

This Saturday the grebes were still in their winter plumage, slim and pale again, the courtship forgotten. They hunted separately on the water, within sight of each other but rarely seeming to acknowledge each other's presence. I stood on the shore and watched them, holding my breath for each dive, unable to match the staying capacity of their lungs. Each time I would be forced to take another breath well before the bird I had been tracking bobbed buoyantly up to the surface again. It would float for a moment on the water, gleaming white against its reflection, and then, with a little jumping dive, it would be gone again, back into the depths. I watched them for an hour as they busied themselves with their lives, as they passed and re-passed each other in companionable silence. Then I thrust my cold hands into the depths of my pockets and trudged back to the empty waiting house.

Ever since university, the first Monday of every month had always been spent in the pub with the rest of the gang. Now as I wandered round the house, room after room, trying to summon the will to cook myself another solitary supper, I didn't know what to do with myself. I thought I had made a life here, settled like the grebes for this place, for this cold and unpromising country, and made the best of it. Zannah talked about home, these days, and meant Africa. I stared out of the blank and empty sitting-room window and wondered where home was now for me. Only my face stared back, telling me nothing.

As I waited for my supper to heat up, I stepped out for a moment into the cold of the garden and looked up. The night had cleared and the chill was growing, a hard frost threatening, sucking the last life out of the winter foliage. The wrong stars looked back at me: weak, few, struggling against the street lights. My father had once tried to teach me how to navigate by the night sky, how to find my bearings and set a course, but had grown frustrated and given up because the constellations he remembered weren't there in the glittering southern skies. Only Orion, whose belt hung above me now, was familiar to us both. These stars, so distant and faint, were the ones he had been seeking, but I knew no names for them, and he was dead now, and couldn't tell me.

I looked in through the window at the brightly lit kitchen, the dark emptiness of the house beyond. I wondered what would happen if I simply walked away, where I would end up, what would become of me. I must have stood there wondering for a long time, with no sense of time passing, lost to the world.

I hadn't even had a chance to look properly at the others' year lists, how mine compared. I thought about them all sitting in the warm fug of the pub, Alan with his furtive cigarettes, Will joking, Tom silently musing. Gareth would be the bright centre, as usual, the sociable one. She would probably be bored. I wondered if he'd even looked at his own life list yet, seen what I'd done. Tom would have noticed, though. He had looked up from the list for a moment just as I was leaving and our eyes met, and I thought I saw him nod, just once, as though in approval.

I smiled to myself a little as I ate my lonely meal. I'd been reminded, as I went through his list, just how many birds Gareth had that would cause rolled eyes and exchanged glances in the pub. Like the Aldeburgh Icelandic gull, and the capercaillie that had appeared – briefly, beating through the Scots pines – while I was behind a bush having a pee. And the golden eagle that everyone else thought was probably a buzzard. We all see, some of the time, what we want to see. It's just that Gareth was better at that than anybody else. So it was for his own good, really, that I'd carefully removed them all – every last dubious one of them – from his life list before I handed it over.

DUNNOCK

Prunella modularis, family 'Prunellidae'

A couple of weeks later I was startled by the phone ringing on a Friday evening. Zannah's day to ring was Thursdays; after she'd watched *EastEnders* and before she sat down to eat. I could set my watch by it. She would fill me in with her boss's latest atrocity, and I would dredge up some incident from my week that would demonstrate that I was still getting up and going to work on a daily basis and not, say, lying in a warm bath with both wrists slashed. On Fridays Zannah went out. On Fridays I ate my solitary meal in front of the television in the still-uncurtained sitting room and planned my weekend. It was somewhere between the end of the gardening shows and the beginning of the American comedy imports that the phone rang. If not Zannah, then who? I picked up the phone.

'Gareth?' It was Tom.

'Tom, he left me. Six weeks ago. Remember?'

'Oh,' he said. 'Shit. Sorry, Manda. I was going to update my phone.'

The silence lengthened between us. I wasn't about to help him out. I was still bitter about his betrayal that night in the pub, the way he'd failed to stick up for me, the fact that neither he nor any one of them, not even Jenny, had contacted me since. Still, something prevented me from simply hanging up on him, and as the silence extended between us, I relented.

'Do you need his number?'

'No, no, I have it.' More silence. I imagined Tom squirming a little on the other end of the line and I found I was enjoying the moment.

'Was it something I can help with?'

'Oh, well, I was wondering what hour Gareth was going to do for the garden birdwatch weekend.'

When I first met Gareth, garden birdwatching, and bird feeding generally, was considered pretty lame, the sort of thing your parents would do. Luring birds to the artificial habitat of the back garden seemed somehow cheating compared with going out and finding them in the wild. But once the RSPB garden survey got to be big, and they discovered they could submit a *list*, the lads' interest was piqued and the whole thing got a bit competitive. Our flat fenced square of builders' rubble thinly disguised as a lawn suddenly sprouted plants: berries for the birds, flowers for the insects the birds ate, teasels for the finches, a pine tree for the goldcrests and coal tits. Pointing out that the whole event was supposed to be a scientific survey, not a territorial pissing competition, fell on deaf ears. The problem was that while the count could take place at any time during the allotted survey weekend, it had to be completed within an hour.

'I don't know, Tom, you'll have to ask him.'

I twisted the phone cord as I listened. Tom seemed to have forgotten his embarrassment now, had forgotten even that he was talking to the wrong person, and was warming to the theme.

'Only, if I pick, say, seven a.m., I'm likely to get the woodpecker in on the fat ball. But I won't see the coal tits. If I wait till later, I might even get the sparrowhawk, or a buzzard.'

'Jenny told me last year that Alan spent pretty much the entire weekend watching out of their kitchen window. Then he worked out which sixty-minute time span gave him the best number and used that.'

There was a long pause while Tom digested this. 'Don't tell Tom,' Jenny had added as she told me, giggling. 'You know what he's like about lists.'

'Well, at least he still sticks to the hour,' Tom said finally.

'You're tempted, though, aren't you?' I asked. 'Go on, admit it.'

'What do you think Gareth will do?' Tom asked.

'Gareth will do what he did last year, write down every bird he's ever seen in the garden and a few that he wishes he had.' I felt a small twinge of disloyalty at this, quickly suppressed. The evening stretched out endlessly in front of me, and I was enjoying the brief moment of human contact.

'And you?'

Ah yes, and me. My fleeting cheerfulness vanished. I'd been avoiding looking out of my kitchen window for the last few weeks since returning from Zannah's. It wasn't just the maps Gareth had taken, and the bird books, and the rug. All of the feeders had gone, and their bare hooks, and the empty nail where the bird box had hung, depressed me every time I caught sight of them. The life had gone out of the garden, leaving behind only a vague feeling of guilt at not feeding the birds; one more thing I ought to be doing and wasn't. I made a vague and non-committal answer, but Tom wasn't really listening any more. He had returned to Alan's idea and was chewing it over, squaring it up with his conscience, more tempted than he wanted to admit.

'The thing is, I'm working on Sunday. I can't cover the whole weekend.'

I sighed and shifted the phone from one ear to the other, peering out into the dark of the window and seeing only my own face glaring palely back at me. 'Why don't I spell you in on Sunday? If you trust me to get the birds right, that is.'

After I'd put the phone down, having made arrangements to meet, I didn't return immediately to the TV but sat on for a moment, staring out at the invisible garden while canned laughter blared out behind me. I didn't need its dulling stupor. Tom's call had reminded me I had things to do, and more than that, that I had a whole life out there, a world I belonged to, with its rules and its in-jokes, and it was time for me to rejoin it.

I snapped off the TV and headed upstairs to the computer, logging into the club's website. *Birding, Berks* – named by Will, naturally, and usually losing that vital comma – had grown out of the regular Monday night sessions in the pub but was now bigger than the original group. It sat on a semi-official corner of the university web server, a minor perk of the job. As long as I didn't work on it during office hours and kept it free of anything defamatory, my boss turned a blind eye. It had started as a place where we could keep our lists and our photos and had evolved from there. Now anyone in the local area could set up an account, keep a list, alert others to unusual sightings, fill in trip reports, plan itineraries, ask advice. Half the accounts belonged to people I recognized, the rest were strangers, some using nicknames to maintain their anonymity. Somehow over the past couple of years this site had become a community of sorts, filled with semi-strangers whose on-line lives were more vivid to me than some of the people I knew in real life. I spent an hour or so setting up a new page for the big Garden Birdwatch, to allow people to submit their lists to us as well as to the RSPB. And then I spent the rest of the evening wandering invisibly around my domain, eavesdropping on conversations, looking at lists, the benevolent keeper of my own little world.

Two new accounts had been created since I last checked. One had a university address, *stillhunter*, with New Year's Day sightings for Selsey and Pagham Harbour. 'Cattle egret!!!' it had as its first bird, black-tailed godwit the second, and I smiled to myself, imagining Tom's response if he encountered it. *Ruthie_d* was the second, and the email address was instantly familiar, causing a sick lurch to my stomach. I was surprised she hadn't used a different one, surprised Gareth had even suggested she join, knowing as he must know that I would see it there. My hand hovered over the delete key, poised to wipe her account out of existence, but I resisted. Just knowing I could remove her whenever I chose was power enough.

*

I woke up the next morning determined to go out and replace the bird feeders Gareth had taken from the garden. One good thing about living in suburbia: you didn't have to go too far to find a garden centre. There was one right on the corner of our road. I stopped in but the selection of feeders wasn't very inspiring. I looked at the price stickers in despair. A letter had arrived from Gareth's solicitors – he had solicitors now. Or maybe they were hers. A decision had been reached about the house in my absence. I was to buy him out. Generously, I had been given until April to arrange this. Less generously, it would be at the current market price. Essex Girl's voice on her answering machine had asked me to leave a message. Halfway through my carefully worded suggestions of where they could stick their letter, and their solicitors after it, Gareth picked up the phone.

'Manda, you're scaring Ruth. And you're not doing yourself any favours.'

I put the phone down. Added to my list. Find lawyer. Get house valued. Find an enormous sum of money I didn't have.

The cheapest bird feeder was plastic and acrylic. It didn't even pretend to be squirrel proof. Lightweight and gaudy and cheap. I put it back, picked up a more robust version.

'That's a very good bird feeder,' said an unctuously familiar voice behind me. I turned, almost dropping it. David.

'What are you doing here?'

'I work here,' he said, acting hurt. 'Saturday job. I'm at the university.' He wasn't wearing the turquoise jacket now and his manner was a little more subdued; he'd lost some of the bumptiousness I remembered. I hadn't had him down as a student; there was something in his face that didn't fit, a wariness behind the clowning manner that the students didn't share. He had approached behind me so quietly that I had been completely unaware of his presence, but now he was suddenly too big, too close, to be ignored. I felt that if I stepped away from him he would follow, that I could find myself cornered. Looking around I realized that there was nobody else in the shop; the other few customers lingered outside, poking through the shrubs and pots.

'Bit old to be a student, aren't you?'

He shrugged. 'Did some other stuff first.' He didn't elaborate and I didn't ask. 'I'd have thought you'd have a feeder by now.'

I spoke without thinking, my mind on other things. 'I did, several. Or rather Gareth did.'

'Wow, he took the feeders.' He did a silent whistle, shaking his head, but with a half-smile of amusement playing about his lips, and I could have cursed myself for giving him the opening. 'Harsh. That's harsh.'

I walked slowly down the aisle, trying to concentrate on the job in hand with David trailing behind me, still shaking his head and talking. None of them seemed right – the solid ones were too expensive, the rest were just toys, flimsy things that wouldn't last a winter. Finally I gave up, and picked up a packet of bird seed, thinking I'd buy a feeder in town.

I felt it taken out of my hand. 'I'll get this,' he said.

'I'm sorry?' I said.

'My treat. My gift. To you. To make it up to you. To show you that some men know how to behave.' He leaned forward, looking around, dropping his voice in a parody of discretion. 'And I finish my shift in a minute. I can even help you carry it home.'

'Please,' I said. 'Don't.' I didn't have it in me to play along with his joke. He was smiling, head on one side, a ridiculous expression on his face that I supposed was meant to be appealing. 'Please, David, I'm in no mood. I wish you'd just leave me alone.' The smile vanished and before he could put on a puppyish expression of disappointment I thought I saw a flash of anger, lightning in a summer sky.

'Your loss,' he said simply, handing the seed back, and I dragged up from somewhere a few words of thanks. I hurried over to the till, feeling his eyes on me long after I'd woven through the high maze of shelving and found the counter where I could pay. Once I'd got outside the door, my mind on the next set of errands, something – that uneasy feeling of being watched – made me turn round again. There was no one in sight, just the shrubs and the bedding plants, the racks full of pots and containers, square bags of compost and mulch stacked high on pallets, blocking my view. I waited for a moment, listening to the quality of the quiet that surrounded me. Sometimes the best way to see a shy bird is to walk on past it, looking behind you to see it emerge when it thinks that the danger is past. I set off again, two brisk steps, stopping and turning abruptly, sure I'd caught a peripheral flicker of movement out of the corner of my eye, a tall figure ducking down behind a half-assembled shed. I set off again, sauntering this time, easing my pace, pulling out my mobile as I went and then stopping to sit on a low wall by the car park. David had no choice but to walk past me, and keep on walking as I mimed a wave, lost in my conversation, uninterruptable, safe from his approach.

I sat on for a good while, ignoring the cold, making sure I had shaken him off completely. In front of me was a small tree, planted in a tiny circle of brick paving. It was staked to a post, the ties already digging into the bark, caged in by an iron railing. Despite all this protection, one of its branches had been broken off and was trailing on the ground, last year's dead leaves still clinging to it. At the very tip of the tree sat a blackbird, loudly advertising his territory, working his way through his repertoire of whistles and calls.

Threaded through his song I heard a distinctly familiar combination of notes. A passing man unconsciously patted his pocket, checking his phone. The Nokia ring tone. Gareth's phone had the same one – hardly surprising, it was the default setting. The blackbird must have heard these notes a hundred times. Even on this cold and quiet Saturday morning I could see three or four people clutching phones to their ears. Husbands calling wives, checking their purchases. Men taking advantage of the brief moment of solitude to call their lovers. The blackbird had casually picked up the cheery little tune, not unlike one of its own, and was using it to impress its drab brown mate. She would be crouched somewhere less conspicuous, listening. So too would any young male blackbirds without a territory of their own, alert for any hint of weakness in the voice, ready to muscle in. And there might be other females too, still looking for a mate, uncaring whether he already had one, whether he had a brood of his own. The blackbird sang on lustily, his eye ring and beak bright orange, advertising his health, his excellent diet, apparently uncaring, just full of the joys of the coming spring.

I got up, abandoning my pretence, flipping shut my own mobile and sending the blackbird fleeing in alarm. I had forgotten to recharge my phone three days ago, but that didn't matter. It sat mute in my pocket anyway, charged up or not. No one was singing for me.

Tom's house – more of a cottage really – sat in the nearest thing to a wild wood Berkshire could offer. Straight out of his master's course in ecological science, Tom had landed a job as a forester at a private estate that had somehow survived among the motorways and suburbs of the county. A nature reserve but without the pesky addition of any visitors, he lived among hundreds of acres of trees which were technically accessible only to those people living in the few houses scattered around the estate. The pay was terrible but the duties few and ill defined. As long as the bridle paths remained open and no rotting tree branches landed on anyone's head he and his boss were free to manage the estate as they felt fit. When I arrived on Sunday morning he was preparing to go out and clear the rhododendron that spread through the forest like a cancer. He threw his chainsaw and helmet into the back of his truck.

'Make yourself at home. List is on the kitchen table. I'll be back round four.'

I pushed open the door. I had never been inside Tom's house in the five or six years he'd lived there. It was surprisingly tidy, the kitchen spartan. A single mug, plate and knife on the dish rack, a scrupulously clean tea-towel hanging from the cooker door. Books – not just field guides and forestry manuals, but a whole library of bird books and ecological studies – were neatly marshalled along shelves on the dresser. More books filled a case in the hall. Pushing open another door I found a sparsely furnished sitting room. Two easy chairs faced an empty grate but a third was pushed up against the window, and an ancient pair of binoculars hung by their strap from the window catch. A third door led to a bathroom, also furnished with a pair of binoculars. Tom obviously made sure he didn't miss a thing. Looking up, I could see a telescope set up on the half-landing. Tom had told me once he'd felled three trees to make sure he could see the tree where he suspected a pair of hobbies were nesting. Peering down the eyepiece, I could make out an old bundle of sticks in the crook of a distant branch but saw no movement.

Back in the kitchen I could see that Tom had been up since dawn. Each bird was entered in neat block capitals with the time seen to the minute. I settled down by the window with a cup of tea and my binoculars to hand for a long quiet day of observation. The first birds I saw, gleaning the scattered seed, were a pair of dunnocks. Two little brown birds, subtly streaked with grey, they appeared unremarkable and demure as they peaceably pecked and hopped side by side. There had been a time – back in the early days – when Gareth's nickname for me was Dunnock. When I finally broke down and asked him why, he laughed and ruffled my hair and said, 'Because you're little and brown and unobtrusive.'

'Oh, thanks,' I'd said, not very pleased, trying to flatten my hair back down against the onslaught of the wind. We were sitting on the beach at Selsey at the time. Alan had driven us all down to look for a group of red-necked divers that had been reported a week earlier. Tom had immediately disappeared off to Selsey Bill to watch for passing seabirds. Gareth and I were technically sea-watching too but somehow we had found ourselves just sitting on the shingle watching the endless cycling of the waves and huddling together against the biting April breeze. When I turned my head away from the sea to try and get the short strands of hair out of my face for a minute, I could see Alan and Jenny doing much the same a few yards down the beach. I focused my binoculars on them for a second, catching Jenny in mid laugh as she comfortably settled herself against Alan's back.

'Completely misleading, of course,' he said, as though it were a change of subject. 'They are famous for their adultery.'

'Who, Alan and Jenny?'

'No, silly, dunnocks.' I kicked him, and he kicked me back and tried to wrestle me down, but I was intrigued and persisted.

'So why me? Why call me a dunnock, then?'

He looked away for a moment, then back at me and his

eyes were slaty blue, opaque as washed pebbles, unreadable as the sea.

'I was reading about it. They are supposed to be monogamous but sometimes the male takes another female – which is nothing unusual, I suppose – but what's more unusual is that the female will sometimes mate with another male, the minute her own mate's back is turned.'

'Seems fair enough to me.'

'Yeah, but then he comes back, catches them at it, chases the other male off, the beta male, and mates her again, just to make sure. All season they're at it, shag and counter-shag until she starts laying eggs. Then both of them – both males – help feed the chicks.'

'And that reminds you of me, does it?'

'I've seen the way you look at men.' And then I knew he was joking, for I had eyes only for him, and he knew it. 'Tom, Alan, Will, the guy in the newspaper shop . . .' We gave up all pretence of interest in the birds and rolled like children on the shingle, tasting the salt spray on each other's mouths. And when we stopped, breathless with laughter, there they all were waiting: Alan and Jenny and Will, and Tom, stood apart from the others, up on the road, arms folded, fixing us both with a level gaze.

Now here I was, alone, watching dunnocks in Tom's kitchen, and I saw another way of interpreting Gareth's words, one I had missed up to now. For it isn't just the female dunnock that plays fast and loose with the pair bond.

*

Whatever his meaning, Gareth had taken to winding Tom up – or maybe it was me – pretending he thought Tom fancied me. It had started around a year after I had left university. Tom was at Bangor, doing his master's, down visiting us for a weekend. Gareth had just bought our first car, we were renting a two-bedroom flat, and Tom, for once, was the one to do the teasing.

'Ooh, washing machine! Microwave! All the mod cons,' he exclaimed sarcastically as I showed off our little kitchen, the spare bedroom which I had hurriedly prepared the night before.

'It's only Tom, Manda,' Gareth had said, as I hunted the cupboards for a clean towel and matching sheets, but he was our first real guest and I was measuring myself against some forgotten or imagined standard of domesticity, dredged up from who knows where. That night I cooked supper while they talked, throwing a remark or two of my own into their point and counterpoint of reminiscence. Some of their stories I knew so well from long repetition I could almost join in in their telling. We ate with our plates on our knees on the sofa because the table was crowded with maps and notebooks, our plans for our first birding trip abroad together. Tom stood and surveyed them, threw in a few suggestions and then, finally, a curt nod of approval.

'Should be good,' he said. 'Wish I was going myself.'

'Sorry, mate,' Gareth said, giving me an affectionate squeeze. 'Couples only, know what I mean?' I leaned against him, at home in the warm enclosure of his arms. Afterwards Tom and Gareth went to wash up in the kitchen and I remained curled up on the sofa listening to the rumble of male voices through the doorway, no longer paying any attention to the words. It had become simply a background noise, the soundtrack of my contentment, and I remember thinking then that this was it, that I was happy.

We spent the whole weekend driving round all of Tom's old favourite birding spots, ending in Burnham Beeches on the Sunday afternoon. He was due to get the train back to Wales that evening, but we just had time for one final wander through the spring woods looking for birds together. We headed down, away from the crowds of dog walkers and family groups on constitutionals, past the ponds and into the scrubbier woods where beeches gave way to oak and holly and everything was tangled with old man's beard. We had stopped to watch a party of long-tailed tits as they flitted through the bushes, calling constantly to keep in contact. They were feeding near a dense stand of holly, which hollowed out into a little covered clearing, and Tom leaned down, watching the tits but also beyond them, into the bushes, always alert to the chance of something else, something interesting.

The tits flew off and Gareth, bored, wandered after them along the path of a small leaf-choked stream. Tom paused me for a moment with an imperious gesture of the hand just as I was about to follow.

'Watch this,' he said, and I leaned down to look through the branches towards the ground where a small brown bird foraged busily among last year's dried leaves.

'It's a dunnock,' I said, curious as to why Tom would be

directing his attention to such a commonplace little bird.

'Yes, I know, a female,' he said. 'Watch.'

I watched. The little bird foraged on, oblivious. Tom squatted down, getting comfortable against the trunk of a tree, and I sank down slowly too, resting my elbows on my knees. Gareth's footsteps faded away and soon I could only hear the dry rustles of the bird's movements, Tom's breathing, and my own.

'What are we watching for?' I said at last, in an undertone. Tom didn't respond for a few moments, and I thought he hadn't heard until he put his finger up to his lips and then pointed beyond the little female to a branch a few feet above her, where another, apparently identical, bird was perched.

'Wait,' he said, and as we waited we saw her crouch down and twirl her tail in invitation at this skulking male. Behind and above us I heard a fractured song, and as I turned to look, Tom breathed in my ear, 'That's him, behind us.'

'Who?' I said, confused, and almost missed the brief second's frantic mating as the first male flew down from his concealed perch and barely hovered behind the crouching, waiting female.

'The other male,' Tom said, and as he spoke there was a feathery whirr as a third brown bird flew into the little clearing, seeing off his rival. 'The mate. The alpha male.'

His rival may have gone but the female remained, still crouching and submissive as her mate pecked brutally at her cloaca, then mounted her himself, just as briefly.

'Ouch,' I said, but Tom just laughed.

'That's evolution,' he said, and we started to scramble back out of the concealing bush. I stood up too quickly and I felt as much as saw the rising tide of blackness as the blood rushed downwards – the world fading out into nothing – and my hand reached out instinctively for support. It met scratchy wool and warmth and I steadied myself briefly before sound and vision returned and I saw Gareth's bright face before us, darkening briefly to a frown as he approached.

'What have you two been up to?' he said, reaching for jokiness in his voice.

'Watching dunnocks,' said Tom, and I took my hand off his shoulder and put it through Gareth's arm, sneaking it down into his jacket pocket and insinuating my fingers into the warmth of his palm.

'So that's what they call it these days, is it?' he said, picking a dead leaf out of my hair with his free hand, but this time the laugh was unforced. 'Watching dunnocks? Hands off my bird, Tom.' We started back towards the car, Gareth and I together, Tom off to one side.

'*Ménage a trois*,' Tom said, ignoring Gareth's last remark, and I could feel Gareth's stride hitch for a second before he continued walking easily on. 'The dunnocks, I mean. The female was having a sneaky little shag with her lover in the bushes.'

'You saw that?' Gareth said. 'Wow. So you won't be impressed with my tree creeper then.'

'Ah, bastard, I haven't had that yet this year. Wait up, will you?'

As Tom headed back to get the tree creeper, Gareth

wound his hands behind my back and pulled me close. 'No sneaky shags with my rival, right?' he breathed, and it was my turn to laugh.

'Tom? Give me a break.'

'I know, I know, credit the girl with some taste, eh?' His mouth was on my face, my ears, my neck, nuzzling through the wool of my jumper, his hands pushing up against the skin of my back, down into the waistband of my jeans. But he didn't forget – wouldn't forget – the incident; and for a while afterwards he went back to calling me Dunnock on occasion, catching my eye across a table or a room, especially when Tom was around. It wasn't a private thing now, but a public one, done with a heavy-lidded stare at me as he said it, as though challenging the assembled company to ask him why he called me that. He knew I'd flush and look away as he threw it into the conversation and then as often as not moved on, leaving me confused and stumbling for the next word. Those would often be the nights that he'd grab me even before we reached the car, pulling me into doorways, kissing me roughly as I half protested, half acquiesced, even after he'd spent a whole evening alternating between baiting and ignoring me.

But he did it less often as things cooled between us, when whole weeks might pass without us so much as touching, when I went to bed, pleading exhaustion, at nine and feigned sleep, back turned, when he stumbled up after midnight. Our nights out together became fewer, anyway, as he found work colleagues to drink with, other places to go without me. I began to hate the nickname and everything it stood for; it reminded me too much of a time when we had been happy, especially when others picked it up and used it unknowingly, long after Gareth had stopped bothering to tease me any more, had stopped bothering about anything at all.

I shook my head at the memory and banished it. The birds had flown, anyway, replaced by a flock of squabbling sparrows which looked crude and scruffy after the dunnocks' muted elegance. Gareth had bored of the joke in the end. He still liked to taunt Tom about things – his solitary life, his seriousness – but Tom, like me, put up with the teasing. It was the price we paid, with Gareth, for his attention.

I made a note of the sparrows and watched on. Tits – blue tits, coal tits, great tits – busied themselves at the peanut feeder. A pair of collared doves sat bowing in a tree. I sat and watched and noted, my tea cooling beside me. Only the constant checking of the clock as a new bird flew in gave me any sense of the passing of time. It was long past four before Tom showed up, and the last birds were leaving for their roosts. Only a blackbird sang on in the dusk.

I didn't mention the dunnocks to Tom, in the end. It seemed like it would open a whole conversation I didn't feel like having. Instead, I told him about the ring tone call of the blackbird in the car park. 'Normal or polyphonic?' he asked.

'Normal, I think.'

'I remember when I was a boy, they all started doing the trim-phone ring. Remember those phones?' I shook my head. Something else I'd missed. 'And then it was car alarms. They'll be doing polyphonic by next year, I bet you any money. The new young ones coming through. Those trim-phone blackbirds are all dead now.'

He sat down to pull his boots off, then leaned back and closed his eyes. His face was marked slightly by soot from the bonfire I could smell on his clothes, and his throat stood out white against the dark wool of his jumper. Without the usual penetrating gaze his face was softened, blurred by tiredness. It only lasted for a second and then he was back, instantly alert.

'Where's that list?'

Later, over bacon and eggs, I finally broached the subject that had been bothering me for a fortnight.

'What was she like then?'

'Who?'

'Essex Girl. You know.' I didn't want to dignify her with a name. 'Gareth's new . . .'

'Ruth? All right.' He shrugged. 'Haven't you met her?'

'Barely. When Gareth was sleeping with her behind my back he spent quite a lot of energy keeping us apart. And after I found out, I wasn't too keen to socialize.' I regretted the words the minute they came out of my mouth. The light tone I'd aimed for hadn't quite made it past the bitterness in my throat. Tom looked uncomfortable, started clearing up the plates, and I found I was dreading the end of the evening, the return home. 'All I know is, if her text messages are anything to go by, she can't spell.' He laughed, sat down again.

'Well, OK, she didn't strike me as the sharpest tool in

the box. I don't think she'll be back in the Bird in Hand either.' He paused, cleared his throat, and the next sentence came out of his mouth almost sideways. 'In my opinion, Gareth has made a big mistake.'

I looked at Tom but he had turned his back, taking the plates to the sink and scraping them busily. For a moment I thought he meant there was a possibility that Gareth and I could go back, right back to the way we had been, as though he hadn't done what he had done, as though I hadn't done what I'd done, as though nothing had happened. I could suddenly see the five of us sitting round the pub table as we had done for years. We would be laughing. Laughing at one of Gareth's witticisms, or Will's terrible jokes, it didn't matter. Listening to one of Alan's long drawn-out stories about a birding trip involving uncomprehending foreigners. Arguing about whose turn it was to get the next round in. Drawing up our top-ten list of all-time great birds. We could sit in the warm circle of our own making and exclude the rest of the pub, the rest of the world. And this time maybe I wouldn't pick up that gleaming little Nokia with its cheery ring and idly page through the messages received box. Wouldn't ask, when Gareth came back from the Gents, who 'R' was. Wouldn't feel that cold sinking in the pit of my stomach, the pounding heart, and the shaking hands, as his eyes shifted away, and he cleared his throat, and the rest of the table gradually fell silent.

'You reckon? Do you think he might come back?'

Tom paused in the act of turning from the sink, a plate

in one hand. His face was unreadable, but I thought I saw pity there, pity and pain. He didn't say anything, but turned back to the sink, scraping the plate with what seemed like unnecessary vigour, blasting it with the tap so it drowned out my words.

'Ah, no, stupid question,' I said to his back. 'Forget I asked it.'

For five days, as January crept over into February, I rose and left for work in the dark, and returned in the dark. On the Friday evening I finally got around to updating my own list from the weekend's birdwatch. Tom's was in already, and Alan and Jenny's. I was half expecting a panicky phone call from Will wanting to know what his password was. A few others had submitted too. I pulled my list up off the database and logged in myself.

Twenty minutes later I was still cursing at the computer. Every time I tried to transfer my list up, it complained that the file was already there. Five days of sorting out other people's computer problems had left me dull-witted and slow, and it was another ten minutes of trying various combinations of key strokes and muttered swear words before I had the wit to check the entry under my own name.

'Manda Brooks', the computer obediently displayed, followed by my address. And a list, for 11 a.m. on Sunday: Blackbird, two, male and female (male with single white tail feather). Wren. Great tit. Coal tits, three. Blue tits, two. Mistle thrush. House sparrows, five, two males. Robin.

Collared doves, pair. Wood pigeons, pair. Feral pigeons (overhead). Pied wagtail. Magpies, three, mobbed by sparrows. Crow (overhead). Starlings, five plus. Chaffinch, male.

It was an unremarkable list. One I could have made on almost any day in winter in my garden, or any other. But it wasn't my list – I'd been at Tom's at the time, had done my list earlier. And besides, at the end there was a final observation. 'Dunnock, three. Female entertaining two males, the little tart.'

At the time, I dismissed the posting as a joke. I replaced the list with my own, which wasn't much different, and made a note to investigate it when I had a chance, then went to bed and slept the dreamless sleep of exhaustion.

The next morning I woke with the feeling of having been snatched awake by something – a noise, a disturbance – but, listening, could hear nothing but my own breathing and then, as my ears tuned in, the sound of birdsong. It was early but I got up, pulled on some clothes and went to put out the bird seed which had been sitting reproaching me on the kitchen counter all week. I was still dazed from my abrupt awakening and not paying attention as I pushed my feet into my shoes and unlocked the kitchen door, not even looking out of the window as I went. I was greeted by an uprush of feathery panic, the whole garden suddenly alive with birds fleeing from my approach. I stopped and stared. Bird feeders hung everywhere: from all the hooks and nails, from every tree branch and even the washing line, some still swinging from the birds' abrupt departure.

Only the blackbird remained, and I could see now he

had a single white tail feather, shining translucent in the early morning sun. I crouched down on the step and scattered some of the seed; waited until, after a pause, he ran forward with his hunched and scuttling gait and took it.

'Who's been watching you, then?' I asked, quietly and evenly so that he wouldn't take flight. He simply ignored me, and around him the other birds began to filter back into the edges of the garden, torn between feeding and fear. 'Who's been in here?' I asked them, but there was no answer.

STARLING

Sturnus vulgaris, family 'Sturnidae'

'Do you ever ask yourself why we do this?'

'Constantly.' Jenny eased herself between two strands of barbed wire as she spoke. 'Especially when – eurgh – I have one hand in some sort of a puddle and one knee in what looks like a very fresh cowpat.'

'So why do we do it?' I persisted as I followed Jenny through the fence, feeling the sharp barbs catch and tug at my hair. 'Any ideas?'

'Nope, I'm drawing a blank here.' Jenny shouldered her scope and thrust her hands into her pockets, hunching her coat up around her ears. I wondered if my nose was as red as hers. 'No idea at all.'

Four or five other figures were trudging through the mud ahead of us, and there was a queue of at least three waiting their turn to scramble through the fence. Standing on the verge, surrounded by the haphazardly parked cars that stretched along the lane in either direction, stood the owner of the field, a shabbily dressed farmer who was getting a crash-course introduction into the logistics of a medium-size twitch. He'd long since stopped trying to prevent the steady stream of birders from getting onto his land and was reduced to scratching his head in bewilderment.

'What did you say it was?' he asked.

'A hoopoe,' said Jenny, always ready to take a novice under her wing. 'It's like a – well, it's about the same size as a pigeon, but sort of pink – it's got a crest . . .'

'Right,' said the farmer slowly. 'A pink pigeon. You've all come to look at a pink pigeon.' He shook his head, surveyed the muddy wreckage of his field. 'You know what?' he asked, mainly addressing Jenny and me, but encompassing the whole scene with a wave of his hand. 'You lot are all absolutely bloody cuckoo.'

Jenny gave up on him and turned to face the hill. 'Shall we?' she asked, indicating upwards.

Jenny had dropped round one evening a few days before with a couple of maps that we had lent them for a trip and had stayed for a drink once I'd rounded up a couple of clean glasses and some wine. Alan was looking after the children and she confessed she was in no particular rush to get back.

'This is civilized,' she had said, leaning back against the kitchen counter, ignoring the chaos of takeaways and unwashed plates. 'Nobody's asked me to do anything for, ooh, twenty minutes, now. And listen to that.'

I listened, and heard nothing. 'What?'

'The silence. No radio, no TV, nobody yelling for their clean socks. Nothing.'

I swirled the wine in my glass and watched it ripple and settle. 'Sometimes I turn the TV on in the next room, just so it doesn't feel so creepy at night.'

'You should come over to us.'

'Yeah,' I said, knowing she didn't really mean it.

'Or come out with us. God, I haven't been birding for ages, not properly. The kids won't. Or not for longer than twenty minutes, and then they're cold, they're bored, they want sweets, they need a wee.'

'Leave them behind. Let Alan look after them.'

'You're right, I should,' she said, sighing and closing her eyes as though I had suggested some unpleasant duty. 'It's his turn after all.'

Two days later Jenny had emailed me to say there was a hoopoe in a field outside Cookham Dean, that Alan had seen it already, that it was still around and did I want to come and see it with her? She picked me up, bubbling with her usual enthusiasm, like a child released from school. I felt some of the deadening exhaustion of the week lift as I shut the front door behind me and scrambled into the car.

'Haven't been on a good twitch for ages,' she said. 'This one's not exactly your semi-palmated sandpiper, but a twitch is a twitch, after all.'

Following what was by now a fairly well-defined path, we walked up the rise to a ridge where a few trees sheltered a semi-circular hollow. Finding the bird is never a problem in situations like this. Around a dozen people were all staring fixedly in its direction. A few of them looked round at our approach, greeted us with a nod. Most of the rest continued to look through the telescopes which were trained on the bird. The hoopoe itself stood largely unconcerned about twenty yards away, probing the ground occasionally with its bill. Every so often it would look up and raise its crest a couple of times as though displaying for its audience. A sigh would pass through the crowd, an undertone of muttering. Every minute or so another person, or couple or group would join the cluster, shuffling round to find a gap so that a loose, evenly spaced circle of birders was formed around the bird.

'Fantastic,' breathed Jenny.

'I don't know,' I said. 'It depresses me, sometimes, this sort of thing. A lost bird that's been blown too far north too early in the year. Which might, just, if it's lucky, survive the winter only to die a lonely death because there are no other hoopoes about for it to mate with.'

'It's a first for Berkshire in February,' Jenny said, having got her scope set up and peering down the eyepiece, 'and – wow, look at that.' The bird raised its crest again, hopped up with a loose flutter of its black-and-white wings, before settling down again to probe in the mud with its bill.

'Come on, though. If you were on holiday in France, you wouldn't even get out of bed for a hoopoe.'

One of the more devout-looking couples, bent reverently over their matching tripods, turned crossly to look at me.

'You're missing the point.'

For Jenny, I supposed, this was the point. Not the bird. The twitch itself. She was already looking beyond the hoopoe at the crowd, smiling at people she recognized, passing a few muttered comments to me as I peered through my binoculars at the doomed bird. Its cheerful feathers looked wrong against the prevailing colours of an English winter. It had hunched them up against the cold and its lowered crest feathers blew loosely in the wind, giving it a cockeyed look. It was probably young, a first-year bird, too inexperienced to navigate its way back to the warmer lands where it belonged.

'Hey, Manda, don't look now, but it looks like you've got a secret admirer.'

'Where?'

'Got him in the scope for you. Handsome, too, if you like them tall and dark and a bit Mr Darcy.'

I groaned but, unable to resist, looked to see David staring intently across the field to where we stood. His Leicas were slung loosely round his neck and he was just staring, pausing occasionally to make a note. Jenny kept up her running commentary as I watched.

'He was looking right at you. Oh, no, now he's on the move – working his way round towards us . . . nope, he's stopped behind those people – taken something out – can't quite make it out, a book?'

'His notebook.' I was following his progress with the scope, nudging it round with my free hand as he moved. Around us, a couple of people were following the direction of our gaze, thinking we'd seen something interesting.

'Who is he? He looks familiar.'

'Oh, God, Jenny, he's . . .' I struggled to put it into words. My garden still hung with bird feeders and the sight left me uneasy every morning. I found myself looking over my shoulder at odd times, pausing in the doorway of the house to see if the coast was clear. I hid behind my answering machine, the tape every evening filling up with clicks and sighs and silences. At work, the knots of students I saw passing across the campus or coalescing around the various computer rooms and labs had become something to steer well around. Whenever I saw him, when he grinned broadly at me, or waved, or winked as he passed, I found myself cringing, accelerating away as fast as I could. But it was when I didn't see him that I really worried, sure that he was watching me from some hidden vantage point, planning his next move. In his presence I could dismiss him as a clown, a buffoon, irritating but not dangerous. But when he wasn't there, the thought of his persistence worried me, the single-minded determination of his pursuit. And now he was here, not allowing me even the simple pleasure of this bird, ruining everything.

'You could do worse.' Jenny was still scanning the crowd, oblivious, not registering my lack of response. 'Where has he gone to now . . . behind – God, is that Emily? I should go and say hello.'

'Please, don't do that – don't leave me.' But Jenny was gone, threading her way through the clumps of people, leaving me defenceless. David was on the move again, slipping behind people, a ripple of disturbance marking his passage. I thought about moving too, but I was damned if I was going to run from him, be driven away by his persistence. A blast of wind left us all hunched miserably against the cold, and a thin and seeping rain had begun to drift down. Some starlings, driven to the top of the nearest trees by the disturbance, set up a metallic chorus of complaint. The crowd turned up their collars and leaned back down towards their scopes and resumed staring at the lost hoopoe. I leaned back down too, standing my ground, waiting for his approach.

I was fifteen when I first encountered a big twitch – a really big one, this time – on a school trip to the Dorset coast. We all piled out of the coach while the teacher tried to marshal us into groups, handing out clipboards. We were supposed to be examining rock strata. Sixteen girls in a state of suppressed hormonal turmoil. And me. Seventeen girls didn't divide up neatly into twos, wouldn't divide up neatly into any combination, as the teacher quickly worked out. The rest of the class had sorted themselves out already, pairs of glossy blonde and brunette and auburn heads, bent over their worksheets, plotting their quick getaway into the nearest cafe, and hopefully male company. How to explain to any one of them that I was actually interested in rock strata? The teacher looked uncomfortably at me. She didn't want to pair up with me either. She wanted to head behind the coach for a cigarette.

'Manda, why don't you go as a three with Becky and Rachel?'

Becky and Rachel rolled their eyes. 'Aw, miss . . .'

'Samantha? Holly?' They all did a good impression of not hearing. 'Miss' looked at me helplessly. She was the sort of teacher who preferred to be popular, saw herself as our friend. Foisting me on any one of this lot wasn't going to help her. Unfortunately the only girl less popular than me, Fat Phoebe, my normal pair on these sorts of occasions, had got out of the whole humiliating experience by sticking her fingers down her throat after breakfast and throwing up on the house mistress's shoes, instead of discreetly down the toilet like she normally did.

'I'm fine on my own.' I picked up the one remaining clipboard. The teacher gave me a weak and grateful smile. I trailed after the other girls, who were racing through their questions with barely a glance at the rocks we'd come to see. I didn't mind being on my own. I felt relieved not to have Phoebe stumping along in my wake, complaining about her feet, her weight, and the fact that everyone hated her. It must have been early March, but I remember it being almost warm, and sunny, and I could hear the shrill cries of Becky and Holly and Rachel and the others as they rolled down their school socks and hitched up their skirts with their sashes. They reached the cliffs and turned left, towards civilization and boys. I checked my watch, looked round to see that the teacher was safely flirting with the coach driver, and turned right.

I thought I'd come across some Hollywood star or paparazzi shoot. Twenty or thirty men on a slight rise overlooking the shore, all peering through what I took to be cameras resting on tripods. But the spot on which they were all focused was apparently empty. They stood rapt, staring at nothing.

Intrigued, I sidled up to the nearest, younger than the rest, who didn't have a tripod, just a pair of binoculars. Rock strata forgotten, I finally plucked up the courage to ask him what he was looking at. His companion, an older man, straightened up from his telescope and motioned me forward to have a look. Covering one eye, I peered through at a stocky little bird, brown and white and grey, that was moving slowly along the shore, probing occasionally with its beak.

'See it?' asked the younger lad.

'I think so.' I saw only a bird. 'What's so special about it?'

'Semi-palmated sandpiper.' He said it with reverence.

'I'd have expected something fully palmated, the amount of fuss you're making.'

He laughed, then stopped abruptly when the bird, startled, paused its probing of the muddy foreshore. I looked up and saw his hand clapped over his mouth.

'Is it rare?'

The older man spoke. 'Not in America, where it's from. But they're rare here. This is probably the first one in Dorset in a decade.' He took up his position at the telescope again.

The lad handed me his binoculars and I struggled to find the bird again. 'See its feet? How they're a little bit webbed just up between the toes?'

'Sort of,' I said. I was looking at a bird, not entirely sure that it was the right one.

'That's what makes it a semi-palm. It's the first time I've seen one.'

'Me too.' I was being sarcastic, but he nodded seriously, and when he smiled his thanks as I handed him back the binoculars I suddenly didn't feel quite so clever. I wanted to take the binoculars again, see those almost webbed feet. I smiled back.

'You on the lam from school?'

'No. Field trip.' I pulled the clipboard out from under my arm. 'Rock strata.'

'I remember them.'

I realized he wasn't that much older than me. 'So, are you on the lam yourself then?'

He grinned. 'It's educational, isn't that right, Dad?'

His father stood up, began to pack up his kit. All around us others were doing the same as though responding to some signal I couldn't hear while the bird probed on, unmoved by the loss of its audience. 'Educational is right, Eddie. And now I'm bloody gagging for a cup of tea.'

As, one by one, the birders moved along the beach towards the town, I simply joined their slipstream. Eddie took my clipboard from me, began filling in the answers.

'We had this worksheet last year. The very same one.'

His dad bought me a cup of tea and we sat, squashed up around a small Formica table, as Eddie and his father reminisced about other trips they'd been on. There was a bantering intimacy between the pair of them and with the others queuing up at the counter who inched past the table. I sat and swung my legs and blew on the hot tea and let the warm flow of words wash over me. Half of it I didn't even understand, but I laughed when Eddie laughed, and some-times he'd explain something and I'd nod as though that helped.

Out of the corner of my eye I could see Becky and Holly and Rachel, their shared pack of Silk Cut not too discreetly hidden in Becky's blazer pocket.

'Hey, remember Studland, last year, the yellow-browed warbler on the nudist beach?'

'Trying to explain to the guy we really were trying to look at birds . . .'

'. . . the feathered kind! And the look on Del's face when he realized he'd set his scope up looking straight at that woman.'

'The one who thought he was a peeping Tom.'

'I almost died.'

'It was Del almost died when her husband showed up.'

Eddie was pointing out Del to me, but Becky and Rachel and Holly were making their way out the door. I looked at my watch, knowing it was time to go, time to tear myself away from the warm circle. I stood up.

'Thanks for the tea.'

'Bleeding hell, Ed, it's almost dark out. See her back to the coach, why don't you?'

We walked out into the dusk. As I turned towards the car park, Eddie took my elbow and stopped me.

'Wait. I want to show you something. Look.'

I turned and followed his gaze. Out towards the setting sun, over the sea, hundreds of birds were circling in perfect unison. They flew in a dense formation, turning as one; the flock darkening when they tipped their wings, thickening then thinning as they flashed against the beaten gold of the sky. Even as I watched, a smaller group came in and shot towards the cloud and was absorbed into it. Another group and then another flew in, each merging imperceptibly with the mass, which circled on without missing a beat. Hundreds became thousands became uncountable. The flock circled in and flew inland and I heard and could almost feel the rush of their wings against the air as they swooped and turned and beat out again over the sea, pouring over our heads.

'Starlings,' Eddie said, 'gathering to roost.'

I didn't want to know what they were, or what they were doing. It was enough that I was watching. The cloud of birds seemed to me to be a thing in itself, a living entity, forming shapes; a rolling river of birds snaking over the water low and fast transformed into a blunted mass, high and slow. It rose and fell, started to drift off slowly along the shore, all the time pulling in the smaller groups that flew towards it as though drawn by a magnet.

I was expecting the usual ribbing on the ride home. Generally, my tactic was to keep myself well out of the orbit of those three, hoping to go unnoticed. I made my way to my solitary seat, and watched as the coach pulled past the warm steamed-up windows of the cafe. Becky, Rachel and Holly plumped themselves down around me, Holly in the seat in front, Rachel across the aisle, Becky behind, her blonde head poking through the seats. I was surrounded.

'What?' I said, without turning my head from the window.

'Well, go on then, did you snog him?'

I turned my head slowly to look at them. There was only avid curiosity in their faces. 'Did you?'

I just smiled, folded my arms, closed my eyes as though to sleep. I knew not knowing would drive them mad and I relished the thought. As the coach rocked on through the twisting Dorset lanes I let their voices merge with the harsh remembered calls of the birds I'd seen and saw again against the darkness of my closed lids the swirling specks of starlings, gathering to roost.

*

'Penny for them?' David had his by now familiar foolish grin on. I looked at him, trying to see past the smile to what I knew lay underneath.

'What are you doing here?' I no longer had the energy to be polite. People turned to look at me again, disapproval in every line.

'You know, I could point out that I am a birder' – the word sounded all wrong somehow in his mouth – 'and that this is a bird, and I'm perfectly entitled to be here watching it. But actually, as you know, I'm here mainly because I thought I might see you.'

I wanted to put my face in my hands, to rub the whole situation away. 'Please leave me alone.'

'Manda,' he said, and he caught my elbow. 'Don't you see? I just want to make you happy.'

It was too much. I jerked out my arm from his grasp. I hated to be held like that, detained, arrested. Too many memories there. I pulled out my arm too hard, too fast, uncaring in my panic, the violence of the movement spooking the bird. A great sigh went up from the crowd as the hoopoe lifted up and flew, beating west, vanishing over the trees. Then every eye seemed to turn from the space where it had been, and lighted on us, on me, accusingly.

I turned round to David, still rubbing my elbow, feeling the ghost of his grip like a print on my skin. But there was no one behind me; he had gone, slipped out through the crowd and vanished as swiftly as the bird.

Jenny caught up with me at the bottom of the hill.

'What was that about?' she asked.

I shrugged.

'I guess he's just not your type,' she said, smiling a little, raising her eyebrows, trying to lighten the mood.

I didn't answer but I slowed my pace, letting her keep up beside me without breaking into a jog. My heart rate was returning to normal. I realized I was still rubbing the spot on my elbow where his hand had been and I stopped that, putting my hands into my pockets instead.

'Sorry,' I said finally. It was something I seemed to be saying a lot these days.

'Cup of tea?' she said. 'You look like you need one.' We stood by her car for a moment and I got the impression she was waiting for something, an explanation, an answer, something I couldn't give. All I could offer her was a weak joke, pretending normality.

'At least we saw the bird, before I scared it off,' I said. 'And you know what? I don't think Gareth's seen it yet.' And we laughed and the moment was past.

Jenny's house was empty, for once.

'Alan and the kids still out, looks like,' she said, pushing open the door into the hallway. 'Will said he might drop round later, pick up an old scope of Alan's for his trip.' I'd never seen their house so quiet or still. We settled in the kitchen among a slew of half-finished school projects and abandoned toys. Jenny made tea, chattering through the sound of the kettle boiling and then the dishwasher rumbling into life. I could barely hear what she was saying, but it didn't matter. She was talking as she always did, just filling the silence, hopping from subject to subject.

I watched her as she moved around the kitchen, beginning to clear up the mess, happy to be still, half listening, half not, drifting along with my thoughts.

Gareth had sometimes pressed me with questions, seeking some version of my past that might make some sense of my behaviour. Why I could not stand hospitals and clinics, police stations, waiting rooms of any kind. Why my own father was dead to me, my mother not spoken of, my sister seeming to need to keep me close, tracking me down, checking I was OK. His childhood seemed like some sunny dream to me, out birdwatching with Tom in the woods and heaths of Surrey, something from a book. I found it hard to frame my own in a way that would make sense to him, or to me for that matter. The few bits and snippets that I'd inadvertently dropped seemed to shock him, and I backed off, not wanting to drive him away. His parents were alive, well, stolid in their neat brick house, and talked of dogs and roses and the prospects for the weather. Sitting in their cheerful sitting room, surrounded by pictures of Gareth as a baby, Gareth as a boy, with Tom, with his dog, with his parents, even with me, my own memories seemed somehow improbable, unmentionable in this cosy world. I gave them the bowdlerized version, stories from my early childhood, when I thought we had been happy. I told them what they wanted to hear, about safari trips and coral beaches, taking a dhow to Zanzibar and watching my parents wander hand-in-hand through its crowded ancient streets while Zannah and I trailed behind, hand-in-hand too, worried we might have been forgotten.

The rest I left unspoken, and his parents didn't ask.

Only Gareth persisted, coming upon me late at night when sleep had proved elusive, sitting in their dark conservatory, warding off the rush of memories my half-stories to them had triggered. He'd tuck my chilled feet into the warm space between his arm and his chest and try to talk about my past, about the things I wouldn't tell him. And I'd sit mute and unyielding, wishing I could tell him everything, but not knowing how to begin. We would sit like that as the minutes passed, and the silence stretched out between us, my feet icy against his skin, never seeming to grow any warmer. Then he would sigh and disentangle himself, pull me up and lead me back up the stairs to bed. One night, one visit, he stopped coming down. I sat on through the small hours anyway, not sure if I was waiting for him to find me or not, not certain if I even cared.

With the tea made, Jenny sat down at last, handing me my mug, taking her own and clasping it, head on one side.

'Are you OK?' she asked finally, when a long minute had passed on the kitchen clock and I had not spoken. I revolved some answers in my head, but it didn't matter, she filled up the silence with her own answers. 'Gareth's leaving must have hit you harder than I thought. Tough after so many years.' She paused to let me answer, then when I didn't, continued on without me. 'But, you know, there's other fish in the sea, Manda. Gareth and you, well, maybe it wasn't meant to be.'

She stood up again – Jenny was never one to sit for long – hunting for something in a cupboard, then, distracted, starting to fold a pile of laundry that stood in a basket on the counter.

'I should be going,' I said. It was growing dark while we were sitting there, and I still had to walk home.

'Don't go,' she said, but then the phone rang and she went to answer it, chatting to Will as easily as she had chatted to me, switching her tone from concern to animation without skipping a beat. I looked around and saw I didn't belong here, wouldn't be missed. This was Gareth's world. I put down my untouched tea, relinquished its warmth, and slipped out quietly through the front door while she was still on the phone. Jenny meant well but I hadn't the energy any more to pretend, to keep up the front that I was OK.

I had forgotten all about semi-palmated sandpipers, and Eddie, until I got to university. After the death of my mother, and the eight years of misery I had endured at school, I arrived determined to make this a fresh start. But by the first week I already felt my nerve failing, my resolve slipping. The student bar had been intimidating, and the girls in the corridor of my hall of residence seemed no different from the ones who had tormented me at school. So far we'd exchanged only names, subjects, polite smiles, but I worried that whatever it was that clung to me, whatever air of defeat or desperation or madness, would soon be sniffed out and I would spend another three years as an outcast.

Determined to forge some life for myself beyond lectures, I stepped into the echoing hall where the freshers' fair was held. The student societies had laid out their wares and were displaying in front of them. Every stall was a bustle of hope and enticement. I saw a block of girls I recognized – three friends already – tilting their heads and flicking their hair at two older boys who were trying to interest them in rugby. Drama students postured, musical ones sang, there was an inflatable boat swaying precariously above the scuba diving club. The cacophony almost drove me back, but the throng had pushed in behind me and the only way out was forward, through the hall, and out the other side. Sidling past rowers and debaters and Christians, I found a gap in front of a quieter stall and paused, bracing myself for my next move. I didn't even see what club it was, saw only a familiar typeface, leaping out from a row of books laid out for sale on the table. The *Field Guide to East African Mammals*. Unable to resist, I picked it up.

'Bit old, that one,' said a male voice. 'Bought it for my year off, couple of years back. It was out of date even then.'

'The mammals don't change, though, do they?' I said as I flicked through the pages, all of my old friends springing to life. I looked up properly, saw a tall, handsome blond boy smiling at me with blue eyes, and noticed their sign. 'Funny thing for a birdwatching club to sell, though.'

'We're raising funds to build a hide.'

I handed over my fifty pence and turned and looked at the crowd despairingly, trying to see a route out.

'Gareth, you're supposed to ask her to join us.' I noticed beside the blond boy another stockier lad with the anxious brown eyes of a teased dog. He had had a T-shirt printed, I noticed. 'Birds – the feathered kind!' was written on the front. *The feathered kind.* Something in the phrase tugged at my memory.

'She's not interested, Will.' But the blond boy, the one called Gareth, smiled even as he dismissed me. 'Are you now?'

'I might be,' I said, suddenly unwilling to be brushed off so easily. 'What makes you think I'm not interested in birdwatching?' There was something in that smile, those blue eyes and the warmth they gave off that kept me standing there, the book's familiar weight in my hand.

'It's not just about bloody robins,' said a third voice from behind the pair of them. I hadn't seen the figure who sat, his chair tipped backwards nonchalantly against the wall, a half-dismantled tripod in his hands. Through the gap formed by Gareth and Will I could make out only dark cropped hair, a cold gaze. 'Name one interesting bird you've seen, then.'

'Semi-palmated sandpiper.' The words came out unbidden. 'Dorset, 1991.'

The chair legs came down to the floor with a crash. 'Fuck,' he said.

By the time they worked out I was bluffing I was well ensconced in the pub with them. Tom, the tripod dismantler, was seated in the corner, silent for the most part, except when appealed to on some point of identification or birding etiquette. Every so often I'd turn and catch him watching me, his gaze cold, assessing, and I'd look away. I wasn't interested in him. Gareth was seated to my right, with his warm thigh pressed against mine, under the table.

Will was regaling Alan, an older postgraduate student, with the sandpiper story for about the third time. The banter flowed over my head and I sipped at my beer and felt like I'd come home. The girls I knew came past, bored of the rugby players, and greeted me warmly, eyes wandering over to where Gareth sat, barely according the others a flicker of a glance. I nodded at them and turned my attention back to the group: to Will, to Tom's brief intervention, to Alan's shout of appreciative laughter. But above all to Gareth, as he turned his gaze towards me more and more until we seemed almost alone together, lost in each other's presence, our fingers now entwined under the table, both of us smiling and gradually falling silent.

I didn't really know how it had come about, what unspoken words had made this happen. We stepped out of the pub together while it was still almost light, leaving the others behind, and both looked up into the warm October evening. Above our heads the starlings were gathering to roost, to sleep together for warmth and safety in numbers. The air was full of their metallic cries as he turned my face towards his. I could have fallen in love with him then, from that one gesture, as he cupped my face with his warm hands and told me I was beautiful. But it was too late. I was in love with him anyway: had been since I'd sat in the pub with them all, in the circle of faces, included.

I stepped out into the calm of the late-winter suburban dusk. There was no one around on the street. The doors of the houses were tightly shut, but their curtains were open so that each window presented a display, a tableau of happy family life. I wondered when Jenny would notice I was gone, and what she would do. Phone Gareth, I thought bitterly, or Will, or tell Alan, spreading the news. Manda, poor Manda, she's gone a bit strange, always thought she was odd, she's losing it now, the poor dear. And then they'd forget, move on to the next thing, the next bird, the next story, and I would be left in peace.

I looked up at the sky where the last light lingered over the rooftops. The starlings were doing their gathering flight. Just a few tens or dozens, swooping high and then low, seeking the comfort of each other before settling down to their roost. They might find safety in numbers, but not me. I turned up my collar against the raw wind and set off for the long walk home.

FIRECREST

Regulus ignicapillus, family 'Sylviidae'

I sat on a bench near my office, flicking crumbs from my sandwich towards the scrambling sparrows, and tried not to think about the long stretch of the afternoon ahead of me. March, which had roared in on a raw east wind, had now relented and offered its first painful day of spring. A blue sky gleamed behind thin clouds and the sun touched my face with warmth as well as light. Somebody, somewhere, had mown the grass and released the sharp green smell of summer. Everywhere there was a loosening: of jackets, scarves, coats; and of the faces I passed in the streets, no longer pinched against the cold. The birds were feeling it too, had been for longer, their own internal rhythms telling them now was the time to fly, to fight, to breed. Even in this scrap of green space the air was loud with birds. A male chaffinch, with blush-pink chest puffed out, was doing his brisk arpeggio, and above the softer sweeter coloratura of the robin I could hear for the first time this year the repetitions of the chiffchaff's call that signalled its return from Africa. The south-westerly gales had blown in more than the warmth, they had brought the first wave of migrants. It was a time, in short, to be out birding.

Just as I was crumpling up the wrapper from my lunch

my phone rang with its own electronic warble. Tom. I had shaken everybody else off, it seemed, but not him.

'Firecrest in Deal.'

'I know.' I'd seen the email in my inbox already. It had flashed up just as I was leaving for lunch. Tom knew I'd been looking for a firecrest for years; it had become a standing joke among the group. It's not as though it was a particularly rare bird, nor even a particularly elusive one, unless you happen to be me. But every birder's got one bird like that: the one that they haven't seen, that they should have seen, that everyone else has seen. The one that's just flown the minute you get in, the one that was showing beautifully yesterday, the one that was all over the shop, last year, you should have seen it. Probably even Tom.

Deal was both tantalizingly close and impossibly far away. By the weekend the bird would be gone, and it was impossible for me to take time off from work. Our office was piled with boxes of unassembled kit. We were walled in with them, trapped by the constantly ringing phone and the hovering presence of university staff members who had taken to haunting our doorway. Deal was impossible.

'You're going, right? Come down with me.'

'Tom, I can't.' The sun was dimming as the soft breeze blew in clouds. The sparrows fled the shadows they made. Tom didn't respond. 'My car needs servicing.' More silence. 'It's mental at work just now.' He waited. I'd been looking for a firecrest for ten years. I ran out of excuses. Tom let his silence do the talking. I sighed.

'Ah, Tom. Don't you start giving me a hard time.'

*

I walked back to the office with dragging feet. The sun was still warm on my face but the joy had gone out of the day. Tom was right, of course, he always was. It was spring already and I was falling behind. Janet, who operated our help desk, handed me three slips as I walked in. Three more jobs to add to the stack. Setting them aside, I checked my email first. Tom again. The firecrest had moved, according to the latest bulletin, and was now in a supermarket car park on the outskirts of Dover. He'd be going down there anyway whether I joined him or not. I sighed. A supermarket car park was excellent for viewing but a sign that the bird was restless, hunting for territory. It wouldn't stick around in a car park for long. By the weekend, when I was finally free to seek it out, it would be gone. The phone rang, and I picked it up, half concentrating, half thinking about the bird, pulling up a map of its new location on my screen as I answered.

'IT support.'

David's voice broke into my abstraction, startling me. 'I have a problem with my computer.'

I glanced over to where Janet was sitting and watching me closely. She had taken to doing that these past few days as the work piled up around me and I fell further behind. I said through clenched teeth, 'What sort of problem?'

'My emails keep bouncing. My emails to you.' They had filled up my inbox before I could filter them out, arriving faster than I could delete them. 'I'm worried that you may not have received my invitation to dinner this evening.'

I closed my eyes, ignoring Janet, breathing in and counting slowly down as I exhaled. Then I put the phone down, softly and gently, settling it down in its cradle as though that might keep it quiet for the rest of the afternoon. My hands, I noticed with some detachment, were trembling slightly. I returned to my computer, looking down at the slips scattered around my desk, picking up the first one, and trying to concentrate on it, wishing I hadn't been so rattled by the call. My phone rang again and I jumped at the sound, barely able to muster a coherent response to a query from Finance, my eyes fixed on my monitor, functioning on autopilot, taking very little in. Up until now, David had provoked mainly irritation in me, irritation and an underlying current of unease. But he was turning up too often, in too many places. Once or twice I thought I saw his car, just at the bottom of my street, always pulling away when I went to investigate. Other times he was just there, shopping where I shopped, walking where I walked, always around. Each time he kept up his act of baffled friendliness, as though this were some chance encounter, no more than coincidence. But something had shifted in my mind, like a wall giving way under steady strain; a slow and unnoticeable creep suddenly and catastrophically transformed. I could no longer ignore it. I was becoming afraid.

I got rid of the caller from Finance and tried to return to my job. It all seemed so remote. On the screen I could see pictures of the firecrest posted by people who'd been down to see it already. It was hunkered in among the bright orange berries of the trees that seemed only to grow in supermarket car parks, its feathers fluffed defensively into a ball. It looked startled and hunted, ready to flee, unsettled by all the attention. I know how you feel, I thought. The sight of it triggered a hunger. I wanted that bird on my list.

My phone was ringing again. I stared at it but didn't pick it up. Six rings, seven, eight, nine and it went to voicemail. In the respite of silence I tried to focus. I knew I ought to be working but I granted myself one more indulgence before buckling down. With an action that had become too habitual these days, I went in to check the others' lists. Gareth's hadn't changed yet – not since I last checked, an hour ago. Tom had updated his list over lunchtime, as he usually did, using the computer in the forestry office as he didn't have one at home. Owls, he'd added. He must have been out spotlighting for them in the evening. Alan and Jenny were in Norfolk with the kids – their joint list full of avocets and marsh harriers and thousands and thousands of waders still overwintering in the marshes. 'Bittern booming?' Jenny had added at the end. 'Alan *claims* he saw it . . .' I could imagine her writing it, him leaning over her protesting, laughing, but in the end allowing the disbelief to stand.

The phone rang, stopped ringing, paused as though for breath, then rang again. I stared at the screen. The site had been hacked, I knew that. Ever since my list had been tampered with I'd had a sense of someone else in there, someone besides me, leaving a trail of small changes. There was a pattern among them, too subtle to notice unless you were looking for it. Most were merely random, but others recurred. Ruth's list, for instance, lost a few birds overnight whenever she updated it. Someone kept changing Will's password, convincing him he'd forgotten it again, forcing him to ring me up. Wildly improbable birds – albatrosses and condors – showed up on Gareth's list, but only fleetingly, enough to provoke a flurry of interest before they were gone. Only Tom's account seemed immune, Tom's and mine.

When I had first stopped trusting Gareth, I hacked into his email account. It hadn't been hard. Gareth was not a good conspirator; he used the same password for everything. His life was laid out in front of me, open to view, everything he had tried to keep hidden. I read all his emails to Ruth and all hers to him for six weeks before I could make myself stop. The first time I opened one, I felt sick. My hands trembled and I could feel the clammy chill of sweat, my stomach turn over and sink as I clicked on the icon and waited for the text to come up. I should have stopped there, should have walked away, never bridged that hard gap between suspecting and knowing the truth. But once I had started, I couldn't stop. For six weeks, I watched Gareth and knew, knew that I knew and he didn't, enjoying the sense of power I had, little as it was, something snatched out of the wreckage.

Now, staring at the site, looking vainly for clues, I felt that the tables were turned. My world had been invaded, and I didn't know how. Someone was watching what I did, I felt sure, knowing what I had done, adjusting their strategy to stay one step ahead. Somebody had me in their power.

I looked once more through the log files on the server, confirming what I already knew, what I had seen before a hundred times. The latest changes had been made through my account. And they had been made by someone logging in from my PC. I shook my head hard, trying to shake off the thought that I was simply going mad. The only person who could possibly have made those changes was me.

The phone was ringing again, the noise drilling into my thoughts. I picked it up and heard with a sort of dull lack of surprise that it was David.

'Are you avoiding me?' I tried to square the subtle mind behind the hacking with this foolish voice, this open pursuit, apparently so benign. He was still talking, almost pleading, a whining note of entreaty in his voice. 'You're too cruel.'

Sighing, I told him I had nothing to say. I put down the phone and went out for a breather, surprised by the sunlight when I emerged, the warmth of the sunshine still there on my face. I had forgotten about the spring. Soon the clocks would be going forward; a quarter of the year over already and nothing achieved except the dull round of survival. Apart from the hoopoe, and a few migrants that had showed up at the gravel pit over the weekend, I was getting nowhere. During the week I spent the daylight hours buried at work, and the weekends I now spent endlessly walking round the familiar bounds of the gravel pit, unable to tear myself away. I found myself spending hour after hour there, watching the grebes as they danced in their courtship dance, sitting on the raw bare banks at the edge of the water, huddled in an old coat of Gareth's. Each time I put it on I knew I was making a mistake, but I couldn't let go. It was still filled with his presence, still holding his shape, his smell, triggering memories, dragging me back to the past. I seemed to see him everywhere – his walk, his back, the turn of his head, only to look again and see a stranger, or no one at all. Sometimes I wondered if he left his coat with me deliberately, marking his territory, keeping me hanging on. As if he knew that I would wear it, would not be able to resist, and that as long as I did I would never quite be free of the past.

I was filled suddenly with the restless ache of spring, from the thawing of memories I tried to keep frozen. And back in the office, plodding through the next hour, I found I had shaken off all the distractions but one. I forgot about David, about the site, even about Gareth and what he might be doing without me. It was the thought of the year turning, of the precious spring coming and going without me, that preyed on my mind.

At four o'clock I stood up and logged out, reminding Janet I had to leave early. I had another rendezvous, one I couldn't avoid. It was just a short drive from work, something that never failed to surprise me. The events of those days seemed now so remote, so separate from the life I'd managed to forge for myself, that it seemed impossible they could have happened just half-an-hour's drive from my home. Zannah was waiting for me there, and as I pulled up and parked I was struck for a moment by how alike we had grown, somehow, over the years. She had worn black, as she did every year, and her face stood out white against her collar. She seemed drowned by her coat, her hands barely creeping through the cuffs. Only her blue eyes, catching the last of the afternoon sun, seemed to have any colour. She had my walk too, I realized, as we fell into step, the same gait, the same way of raising her shoulders and hunching her neck in the cold.

'You remembered the date,' she said, not quite making it a question.

'I remembered the date.'

Eleven years to the day of my mother's death. It was just such a spring day, too, the kind of day that fills a person with painful hope, too much to bear. And it was hope, in a way, that killed her. My father's hope, taking her out of the nursing home thinking that spring might somehow have changed something. My own hope. And hers, that one of us might have been able to save her. I live with that every day; there's no danger I'd ever forget it. It's Zannah who seems to need to mark the date, make this annual ritual, and I go along. With Zannah, that's usually the easiest route.

We stepped through the graveyard gate into the shade of the yews. Spring had not yet reached here, away from the warmth of the sun, and I envied Zannah her coat. We walked side by side in silence. At the approach to the grave site, I stopped. That was as far as I ever came. That was the compromise we had worked out, Zannah and I, over the years. She walked on without me and I sat down on a nearby bench, not needing to watch, looking away, feeling the chill enter my bones, thinking my own thoughts. I knew she would lay down her flowers, arranging them neatly in the stone vase, clearing the grave. I knew she would lay down flowers for me too, although I have never asked her to, stubborn in her delusion, sticking to her notion of what ought to be done. And I knew she would then stand there in silence, her eyes closed, keeping her thoughts to herself.

As I sat and waited for her, there was a movement in the yew tree nearest me, soft and fast, the quick burr of feathered wings in motion, the thin tseeping call of a familiar bird. The goldcrest is even smaller than its cousin the firecrest; a Fabergé bird wrought in flesh and feathers, with a clockwork presence like a magical toy. Only a few small crucial details tell them apart. This one turned its large dark eyes upon me and seemed to observe me for a second. It betrayed no fear, went on with its business of gleaning infinitely small insects from the yew's branches, its head in constant motion as it cocked it back and forth. Its movements were so fast and sudden that it seemed almost to materialize in each new position, working its way so close to me that it no longer mattered that I had no binoculars with me. I was able to see each individual feather unaided. Its crest, flush with the head, was bright gold against the mossy green, its chest was a pale shade of buff. I waited, unbreathing, watching for it to take off and flee, but it seemed undaunted by my presence. Finally, it came to a rest at the top of the tree, opened its beak and sang a few repeated phrases before flitting off silently into the dusk. It was a perfect sighting.

'What was it?' asked Zannah, behind me. She had come up so silently, stood there so still that it was only her words that alerted me.

'The wrong bird,' I said, turning. She didn't ask me

what I meant, and I didn't try to explain. She had a raw peeled look to her face and I realized she had been crying and I remembered that this too surprised me every year, this grief of hers. I put out a hand to console her, not knowing what else to do, but she had turned before I reached her and if she saw my gesture she gave no sign.

We walked back to our cars without speaking. It struck me that we might look a companionable pair, side by side, keeping our distance, silent in the comfortable way of old friends who know without words what the other is thinking. But I knew that our silence was different. Zannah had long since given up asking me what had happened that day, had given up trying to piece it together to get at the truth, but I knew and she knew her questions remained and the unspoken words seemed to drive out all others. And so we walked without speaking together, until the gate released us to go our separate ways.

An open verdict was returned at the inquest, that convenient fiction. The funeral was sparsely attended, apart from a knot of ghouls at the back who'd come to stare at the closed coffin and speculate about what was in it. We all sat together at the front of the church: myself, Zannah, my father, putting up a united front as the vicar described a woman I didn't recognize, one that he'd never known. It was the last time we would ever all be in one place. As we filed out towards the graveyard my father turned to me, detaining me with a hand on my arm. I saw again the dulled and faded gold of his hair, drifting upwards as the breeze took it. I could see the blue sky reflected in his eyes and the loosening of the skin, softened by the disappearance of the strained worry lines that my mother had given him. He tried to give me a compassionate look, but underneath I saw the questions in his eyes, the nagging undercurrent of doubt.

'Manda, I'm sorry.'

I shook him off and trailed down the steps after him, looking neither to right nor left. However many times he apologized, the words that he'd said couldn't be unsaid, nor could his thoughts be unthought. The congregation formed a phalanx of black coats around the grave. As the vicar intoned the last prayers and my father and Zannah stepped forward to throw the first clods of earth down into the grave, I remained outside the circle. The final hymn rose thinly into the air and I could see the pair of them, father and daughter together, comforting each other. I turned my back and walked on through the gate, into the spring sunlight, and away.

When I got home, I sat in the dark for an hour, turning things over in my head, wondering what was left that mattered any more. The goldcrest came to my mind in all its perfection; the wrong bird. And I realized that the desire for the right one was still there, that that hadn't gone.

And something else too, maybe, if I was honest. Tom had asked me to come and see it, me and not anyone else. And that meant something to me too. It was spring. It was time to move forward, not live in thrall to the past.

The phone number came unbidden to my fingers. He

answered at the first ring, as though he had been waiting for my call.

'Manda,' Tom said.

'Tom,' I said.

'Pick you up at six?'

'You're on.'

SKYLARK

Alauda arvensis, family 'Alaudidae'

Tom, never late, arrived well before dawn the next day. His work Land Rover chugged noisily in the street outside the house and I hurried out before he could sound the horn. As we drove through the sleeping suburban streets I felt lifted by an excitement I hadn't felt for months, maybe years. This was the hour of birding trips, of holiday departures to bizarre locations on bargain flights. On a work day it had an illicit feel. Tom seemed to have caught it too, the fizzing mood of a successful getaway. We roared down an empty motorway, the Land Rover suspension adding a new harmony of squeaks and groans over the bass note of the engine as the needle crept past seventy. I looked at my watch. It was so early, barely time to be thinking about getting up, making the first coffee of the morning, contemplating the grind into work. Instead, I was escaping. I wanted to laugh out loud.

With the outskirts of London safely negotiated, and the rush hour beginning to bite, we switched to the smaller roads and at around seven-thirty Tom pulled over into a lay-by so I could call in sick without having to shout over the noise of the engine. I left a message on the help desk line while Tom climbed out, switched off the mobile and buried it deep in my bag. I got out too and joined Tom, stretching my back.

'What did you tell them?'

'Food poisoning.'

Tom jerked his head at the old caravan that squatted under a faded and frayed St George's cross. 'Fancy making it an odds-on proposition?'

The morning sun was filtering through the trees by now, and, sheltered from the breeze by the boxy side of the Land Rover, it was almost warm enough to sit in comfort while we ate.

'Now I know I'm on holiday,' I said through a mouthful of salty pig fat and white bread and margarine. I was still huddled in my jacket but Tom seemed comfortable just in his jumper, tipping the white plastic chair perilously backwards. I felt conscious suddenly of my unwashed hair prickling under my woollen hat. If the weather warmed up much more I'd have to take it off. I was aware of other things, too: of Tom's square hands wrapped around the fragile cup, of his nearness, of the dark freckles – like moles – that spread across his nose and cheeks. The holiday fizz I was experiencing had an edge to it. I busied myself with maps and routes. For so long Tom had always just simply been there, an adjunct to Gareth, a disapproving look, someone to appeal to. I'd never really taken in his physical presence before, the way he swung back on chairs, the easy way he turned the heavy steering of the Land Rover. He saw me looking and met my gaze briefly until I looked down at the map again.

'Where's the bird now? Still at that big Sainsbury's out-side Dover?' I asked.

'Last I heard.'

'Fantastic. Still, at least we won't be incurring some farmer's wrath. Did you go and see the hoopoe?'

Tom shook his head. 'Not my scene.'

It was true. Tom's list these days was full of the real rarities, the British ones, not the bewildered vagrants blown in on the spring winds.

'I know what you mean,' I said. 'That poor bird just looked doomed. A spectacle in a freak show. Still, it's one more hoopoe than Gareth's got.'

'Oh, Manda.'

I looked sideways at Tom. I wondered if he guessed how much time I was spending watching Gareth's list mounting up. 'I know, it's not about the numbers.' He was looking at his cup now, slowly shredding the polystyrene edge, worrying away at it with his fingers. I looked down at mine, realized I was doing the same thing. 'It's about the birds. It's about getting out there and looking for them, finding them for yourself, identifying them. Enjoying them. Understanding them.'

'You know, Gareth never really got that,' he said. 'He'd always go for the tick.'

'I'm just fiddling about,' I said. 'Wasting time.'

'You're a good birder, when you put your mind to it, Manda. Better than Gareth.' He looked at me, and I had to drop my eyes, ridiculously pleased by the praise, but guilty too, knowing how little I'd been doing. I felt a sudden desire to fill my year with great birds, ones that

Tom would approve of, ones that would earn me his little nod of praise.

'Well, what are we waiting for, then?' I said. 'Let's go get that firecrest.' We flicked the crumbled remains of our cups into the bin and set off.

The car park at the supermarket was suspiciously empty. Tom cranked the window down, accosted the elderly man who was pushing his train of trolleys across the tarmac.

'Seen a bunch of birdwatchers? Looking for a firecrest?'

'Ah, them, mate. Nah, they went. Their little birdie flew. You could try St Margaret's Bay. Get a lot of birds round St Margaret's, you do.'

A younger girl, passing, said, 'The birdwatchers? They all headed to Sandwich. Sandwich Bay, near the golf course.' She gave directions, stood and watched as we drove off. I distinctly saw her lips shape the word 'nutters' and she shook her head and the old man laughed.

At the toll gate outside Sandwich Bay another old man tried his best to put us off.

'It's four pounds to drive in,' he said, as though he expected that to be argument enough.

For Tom it seemed as though it might be. 'What?' he said. 'Four quid?'

'Fine,' I said, reaching over Tom to pass him the money. 'I'll get it.' But the man wasn't finished trying to put us off yet.

'It's a quiet estate, you know. No shops or restaurants.' I wondered what aspect of Tom's battered Land Rover made us look like fun-seeking day trippers. I managed to force the money on him and he gave us directions to the bird observatory, Tom shaking his head and glowering all the while.

In the car park I climbed down and stretched my legs, pulling the strap of my binoculars over my head, ready for action. Tom was doing the same. We squared up to each other, and I felt a momentary shyness.

'So,' I said.

'Well,' Tom said, simultaneously, and we both laughed at the awkwardness. 'Let's do it, then,' and he put his hand out as though to guide me, close but not touching, so close that I could imagine I felt its warmth.

At that moment a familiar shape came sauntering out of the observatory. Bright jacket, bobble hat, and a beaked profile. I realized too late that the only other car there was David's battered brown hatchback. I ducked behind Tom's back but he had seen us already.

'Manda, Tom!' He greeted us like old friends. 'You made it at last. Firecrest has been seen on the golf course, bopping about among the bushes at the far end near the bay. Not since about six a.m., I grant you, but I live in hope. Come on, I'll show you.'

My stomach sank, and I felt a little knot of shame settle there. I cast my mind back hurriedly, checking that I hadn't betrayed in any way to Tom that I had thought this outing was to be something special, something just for the two of us. Of course, Tom had just been looking for birding company; anyone – me, David – would have done. He must have rung round everyone yesterday. It was only that I'd let Gareth's teasing go to my head, had thought I had been singled out. I could feel the red rising up my neck and hung back as David trotted off, confident that we would follow him, over the stile and up the slope towards the golf course.

Tom had hung back to wait for me and reluctantly I shoved my hands in my pockets and set off, striding past him to show as much indifference as I could muster, unwilling to walk beside either of them. Still feeling the prickles of embarrassment, I concentrated on the vegetation on either side of the path, pausing every few seconds as half-glimpsed birds caught my eye with a flicker of movement. They were frustratingly elusive, there but not there, flitting through the thick gorse or calling invisibly from a tree. Two dog walkers soon caught us up: groomed, confident women with ringing voices, well able to call their charges to heel. David had let his banter drop, and Tom, after a few muttered words, relapsed into sullen silence. I was too busy still berating myself for my stupidity to say anything at all. The women chatted briskly as though we weren't there, passing and re-passing us as we made our stop-start progress along the path. Their dogs roamed around us, their noses down and their minds focused on a world of unimaginable smells. The women's conversation was about things that seemed alien to me – local schools, and vets' bills, and au pairs – but at least it served to mask our own awkward silence.

Halfway across the course we were all stopped to let a party of four golfers through. They were prosperous-looking men, well fed and, like the dog-walking women, their voices carried the conviction that they would be obeyed. Having first warned us that they were teeing off, they paused to discuss some pressing matter while we stood and waited. Above them a skylark rode its song flight high into the air, the sound soaring up above the rumblings of their conversation. I tipped my head back and scanned the unbroken blue of the sky. The bird was a tiny speck, so high as to be barely visible among the random dots and floaters in my eye, but its voice was still clearly audible.

'Ah, a skylark,' one of the dog-walking women said to her friend. 'Wonderful.' They were looking upwards, searching for it as it circled. It was still singing, a manic collection of twitters and trills, constantly elaborated as the bird circled.

'There's something so joyful about the song of a skylark,' the second woman said. 'Just sheer joy.'

The sheer joy didn't seem to be communicating itself to Tom. He was muttering beside me as the four golfers still stood at the tee, clubs held loosely in their grasp. I tried to ignore him, absorbing myself in the slow final descent of the lark. Its song was undiminished but the energy had gone out of its flight and it was coming ever downwards as it sang, pulled towards earth like a spent firework. Yet even as it approached the ground, seemingly falling in exhaustion, it disdained to land and flew off. A few hundred yards away I could see it climbing to begin the feat again. With such an extravagant display it should have been monarch of all it surveyed from the top of its climb, but the air around us was full of larks – one at least for every hole on the course – all of them flamboyantly singing to defend their tiny domains.

A sudden shout interrupted my contemplation of the skylarks. Tom was striding across the fairway, ignoring the golfer who had belatedly lined up his tee shot and was now waving his club at his disappearing back.

'What's got into him?' David asked. I shrugged. 'I think he might just be a tiny bit jealous,' he went on. I gave him a look. He winked at me.

'Come on, come on, you might as well all go.' The second golfer was beckoning us impatiently as though it was us who had held them up. The dog walkers tutted. I had to lengthen my stride to catch up with Tom. Small brown birds, pipits, scattered in panic to left and right as he strode on. I felt my binoculars twisting and jumping against my chest. David kept pace easily beside me, and had breath enough to keep burbling.

'It's not like our Tom, is it, ignoring a good pipit.' I didn't like that easy familiar tone to his voice and a pleased smile on his lips as he contemplated first me, and then Tom's retreating back, as though he'd just won me in a raffle.

Abandoning the attempt to catch Tom up, I stopped to check out the pipits, hoping that David would move on and let me recapture some of the pleasure of the morning. Meadow or tree is the question with pipits in this sort of area; a matter of bill size and claw length and more or less weight of streaking on the flanks, and the finer details of their parachuting display flights. One of them had hopped up onto a tuft of grass, close enough that in the dark tunnel of the binoculars it stood out sharp and clear, filling the circle of the lens so that everything around me narrowed down to that one point. Now was the time for the rest of the world to fade into the background, the golfers and the dog walkers, David's smirk and Tom's stiff-necked retreat, my own embarrassment; everything but the bird. But I couldn't concentrate. I could hear David's breathing in my ear, could feel the hunched tension in my shoulders. And in my mind's eye, I could see the way Tom had stalked off, irritation in every step, and knew the day would be ruined. My attention slipped, the bird had dropped back down onto the ground and I found myself staring at an empty tuft of grass.

'Tree,' said David. 'Look at the streaking on the breast.'

'What the fuck do you know?' I asked. The bird shot upwards, startled by the violence of my words. He looked at me almost sadly, then pasted on the silly grin.

'I bow to your superior knowledge,' and, irritatingly, he did bow, sweeping his binoculars in front of him, the other hand behind his back. 'Come on, I want to find that fire-crest before Tom does.'

But Tom seemed to have abandoned the search. He was seated on the shingle bank overlooking the sea when I caught him up. I was expecting something good – an early Sandwich tern would have been nice, for instance – but apart from a couple of young herring gulls there was nothing on the beach, the tide well out, just emptiness in front of us.

'What's up?'

He turned, looked past me, craning his head. 'Who is that guy you're with?' he said.

'I'm not with him. I thought you knew him.'

'I thought *you* knew him.'

'Well, I sort of do. He seems to follow me about like a bad smell. It's not as though I encourage him.'

Tom's mouth twitched slightly, but he sulked on. 'Well, why did you invite him down today then?'

'I didn't.'

'So what's he doing here?'

The sun chose this moment to disappear behind a cloud and it was cold in the wind without its warmth. It was a good question. What was he doing here? I replayed in my mind his lack of surprise at our arrival, the way he'd seemed to be expecting us. If Tom hadn't told him, how had he known? I sat down beside Tom on the shingle, feeling the cold chill of the stones beneath me. David was moving along the seafront, methodically checking bushes. I watched him dwindle into the distance, then turned to face the sea.

Now it was Tom's turn to ask. 'What's up?' He turned to look at me, catching my eyes, frowning in concern.

'I don't like the way he does that. Shows up wherever I go. It's beginning to freak me out. Sorry. Sorry he ruined our day.'

I must have shuddered or something, shivered in the cold, because Tom put his hand out to me, resting it on my shoulder. 'Hey, it's OK,' he said, and almost roughly he pulled me in, enclosing me in a quick fierce hug that was over as soon as I registered it. 'It's OK.' And he pulled away as quickly, standing up, hauling me upright too, so we stood facing each other joined by the warmth of his hands. I couldn't resist a quick glance over my shoulder. David was still peering into bushes, each movement a parody of stealth. Even as I watched, I saw him freeze, then turn and look towards us.

'Oh shit,' I said. 'I think he's found something.' David was waving and pointing into the bush, then started striding towards us. 'What shall we do?'

'Come on,' said Tom, 'let's run for it,' and his smile was as wide as the sea, my hands still caught in his.

We ran, and as we ran I forgot everything except the running, the mad giggling scramble back to the car park. At some point we had dropped hands and just concentrated on running. By the time we reached the car I was still half laughing, half gasping for breath, but I found I was checking over my shoulder again, worried he'd catch us before we were gone.

'Quick, quick, let's get out of here.' I didn't want to be trailed through Kent like an errant-firecrest. Tom pulled out of the car park and we roared off in a trail of half-combusted diesel and exhaust, a clean getaway. Even so, I found myself worrying away at the thought of him chasing us, finding it constantly there at the back of my mind like a loose tooth, something I couldn't leave alone. Tom was still grinning as we shot past the toll-gate man with a cheery toot of the horn.

'Now where?'

'A sandwich in Sandwich?'

'Ah, no, anywhere but Sandwich. I hate places like that.'

'What's wrong with it?' I didn't like to admit that I had found its leaning gabled houses charming.

'Just so fucking perfect. And smug with it. This whole

area. Four pounds to get in . . . "It's a quiet estate, you know. There aren't any McDonald's here for you common scum."' He imitated the guy at the toll booth viciously. I was surprised at his vehemence. 'Golf courses, Labradors, bankers. Makes me sick.'

'OK,' I said carefully. 'Not Sandwich then.'

'It's all right for you, you didn't have to grow up around those sorts of people. People who think they own the place. People who do own the place half the time.'

'No, I just went to school with them.'

'Yeah, I forgot, you're one of the enemy.' But he grinned as he said this, and I grinned back and we shot through Sandwich without stopping, barely even slowing for the narrow streets and sharp bends.

'Is that what pissed you off before, then?' I asked as we rattled out of the town and I could breathe again. 'The county set?'

'Yes. No. Some of it. Anyway, look at this, firecrest in St Margaret's, now.' His phone had beeped with the text while he was driving and he'd wrestled it out of his pocket, squinting at the screen and steering with one hand. I grabbed it, fearful for our safety, and had a look.

'Probably a different one.'

'Probably.'

'Worth a look though.'

'Worth a look.'

We drove on for a while in companionable silence, or as much silence as you can muster in a Land Rover being hurled down country lanes at sixty miles an hour. Up in the skies on either side of us I could still see larks, fighting their battle against gravity, against the imperatives of energy needs and territorial gain, the drive to reproduce even at the cost of survival. People read joy into a lark's song, Shelley's blithe spirits. How could such a springing, extravagant flight be the product of anything else? But the scientists who unweave such mysteries have a more prosaic explanation. Where the poet sees joy, they saw a territorial ritual that evolved in the absence of trees to act as more convenient song posts. In cold hard terms it was no more joyful than a fight outside a pub.

St Margaret's Bay is one of the closest points in England to France, the place where many spring migrants first make landfall, but not the easiest place in the country to see them. The birds are attracted by the steep hanging woods at the bay, the same woods that conceal them once they've landed. We found ourselves bumping down a decaying road and parking among curious cattle in a grassy car park in a clearing above the sea. Here the still air carried sounds for miles. I could hear the ritualized drumming of a woodpecker in the trees below us, and as a small flock of jackdaws erupted from a church tower and flew across the valley, their short metallic calls could be heard even as the birds flew far out of sight. With their passing, silence descended on the wood. It seemed as though the migrants had moved on.

We worked our way down through the trees, looking to see what remained. Usually Tom was a slow and careful birder, rigorous about getting a proper view of something. But this time it was as if he was on fire and he was using fear and speed to flush the birds, identifying them on the wing, pulling me along behind him. We dropped down the slope through a pathless thicket, branches snatching at my hat, birds fleeing before us. At one point Tom caught me by the jaw, turning my head up and round until I could see the whitethroat that I had missed. When I nodded against the pressure of his fingers he dropped his hand abruptly and moved on, wordless, before taking my arm once more, hushing me, and pointing at the skulking shape of a mistle thrush beneath a tangle of dead stems. Both he and the bird were stilled, the bird in fear, the three of us crouching together until the bird calmed and returned to its restless turning of leaves. Then Tom and I watched on, forgotten, feeling no need for words.

By one o'clock, with the lay-by bacon sandwich nothing more than a fond memory, we worked our way back up the hill rather more briskly than we had come down. I could see the sides of the Land Rover gleaming through the trees when I felt Tom's hand once more on my arm. For a moment I thought he'd seen another bird, but he was looking past the Land Rover at another car, a battered brown car. Leaning against it was David, currently looking the wrong way.

'Fuck.'

I didn't know why Tom was getting so worked up about it. 'Fuck, fuck, fuck.' He was drawing me back through the thin cover of the trees, putting the bulk of the Land Rover between him and us. I was annoyed and hungry and in no mood to play games.

'Come on, he's going to see us anyway, he's parked right next to us.'

Tom just motioned at me to keep my voice down. He drew me back further behind a bush, fingers digging into my upper arm.

'Meet me down at the beach. There's a cafe there. I'll get the car.' He spoke in an undertone. David, oblivious, continued to look the other way. I wanted to argue, but Tom's mood all day had been as fragile as spring sunlight and I didn't want to provoke another outburst, or another sulk. He was strung taut now as he studied David scanning the woods idly with his binoculars. I stepped back and watched as Tom moved round the back of the Land Rover and into the thicker undergrowth behind David's back. Even knowing where he was going, I found him hard to pick out once he'd gone a few yards, he moved with such silence through the dense bushes. And even suspecting what he was up to, I did a double take when the first perfectly rendered cuckoo call carried across the car park clearing. David started, and turned towards it, and I shook my head and started off down the hill.

I sat at one of the cafe tables and looked slowly through the tabloid that an earlier customer had left wedged under the sauce bottles. My coffee cooled before me. The paper was full of horror and disaster. I couldn't remember when I'd last read one, last paid attention to the world beyond my own. I was absorbed, looked up only when the sun was blocked out by a looming figure, felt a familiar hand on my shoulder.

'Tom.'

He was grinning, although it was hard to see his face with the sun behind him. He sat down abruptly, his smile still wolfish and pleased with himself. 'You were completely oblivious there.'

'You shook him off then?'

'I think so.' He threw a couple of small metallic objects onto the table. I could see black streaks on his fingers, a small accumulation of grime under one short nail. 'Tyre valves.' He laughed.

We headed back to the car and drove back against the gathering traffic in silence. Only the Land Rover, complaining through the gears, was doing any talking and I let the racket of the engine be my excuse, after a few shouted remarks, for lapsing into quietness. I was still turning over the question of how David had known where I was going, uneasy about it.

I'd tried raising it again with Tom but he didn't want to know. 'Don't you think it's a bit odd, though, him being there?' I'd asked as Tom had sat down at the cafe and started fiddling with the sauce bottles, eager to be off. He was restless, wound up, not listening, the whole table shuddering with the vibration of his foot against the table leg.

'Well, he's stuck now.'

'Yes, but how did he know to come here?'

'Manda, come on, I've managed to move the Land Rover. Let's go home.' He resumed jigging the table with his foot, deliberately now, making my cup clatter on the saucer. I grabbed it before it rolled off and broke. But I couldn't let the question go, turned it over and over, feeling

I was missing something, but unsure of what. I'd told nobody but Tom that I was going down to the south coast, not a single soul. The firecrest sightings were public knowledge, but why this bird, this sighting, today, now?

'Let's go,' Tom repeated, standing up. He wasn't looking at me any more and I had a feeling I'd done something wrong, missed some vital cue. I didn't know the rules of this game. I didn't know how to play it, what to take for granted, what had to be asked, what had to be said. Something had shifted between us, somewhere between the shingle beach at Sandwich and the dark woods at the bay. For a moment we had linked hands and run laughing together and it had felt as though that meant something. But now I didn't know. And Tom didn't take my hand now, didn't laugh, just led the way to the car in silence, his hands thrust into his pockets. I trailed behind him, wondering what I was letting myself in for. I couldn't recapture the happy bubble of expectation with which I'd started the day, but I couldn't quite work out why.

'Penny for them?'

David had said that too. I shook my head. 'Nothing,' ignoring his raised eyebrows and settling into my seat, letting the brisk clatter of the engine fill the silence as the miles rolled out ahead of us. The empty roads and sense of freedom of the morning had gone, replaced by a growing tension as we snarled up in traffic, or roared through brief gaps between the jams. My nose and forehead prickled with early sunburn, the price of a day spent peering upwards, even in an English spring. But the prickling went beyond that. And when I finally, with an effort of will, set the question aside and turned to Tom, he just seemed like another insoluble problem to consider. Instead I let my mind wander over the birds we had seen and must have lapsed into a doze, lulled by the rocking motion of the car. When I woke, it took me a moment to notice that we had stopped, that we had arrived at my house, and that Tom had said something to me that I had missed. He was smiling as he tried again.

'I asked if I could come in for a coffee.'

'Oh . . .' I shut my eyes and tried to visualize the state of the house. Too many late nights at work, and blank days at the weekend, finding it hard to summon the energy to do anything, had taken their toll. And when I opened them again, he was looking away, frowning.

'Sorry, forget it,' he said.

'No, Tom, I was just . . .' The words sounded feeble the minute I uttered them. 'Of course you can come in.'

'It really was just coffee, you know,' he said. 'It's been a long day.'

'I know that, yes, please, come in, Tom.' But the moment had obviously passed, and he was turning the ignition.

'Forget it,' he said, and when I protested some more. 'I said, forget it. It was just coffee, OK?'

I climbed out of the car, scrambling to get my stuff, putting my head back in through the open window. 'Tom . . .'

'Forget it. I said, forget it. Forget I spoke, OK? Just forget it.' He lifted his hands off the wheel in frustration, seemed to check himself, and placed them back down again, turning to look at me, his face blank. 'Go on, go in.'

'Thank you,' I said. 'It was a great day.' But he was

shaking his head, looking away from me, preparing to pull away. I had to step back or be choked by exhaust fumes. I waved, but he just gunned the engine, roaring up the street, and I let my hand drop back down by my side in defeat. 'It was a great day,' I said quietly to myself. It was just that I had let myself ruin it. My binoculars hung heavy on my neck as I trudged up the path, glaring at Mrs Next Door who was peering at me through her sitting-room curtains. I pulled off the itching woollen hat, freed at last, as I scratched my scalp, two-handed, letting my hair stand up on end where it would. As I fished for my front door keys I pulled out instead the two little tyre valves, darkly gleaming.

But that wasn't to be the only gift I got, I found. The next morning a dunnock's body lay broken on my front doorstep. A cat's offering, maybe, although I had no cat. The breeze blew through its soft brown and grey feathers. I picked it up and found I couldn't throw it away, couldn't cast it off among the tea bags and rotting food in the rubbish bin. The eye had barely dulled and it stared up at me accusingly, a dark circle. As I shifted it in my fingers the head swung down, the neck broken, its beak a slack gape. It weighed nothing in my hand as I brought it in and laid it down gently on the kitchen table. It was only as I left the house a second time and felt the ghosts of its feathers against my palms that I felt my skin crawl with a sudden dread. All day I found myself absently wiping my fingers against my legs, and when the screen blanked and I let my mind run free for a moment I could see only the swing of that limp and broken head as it dangled from my hand.

TAWNY OWL

Strix aluco, family 'Strigidae'

That was the night I first started hearing the owl. The call came floating in on the cool night air as I sat upstairs in the spare room, working on my computer. I had gone to bed at eleven but only to lie awake, my mind still churning with half-formed worries. I was haunted by the thought of the dead dunnock and finally I gave up all hope of sleep and went downstairs to look at it again. The bird lay on the kitchen table where I had left it, substantially unchanged, still beautiful even in death. Close up it was possible to see all the subtle colours in its feathers, the browns and the greys. The feet were curled, clenching nothing, the legs retracted under the wings. I picked it up and gently spread out one wing, realizing just how little there was of it, mostly air and feathers. I set it down again, resolving to bury it in the morning.

'It was a cat,' I said to myself out loud, but the words sounded thin to me, and as insubstantial as the bird itself. I'd never been able to despatch an injured bird with a swift twist of the neck, however distressed it was. Their scrabbling panic infected me and when I'd found a cat-caught sparrow in the garden, its wing torn and dragging, I'd had to ask Gareth to deal with it. He and Tom had spent their teenage years netting and ringing birds for surveys and he knew how to handle them. He picked the bird up and enclosed it in his hands so it calmed and didn't struggle but seemed to sit and wait for its fate, resigned and trusting. Then with one sharp movement it was done, the bird gone, the body whisked away. The cat had taken a visible toll then, but this bird seemed superficially unscathed, only the now-dulled eyes and the gruesome flop of the broken neck marring its perfection. Whatever had killed it had been swift and sure and unhesitating; the bird alive and perfect one moment, gone the next.

The thought did nothing to calm my fears. Heading back upstairs, I realized I was still too keyed up to sleep. Instead, I went to the computer and, opening the spare-bedroom window a little to let the night air in, started hardening the security on the website. This I could do. Changing passwords, changing settings, increasing the logging levels and setting up scripts to alert me to intrusions – all things that I could do as surely as Gareth could handle a struggling bird. An hour flowed past like water and when the owl call came, eerie and strange amid the diminishing rumble of traffic, I was just finishing up, my equilibrium restored, tired with the pleasant weariness of a job well done. As I stretched out my back and neck, the owl hooted again, closer. It was definitely a tawny. They are the ones that sound the way owls are supposed to, a haunting noise like something from another world. I leaned forward towards the window and listened again. It seemed to be coming from the area of the gravel pit. That made sense. There were trees there to form a roost, plenty of long rough grass for mice and voles. Leaving the computer to shut itself down, I hurried downstairs and back into the dark kitchen. The moon was up, competing with the reflected glow of the street lights, and the owl would be able to see everything as clear as day. Flying on silent wings, what it couldn't see it would hear, and still itself remain invisible. But the fact that it was calling told me it had other things on its mind, other owls, and that meant I had a chance of approaching close enough to get a light on it and have a look.

I left the back door on the snib and grabbed my spot-light, pulling on Gareth's jacket over my pyjamas and shoving my feet into my shoes without stopping to tie the laces. The owl was still calling from the open ground around the gravel pit. I made my way down the deserted street and into the relative darkness of the trees. Beyond them the moon had won out over the street lights and it lit up the rough grass. The surface of the water shimmered silver in the breeze. I scanned quickly through the trees but could make out nothing that could be the compact rounded body of a tawny owl.

In the dim and unfamiliar light the world seemed different, the trees looming much larger. The traffic had all but gone and I could hear only the continuous whisper of the wind through the fresh spring leaves of the trees. Then that too died down and the world went quiet. A burst of noise – a car door slamming, voices raised in exclamation, dropped keys, curses, laughter – came as a series of retorts, and then was gone. In the trees there was a brief rearrange-ment of the roosting birds – pigeons and rooks calling sleepily, then crashing through the leaves with a clapping of wings. My eyes, adjusting to the gloom, could see the whirl of bats over the water, their cries silent to my ears.

When the owl called again, I stood stock still to listen, turning my head through the sound, willing my ears to tell me the direction of the call. I peered into a different tree, the light of the spot burning through the moonlight. Nothing. I snapped it off. Owls can pinpoint a noise as soft as a scuffling mouse blindfolded. Not me. I felt the human limitation of my senses. A passing dog had spotted me and growled softly, peering into the shadows where I stood until it was tugged on by its oblivious owner, impatient to be home. I was cold, suddenly tired, beginning to feel conspicuous standing out in the middle of a suburb in an old waxed jacket and untied shoes. Slowly I worked my way around the pit, seeing only sleeping birds, hearing only the occasional car on the motorway through the trees, its lights sweeping through the branches and throwing everything around me into sharp relief. My spotlight had started to fade by the time I decided to give up. I hadn't heard the owl calling for a while and I was beginning to worry that someone would call out the police. As I trudged back, stumbling a little on the uneven path, I felt a bone-deep weariness and a chill, my bed suddenly seeming like a longed-for haven.

I slipped in through the back garden. The first thing I heard was a soft staccato bumping, wood against wood, then a loose rustling, a shifting of paper. The back door was open slightly, banging against the jamb in the renewed breeze. Inside, papers had blown around the kitchen – opened post and stacks of stuff brought back from work,

dumped on the counter for later consideration and then forgotten. I looked around, unsure of what among the chaos
was due to me, and what could be signs of an intruder.
Plates and dishes were still piled in the sink where I had
left them, my bag and coat were still lying where they'd
been dropped. A trail of kicked-off shoes marked out
my usual path from the front door to the fridge. An
unfolded map of Berkshire covered half the table next to
the remains of my meal. Nothing obviously disturbed. I
should clean up, I thought wearily; tidy, sort, read, clean,
throw things away. It all seemed so pointless. Crossing into
the dark sitting room, I checked that the red eye of the
television standby light still glowed reassuringly above
the flashing green 12:00 on the video. My mobile charger
winked yellow. No sign of any intrusion there. Moving up
through the familiar spaces of the house I checked for my
computer, the printer, scope and spare binoculars. Everything fine. I sat on the edge of the bed and reasoned with
myself. I'd left the door unlocked, that was all, and the
wind had caught it. Nothing was gone, no sign of any disturbance. It was fine. And I was tired. Every bone in my
body wanted sleep, to sink down into the depths of the bed
and dream of nothing. But something was tugging at the
back of my mind, something missing, something that had
gone. I could feel the tension in my scalp, fighting against
the heavy pull of sleep. Something I had picked up recently,
handled, something I was going to do something with. The
bird. I ran downstairs, snapped on the kitchen light and
blinked in the harsh glare. It had disappeared.

*

I sat up half the night, clinging to the comfort of Gareth's old jacket, wondering what to do next. Even once I had gone to bed I lay awake, unable to stop the endless cycling of my thoughts. Headlights from passing cars scoured the ceiling, illuminating stray bits of the room, shadows jumping out in sharp relief. Zannah would tell me to call the police, I knew, but there was no way I could do that and face their disbelief. I closed my eyes and tried to summon sleep, alternating between tiredness and fear. Each time I started to drift off, I would jolt awake, heart hammering, thinking I heard a sound, some stealthy movement in the quiet house below.

The passing cars got fewer and stopped altogether as the small hours marched on towards morning. I stared into the murky darkness of the bedroom and listened to the quiet. At some point, as dawn began to filter through the curtains, I did sleep, I must have done, for I was back in the police station, reciting my story, with the soft muffled rhythm of the kitchen door banging behind me, trying to make them understand. The bird lay limp and tiny on the table between us, spotlit, the rest of the room full of shadows. Their eyes were full of hard suspicion, their questions harsh and insistent. 'Why did you kill it?' they asked me, over and over, turning aside my denials. 'Why did you kill it? Why did you kill her?'

I woke to the clatter of bin men and broad daylight, long after I should have been up, and got in late for work. The disturbed night had left me keyed up and with a false sense of alertness, light-headed with tiredness. I was still loading up my email when the phone rang, the help-desk line. Janet had disappeared upstairs to make some coffee and the support guys were habitually late starters, rarely rolling in before ten. I could have let the call go to voicemail but I was wearing Janet's patience thin these days, so I grabbed the phone, not concentrating, wondering if Janet would have thought to get me a coffee while she was up.

'Support line, hello.' I tucked the phone under my chin as I simultaneously flicked through the day's crop of junk mail and stretched over to my own computer to see what was in my inbox. I felt an almost reckless sense of clarity.

'Hello?' said a quavery voice down the line. 'Is that IT?' I recognized the voice immediately. One of the older professors, long since officially retired, who haunted his old labs and taught a few graduate students here and there.

I tried to concentrate, focusing on where I was and what I was doing. From somewhere I managed to pull out my work voice, my best help-desk manner. I could see out of the corner of my eye that my email was taking an age to open, usually a sign of trouble as servers splurged out error messages, filling up my inbox.

'I'm sorry, Professor, I didn't catch that last bit.' He had been talking while I had drifted, my mind skittery with lack of sleep.

Janet came back as I was listening to his explanation, carefully balancing two mugs on a tray. I mouthed my thanks at her and dragged her phone onto my desk, still making encouraging noises as I sat in front of my PC. The coffee was instant, black and bitter, scorching my tongue, delivering a kick to the stomach. 'Loading 347 of 2560 messages,' the progress bar said. 'Loading 348 . . .' I didn't mind. I felt invincible.

'. . . and now it's doing the thing where the little hour glass goes up and the little blue boxes get stuck and it says 99 percent completed and it doesn't move.'

I sighed. I knew the problem. He called with the same one every couple of weeks. The only way to sort it out was to go into his computer myself and disentangle it for him.

'Professor Jones, I am going to take over your computer, OK? It will take a couple of minutes.'

I started up Proxy but paused before connecting to his machine. I sat blankly for a moment, watching the clock turn, letting my mind drift. I like to give users a minute or two before connecting, let them clear anything incriminating from their screens. With Proxy I would be able to see and control his whole machine, or any machine on the network. No electronic door was closed to me. The phone was still tucked under my chin and I could hear the professor breathing, but neither of us said anything. My earlier light-headedness was beginning to fade and I could feel the weariness descending. Without conscious thought, I went to my browser and opened the birding website.

I was just about to make the connection to the other PC when I froze, doing a double take as the website finally loaded. Somebody had got into the site again and this time they'd changed the front page. The 'photo of the week' spot, right at the top, had been Jenny's triumphant shot of a bittern crouching in the reeds, almost invisible. A bittern is a tricky thing, perfectly camouflaged, and with the gift of stillness. Even if you know it is there, you can stare for a long time at a reed bed and not see it in the dry shifting patterns of the reeds, forming and re-forming into a hundred different possible shapes. Then the bird can appear like a mirage, perfectly clear where a second before there was nothing but rustling stalks. You can spot it, and then with a soft sight of the wind rearranging the reeds it is gone, leaving you doubting you ever saw it, unable to trust your eyes. The photograph was like that too: the bird was there and then it wasn't, swimming in and out of view like an optical illusion. I'd put it on the front page the previous night, the last thing before I'd gone out to see the owl, and now it was gone. It had been replaced with a photograph of me, sitting at the cafe at St Margaret's Bay, completely oblivious to anything around me. As I took in what I was looking at I could feel my heart start pounding, could feel my whole chest moving with it as it hammered against my ribs. The site had been hacked again and everything I had done to protect it had been in vain.

Behind me I became aware of Janet hovering, wondering when she would get her phone back, frowning at the picture on the page. I minimised it quickly, took a deep breath and forced myself to appear calm. The professor was still waiting patiently for me at the other end of the phone. I took another breath to steady my voice.

'OK, Professor, are you ready? Don't touch the keyboard or the mouse. Things will start moving of their own accord, this is me. OK?'

'Yes, thank you, Ms Brooks.'

His screen replaced mine, a jumble of windows. 'I'm going to close all of these down, OK?' I cleared the windows one by one. 'And now I'm just going to check to see if the database has been corrupted.' I was keeping up a soothing running commentary because the older staff sometimes panic when they see the cursor moving on its own and they try and grab the mouse and fight me for control. And it was calming me, too, just pretending to be calm. My heart rate had returned to normal. I risked a quick glance at Janet. She had lost interest, was checking her own emails.

'That should be fine now, Professor,' I said, hearing his thanks distantly in my ears. I hung up on autopilot, my eyes staring at the screen, seeing but not seeing, the details of the photograph in my mind's eye as though burned onto my retinas. My snatched impression had been of a surveillance-style shot, taken through a long lens or even a telescope. I hadn't been looking at the camera, but downwards, reading a paper, alone at the table as though abandoned, the hillside looming above me. I had no memory of it being taken, none at all.

I realized with a jolt that things on my screen were moving of their own accord, the cursor moving, windows opening and closing. For a moment I watched in horror. And then I realized I hadn't disconnected from the professor's machine, and it was his computer I was looking at through my Proxy session. And suddenly the pattern I had been seeking swum into focus and I could see it clear, the bird standing out from the reeds. I could see what had happened now. I knew how the site had been hacked. And I knew too how David always seemed to know where I was, where I was going, where I would be.

There was a sound at the door and I turned, seeing with no surprise that he was there in the doorway. He had taken up a casual pose, leaning against the door jamb, but the effect was far from casual. His arms were folded as though that was the only way to keep them in one place, one hand clenched over his upper arm, fingers dug in. He was still with the strung stillness of tension. He had lost the high colour that usually flushed his face and he was bone white. When he saw I had seen him, he became if anything more still, all his attention focused upon me. There was no smile now, no greeting.

I closed down the Proxy session, opened up the website. My photograph still there, my face still oblivious, unaware of the threat.

'I suppose that was your work,' I said.

'I haven't the faintest idea what you are talking about.' David's voice was cold and harsh, the usual mock pleading tone he used completely absent.

Janet was pretending to read her email, but she wasn't doing a very good job of it. Her mouse had stalled over the list in her inbox. In a minute she would turn around and stare. In a minute, the rest of the team would come rolling in. I turned to face him.

'Yes you do.'

'You've got something of mine, and I want them back.'

He hadn't moved from the doorway, still holding himself rigid while we spoke. When Janet turned round to have a good look he glared at her hard enough that she turned away suddenly, and started busying herself with the papers on her desk.

'Now *I* don't know what you're talking about.'

'Yes you do.' With a sudden lurch he twisted himself upright and strode forward to my desk. As he reached over to pick up the forgotten tyre valves that I'd left on my desk, I found myself flinching, shrinking away from him and his anger. 'These.'

I said nothing, dropping my head. He leaned towards me, one hand on the back of my chair, one on the desk so that I was trapped. I could feel the rigid tension in his arms transmitted as a tremor through the chair. Unable to stop myself, I looked up, looked right into his glare. He didn't soften. I wanted to close my eyes, to look away, but I couldn't.

'You may not know this, Manda, but you are playing with fire,' he said.

I remained frozen, caught, unable to respond. He brought his face closer to mine, repelling me backwards like a polar magnet, until I could withdraw no further. Then he smiled, and the smile was worse than anything that had gone before, a thin, crazed smile, cracked and meaningless.

'I'm warning you.' And then he was gone, and I was left still frozen, shrunk backwards on my chair, leaning away from the memory of his presence. I breathed out shakily, wanting to laugh it off, unable to find the words. Janet sat almost as stunned as I was, finally lost for words.

'You OK?' she asked at last.

I nodded, not trusting my voice.

'What the hell was that about?'

I shook my head. There was no answer to that question.

I found my voice, finally, switching off my PC and standing up.

'Look, Janet, I'm going home. Tell Don I'm ill. Headache.' It was beginning to be no more than the truth. I barged out past Harry and Mansoor, who were just arriving, and hurried away. As I stumbled down the corridor I could hear their voices, Janet's quick clack of betrayal and then a burst of laughter, cut off by the closing door.

A bittern has one trick, and it does it well. When it thinks it is threatened it freezes, its head and neck thrust up like a reed stalk, its body lost in the tangle of growth. From there it can see the intruder coming, but it won't move. It will stay there, quite still, trusting its disguise, however close you come. They say you can take a bittern that way, if you're swift and decisive, if you can see it in the reeds, and the bird will just sit and wait for you, watching your approach, making no move to escape. I had been still too long, allowing David to get too close. It was time to try another tack. It was time to go on the attack.

I headed for my car but when I got there, I stopped, looking around. The car park was full of cars but deserted of people, the day already well under way. Before I headed home there was something I had to do, something I could only do on the university network. I threaded my way through the cars and dived down a narrow walkway between brutalist concrete blocks, hunting out an empty computer lab. PCs were scattered all around here, always on, usually half knackered and full of stolen music and downloaded games and half-written essays that their owners had forgotten to delete. I found a bank of machines in a side lab occupied only by one lank-haired goth playing a shoot-em-up game with the sound blaring. Finding a PC with a halfway decent keyboard and a working mouse, I tuned out the sound of electronic mayhem and logged in as myself, pulling up a console window and connecting to the web server. All the work I'd done last night had been bypassed with ease by someone who'd taken pleasure in tripping every trap I'd set, prompting the deluge of emails overnight. Someone had had access to enough knowledge, and the new passwords I'd only just set up. I checked the website again, looking at the photograph, checking for other damage, seeing none. Two or three people were logged in already, I could see, making changes, adding information, exchanging comments.

I could see now where and how the intrusion had taken place. Everything had happened from two machines: from my work PC, and my home one. Both of them were connected to the university network almost permanently. I never switched them off. Someone with access to Proxy, someone with a password, could be in there, watching what I did and, when I was asleep, able to access everything I had access to, every machine on the network. Everything I did or looked at would be laid out before them clear as day. Working out where I would be on Wednesday would have been a piece of cake. Breaking into the site would be another. Watching me spend futile hours hardening the security on the server would have been a joke. I smiled a bitter smile.

'Headache better then?'

I turned, realizing only then that the noise of the game had stopped a while ago. The goth had gone, and been replaced by my boss, Don, looking dapper and out of place among the grey furnishings and harsh light of the lab.

'Not really,' I said.

'Can't think this place would help much.'

'No. I would like to go home, I think.'

'Of course.' He cocked his head slightly as though hoping for more. I just nodded. He waited. I didn't get up.

'There's just one thing I need to do here,' I said. 'Then I'm gone. It won't take a second.'

He waited a little longer, realized I was neither going to move nor do what I wanted to do until he left, and then stood up. In the doorway he stopped and looked at me again. 'If there's anything I can help with?'

I shook my head and smiled. He stood there for a while, then, with a helpless little motion of his hands, left. I waited for the door to slam shut and turned back to the keyboard. It really wouldn't take a minute. Then I could go home.

My PC sat mute and unchanged in its usual spot in the spare bedroom, apparently undisturbed. Its screen glowed with a dull light, on standby as always, waiting for the press of a key to wake it up. Beside it the wireless router flashed intermittently, never entirely idle. When I pulled the plug on the computer, it died with a protesting squeak, the room suddenly loud with the silence as its omnipresent background hum disappeared. Booting it up on an emergency

CD I started to format the hard drive, sitting and watching the steady work of the progress bar as it destroyed the files and data and work of a lifetime. Every bird I'd seen, every note I had taken, every photograph and every trip report. I sat there staring at the steady progress, listening to the phone ringing downstairs, wondering at what I'd done.

Will had texted me first, as I walked out of the lab, looking at my phone automatically when it beeped.

'website buggered cant log in pls help will x. PS nice pic but not yr best side!' Jenny had tried calling, then texted too. 'Suppose you know the site is down. A. is suffering withdrawals. Help!' I deleted both messages and switched off the phone. It was the first time Jenny had bothered to contact me for weeks. I'd already removed the email account for the site so any other cries for help would be lost, left to wander around the university server until they were bounced back to their sender.

My PC beeped and flashed up a message. Format complete. It hadn't taken long to wipe itself clean, back to a blank slate. It hadn't taken me long to delete the site either. I had told Don it would only take a second and I was right. Just a few keystrokes removed everything, stripping it clean, gone forever.

My computer's cursor blinked at me hopefully, waiting for me to reinstall its operating system and restore it to useful life. Instead I switched it off again, pulling the plug from the wall. The shelf above it was ranked with CDs – months and years worth of backups. Somewhere in them probably lurked the spyware that had cracked that machine in the first place. How that had got there, I didn't know, but the university network was full of holes, impossible to keep secure, and my PC was almost permanently connected to it. The backups would have to go. Only then would I be safe, free and clear from anything that might be able to track me down. I would drop them into the gravel pit, into the cold dark depths, and watch them sink like silvery fish beyond the reach even of the grebes.

That night was another sleepless one. I spent it sitting at my kitchen window, listening to the call of the tawny owl, no longer tempted to hunt it down. The owl is a specialist hunter, beautifully adapted to the night, not particularly good at anything else. In Europe we have given it a reputation for wisdom and learning that is ill deserved. But in Africa it is a bird of ill omen. Hearing an owl at night, having it land on your house, prefigures a death, usually that of a child. Their silent flight, their calls, the pale wash of their feathers as they materialized out of the dark, made them seem closer to ghosts than birds. Juma could imitate the grunting calls of the eagle owls and sometimes in the evening he would sit on the kitchen steps and, if I pleaded hard enough, call them and sometimes they would answer. We would sit in the velvety dark and wait, the smoke from Juma's cigarette harsh and sharp in the air, one ear tuned for the bird, one for the sound of my father. I wasn't supposed to be out there, out in the servants' quarters, long past my official bedtime.

We heard them often, but we only ever saw one once. It was a night with a slim moon just rising sharp in the clear dry-season sky. It was back in the days when my parents still went out and the house behind us was quiet, Zannah asleep. I was supposed to be in bed. My mother had come to kiss me goodnight, bringing the scent of her perfume into the room, then shutting off the light so she appeared as a faint shimmer of silver in the doorway, caught in the light from the hall. My father called, impatient, worried they would be late, and she vanished without a sound, leaving only her fragrance behind.

I had waited until I heard the car leave, and the gate swing shut, before slipping out and down to the kitchen, bare feet cool on the floor tiles. I sat on the step with my toes curled up while Juma sent forth a deep call, almost like a groan of pain, and we heard it answered, startlingly close, the closest it had ever been. Then we saw it. It was perched up close on the garden wall, and it was no more than a brief paling of the darkness until it turned its orange eyes upon us so they gleamed in the faint light that spilled from the door. It sat still and silent, its attention upon us, transfixing us. I sensed its endless patience. Juma's cigarette burned unheeded. Then with a blink it was gone, the wall empty. Juma crossed himself, then ground out the cigarette harshly on the step.

'Ach, it's a bad bird that one. It will come and take you away,' he hissed as he shooed me out of his kitchen. 'It will steal your soul, and what would the master say then, eh?'

That night I couldn't sleep as I lay in the dark under the ghostly skein of the mosquito net. I heard my parents come back, my mother's laugh, hastily shushed, my father's low rumble. The thought of the owl haunted me, its eyes, its long considering stare. I didn't dare close my eyes for the fear of being taken in my sleep. I crept out of my bedroom once more, seeking the warmth of my parents' bed, willing to pay the cost of their anger. Halfway there, I stopped, hearing a noise coming from down below. My mother's voice, low and caressing, enchanting, sounding a way I had never heard her before.

All of our windows were opened wide to catch the night breezes, and the house was filled with moonlight. I followed the sound of her voice down the stairs, through the wide space of the sitting room, onto the veranda. Her dress seemed to catch all the light.

'Darling,' she said, and I thought she was speaking to me, that it was me she was smiling at with her face soft and open. But then I saw the stretched phone cord, the phone itself tucked under her chin, just as she looked up and saw me too, watching her from the door. My answering smile froze on my face. She fixed me with a glare, her face hardening into anger. She put down the phone with a clatter that made me jump. I felt suddenly cold, very small and defenceless against her. I thought she might slap me or shake me as she advanced, and I could smell the drink now, mixed in with her perfume, sour on her breath. I shrank backwards towards the shelter of the shadows.

She didn't say anything, she didn't have to. Her fingers closed around my arm, encircling it completely. Her eyes were narrowed, shadowed, unreadable. We stood, frozen. Inside I could hear my father moving about, coming down the stairs, calling out for my mother.

'Darling?' he said, and he said it with the same inflection, the same caressing tone that she had used on the phone, but she didn't soften, didn't turn to him, or call out. Instead she stood, stiller than ever, her fingers compelling me not to betray her.

'Darling? Are you out there?'

He stood in the doorway, so close, yet unseeing, and his voice sounded sad now and a little uncertain, as though he knew she was there, as though he knew she was telling him a sort of lie just by saying nothing. I longed to call out to him, but she had me locked in complicity, sharing her guilt, holding my tongue.

I wondered why he stood there, just calling, why he didn't simply step out to where he could see us. Instead he withdrew, and as he did so she sprang back into life, releasing my arm with a little shake, stepping into the sitting room with the phone in her hand.

'I think you should talk to the servants,' she said. 'Someone's been out here, using the phone, look.'

I saw her put her free arm round his waist as she spoke. I saw the relief on his face, as he took the phone out of her hand and put it back on the end table, then clasped both of her hands and drew her near. She kept her face guarded, her eyes down. I slipped in behind her, half hoping he'd see me, but he wasn't paying attention to anything but her.

PART TWO

WREN

Troglodytes troglodytes, family 'Troglodytidae'

I woke uneasily, gradually becoming aware of various things. That my alarm was going off and had been going off for some time. That my groping arm, reaching out for it in order to switch it off, was not finding it, because it wasn't there, because I wasn't in my bed, I was lying, still clothed, on the sofa under a blanket. That I no longer had an alarm clock anyway, and that the one that I had had, Gareth's one, the one that he had taken away with him when he moved in with Essex Girl, was the kind that turned on the radio, rather than making the sort of steady mechanical noise that I was hearing now. That besides, if I did still own an alarm clock, I would not have set it for six-thirty because I no longer had to go to work. Because I no longer had a job.

By this time I was fully awake, sitting up on the sofa in the sitting room half angled in a blanket but still hearing the steady alarm-clock noise which was coming from outside the window, from somewhere in the front garden. I stumbled over to have a look, pulling aside the old tablecloth that was doing duty for a set of curtains. Our front garden had very little in it: a square of paving and the bin, and one small tree, just coming into leaf. Among the tree's branches was a tiny wren, and that was the source of all the noise. Its feathers were fluffed out to their full extent but even so it was still barely larger than a ping-pong ball, and almost as round. Its call was directed at a magpie perching in another branch, head cocked, watching the display with apparent interest. Clearly somewhere the wren had a nest, and the magpie was intent on raiding it. The wren was facing it down armed only with its call, steady and loud, drawing unwelcome attention to the magpie. The magpie itself remained mostly silent apart from an occasional soft rattling chirr as it shifted position on the branch.

It was a standoff. The stakes for the wren were high: its whole family. And the stakes for the magpie were low. Even a whole wren family – eggs or hatched chicks – could not make much more than a mouthful for the bird. But it wasn't investing much in the prospective meal. All it had to do was wait, wait for the wren to be exhausted, to need to feed. The wren continued to pump out sound far out of proportion to its size. The magpie continued to wait. But even as I watched, the wren's calls were beginning to lose their mechanical regularity, beginning to falter, the volume tailing off. The magpie shifted a little closer and the wren checked itself after a second and started again with a clockwork ferocity.

I wondered what was keeping the bird there calling. Its chicks, if they'd even hatched by now, would be naked and blind and helpless, mere begging beaks to the parents that fed them. If the magpie did hold out and raided the nest it was early enough in the season that the brood could be replaced. The parents wouldn't mourn. A sensible strategy would be to cut its losses, move on. Yet still the wren called and called, its whole body quivering with the effort.

I don't know how long I stood there watching. A sweep of cloud shifted to let the sun through, lighting up the magpie, illuminating the brilliance of its feathers, iridescent with blue and green. Nothing else changed. But the wren ran out of defiance. The alarm-clock calls stopped. The wren flicked its wings and was gone. The magpie moved forward, gaining with one buoyant hop the spot the wren had just vacated. This time patience had won the battle.

I turned away, unwilling to witness what happened next, and wandered back to the sofa. I thought about going back to sleep but it was too late. I was awake now, the sun was up and the sofa looked uninviting, crumpled and frowsy. Outside I heard the harsh calls of the magpie, and an answering call from another. My mother used to greet magpies whenever she saw them. I used to think it was just part of her madness till I heard Jenny do it too, under her breath, when she was out walking.

'Oh, you have to do it to turn away the bad luck,' Jenny said, blushing, when I asked her. 'Didn't you know? Pure superstition of course. Absolute nonsense. Don't know why I do it.' But she still did, I noticed, surreptitiously, when she thought I wasn't looking.

'Perhaps that's what I'm doing wrong,' I said, but the sound of my voice out loud just startled me. 'That way madness lies,' I added, trying to make a joke of it, but the jokes were worse and I tried turning on the television instead. The witless morning chatter drove me out of the room, but at least it gave some life to the house. Without it, it felt as though the magpies and I were the last living creatures left in the world.

I had to look at my watch to see what day it was. Thursday. A week ago – it felt like an age – my life had been almost normal, built around work like everyone else's. Now I was cast adrift from all that. I had to think back to see how it had happened, piecing together the events of the days since I had confronted David, and he had disappeared.

Saturday hadn't been too bad. I think that was the first night I'd spent on the sofa. The bedroom had started to seem too full, somehow, haunted by ghosts. And the spare room had the dead lump of the computer, its silence still too loud for comfort. The sofa was a blank, innocent of memories, bought from the previous owners of the house and seeming to sit in the room as neutrally as the carpet. I could sleep there, more or less, and that was all I needed. I'd got up and showered and dressed as normal, packed up scope, binoculars, map and notebook and set off. It was only when I got in the car and sat at the wheel and thought about it that I realized what I was doing. I wasn't looking for birds, not today. I was looking for David. I needed to have things out with him, properly, get him to leave me alone. Only then could I start to get my life back together, decide what I was going to do.

I started at the garden centre, remembering his Saturday job there. Spring had wrought a transformation and it was packed, crowds wandering through the shrubs displayed outside and packing into the cafe. It was a more

complex place than I had first realized, actually several different shops: the main garden centre, a place selling water
features and aquaria, a pet shop with rabbits and guinea
pigs, a big play area. David was nowhere to be found
though – the staff all too harried by customers to help me,
shaking their heads blankly when I asked. Finally, one of
the girls behind the till paused for a second between customers and said vaguely, 'Didn't there used to be a David
that worked in accounts?'

'That was Michael,' the other girl interjected, leaning
over. 'There was a David worked in pets, but that was ages
ago.' Her customer shifted impatiently, eager to be getting
on with her day.

'Last year?' the first girl asked.

'Nah, before then. Short fat guy?' she asked turning to
me.

'No, I'm looking for someone tall, dark hair, blue eyes.'

'Left you, love, has he?' A manager had appeared, alerted
by the pause in the sound of tills ringing up sales. The girls
hurriedly went back to their work, losing what little interest they had had in the matter.

'Do you have his home address?'

'Sorry, love, personnel records are confidential. If you're
lonely, though, I'll break a rule and give you my own phone
number.'

I didn't dignify him with an answer but left him standing
there rubbing his hands and leering while the two girls
smirked. Doing the round of places I'd seen him at before,
birdwatching sites, didn't help either. I got caught up repeat-
edly in Saturday traffic, making slow progress, arriving each

time to find no sign: no brown car, no bright jacket, no irritating grin. Around me people were walking dogs, riding bikes, strolling, enjoying the day. I saw Will from a distance and ducked into a hide to avoid him, not wanting to get into a conversation just yet about what had happened to the website. By dusk I was fretful and exhausted, unwilling to give up the pursuit, unable to think of any better way to find him. I ended up back in the kitchen, wondering what I had in the house to eat, watching the birds take a last evening meal from the feeders.

Sunday was no better. Jenny and Alan's car was in the car park at Burnham Beeches and I saw it too late to avoid them. They waved at me from the queue at the tea stall, Jenny hurrying over to greet me.

'Hey, haven't seen you in ages,' Jenny said, seeming oblivious to the fact that the last time I saw her I had walked out of her house without a word of farewell. 'We've been chasing all morning after some wretched merlin that Alan claims he saw, and I'm absolutely famished.'

She was vague about David, didn't seem to recall who I was talking about. Alan denied all knowledge of him.

'Thought you weren't interested, anyway,' she said, not really paying attention, trying to persuade her youngest to take more than a bite of his sandwich.

'I'm not, but I need to get hold of him.'

'And what did you do to Tom? He's been moping around like a wet blanket. If blankets mope.'

I shook away the thought of Tom moping. Jenny exaggerated these things, said the first words that came into her head. And besides, I had other things to worry about now. I couldn't let myself be distracted by the thought of Tom. I extracted a promise that they'd text me if they saw him.

'I'll ring him into Birdline,' Alan joked. 'Tom or this David bloke. Adult male, breeding plumage . . .'

'Very funny.'

The smell of the food had left me feeling hungry but unsettled. I couldn't stomach a bacon sandwich, the memories it would trigger. Letting myself back into the empty spaces of the house felt like a defeat. The fridge now smelled of something badly off, and contained nothing but rolls of expired film, milk and half a wilting lettuce. The answering machine light flashed. Warily I played the call, expecting silence, or more complaints about the website. Instead it was Gareth. From the moment I heard his slight throat-clearing cough I knew it was him. I stood transfixed by hope, hope against hope, hope immediately dashed by his words.

'. . . just to remind you we need to come to some agreement about selling the house, you can contact us through our lawyers on . . .'

I wiped it off before he'd even finished what he had to say, shaken by the power of the emotion he'd triggered, the sound of his dry recital of facts too unbearable to listen to. Giving up on the hunt for David, I spent the afternoon watching the birds on the feeders, thronging my garden. Some of them would need refilling soon, I noticed. Something else to do. Supper that night was the last of the spaghetti sprinkled with ready-grated Parmesan, dry as dust, that I'd found in a corner of the cupboard. The thought of work loomed over the evening. I fell asleep where I sat with the television still on and woke when the channel switched over to rolling 24-hour news. Distant, repeated disasters saw me through until the morning.

On Monday, I'd meant to go to work as usual. My daily routine – tea, toast, shower, work clothes, car – propelled me as far as the staff car park. It was a drizzly grey morning and my wipers still thumped and squeaked across the windscreen as I sat in the car and tried to summon the energy to go in. I'd have some fence mending to do with Janet and although I hadn't been able to check my work email since I'd wiped my computer, I was pretty certain I'd have a summons from Don to explain properly my disappearance on Friday. And Wednesday, come to that. And the massive backlog of work that had been building up these past few weeks. Around me people were hurrying from their cars to the buildings, heads down, hunched against the rain, looking miserable. Staff mostly – it was too early for the students. I looked around at the wasteland of concrete buildings. Somewhere on the campus I was sure David would be lurking, seeking new avenues to spy on me, thwarted but not defeated. The minute I turned on my work computer I would be vulnerable, open to attack. I closed my eyes, prolonging the moment of security, warm within my car. The engine was still ticking over, almost imperceptible, drowned out by the patter of the rain on the roof. I didn't want to move.

'Manda!' Don's voice snapped me awake. His face

loomed through the side window, looking oddly distorted through the glass.

'Amanda? Are you OK?' A woman I didn't know was mouthing at me through the passenger side window. I pressed the button to let the window down on my side to talk to Don, and felt the blast of cold damp air as some of the rain blew in. I ignored the woman on the other side, hoping she'd go away, but she was persistent, going for the handle of the door, almost quick enough to get to it before I hit the central locking.

'Come on, Manda, we need to talk. Preferably in my office.'

'Here's fine.' Don had a webcam in his office, one of his little experiments that he'd set up a couple of years ago and promptly forgotten about. I found its winking red eye unnerving at the best of times. This wasn't the best of times.

'Can we get in the car, Amanda?' said the woman, her air of sweet reason rather diminished by the need to shout above the noise of the wipers and the rain. 'A bit more private, maybe?'

I considered this one. She had a point there, I had to concede. 'OK. Don in the front though. You can get in the back.' The locks snapped at my command and she clambered in awkwardly, tipping the passenger seat forward. Then Don folded himself into the front, sliding the seat back as though to make himself comfortable for a long drive.

'Well, this is cosy, Amanda.' The woman poked her head through the seats and smiled brightly. I deduced HR. I raised my eyebrows at Don.

'Two days unauthorized absence due to illness isn't exactly a disciplinary matter, Don.'

'Do you think we can turn the wipers off, Amanda?' She kept dropping my name – long since not my name – into her sentences, as though she was showing off the fact that she had memorized it.

'I need to be able to see out,' I said. I was still hoping to catch sight of David. Three warm bodies in the car had begun to fog up the windows and I switched on the fan to keep them clear. HR woman and Don exchanged glances. Don raised his voice a little over the new noise.

'Manda, as well you know, this is not about discipline. You're not in any trouble. I just brought Judy here along to give us some advice. On . . .'

'I'm the staff welfare officer, Amanda,' Judy said brightly.

'I'm Manda,' I said. She smiled and stuck out her hand, reaching round awkwardly over the head rest. I ignored it. 'Not A-manda.'

Don gave her a look that I hoped meant leave the talking to him. Don I was prepared to listen to, not some blow-in from Personnel. We went back a long way, Don and I. We had built up a lot of the current IT infrastructure from scratch. It was only as the needs of the university got bigger, as we'd taken on more people and more projects, that he'd retreated to his big office and his budgets and left the work we'd used to do together behind. I'd stayed on doing what I did best, uninterested in advancement. He had always been an inveterate fiddler, a poker-about, even now opening the glove compartment and rooting around.

He pulled out my spare binoculars, wound down the window, peered through them.

'Pretty nice, these,' he said, scanning the car park. 'Sharp. Lovely and clear. Still watching the old birds, then?'

'Yes.'

'Deleted that whole website, though, didn't you? On Friday.'

I shrugged. 'Isn't that what you wanted me to do?'

'One minute there, the next minute gone. Boom. I had some distressed birdwatcher ring my office, this morning.'

'Sorry.'

'Don't be.' Don had never really gone in for fatherly concern as a boss. It took me a while to recognize than that was what he was trying to project now. 'It took you a long time to build up that site, didn't it?'

'I never did it on work time.'

'Manda, that's not my point.'

I refrained from asking him what his point was. In the confines of the back seat Judy was shifting impatiently, flicking awkwardly through a file. 'You have an excellent attendance record, Manda,' she said, and beamed, like a child delighted at getting my name right. 'Not a single day sick until this last week.'

'Do I get a prize?'

'It means you get some slack cut, Manda. It means we go the extra mile.' Her smile had teeth in it, and so did her voice. 'We think you need help.'

It was Don's turn to shift impatiently now. 'Manda, I know you've had a tough time since – er, since Gareth left.

And up until a few weeks ago, you seemed to be coping. But sometimes there can be a delayed effect . . .'

'You may not have realized how hard you have taken it, Manda . . .'

'. . . not concentrating at work, long hours, lack of sleep . . .'

'. . . classic signs of depression . . .'

'. . . the rest of the team are carrying you, to some extent . . .'

'. . . and with your family history . . .'

'Who told you that?' I turned sharply to look at Judy, whose hand had flown up in front of her mouth. I glared back at him. 'Don?'

'It came up,' he said, and had the grace to look away, embarrassed.

'It came up,' I repeated, feeling the knife twist of betrayal.

I had told him about my mother's death in confidence, a late-night conversation we'd had, years back, when it was just the two of us working alone in the server room. I had found I could tell him what I couldn't tell Gareth, letting off the pressure of unspoken words, trusting to his ultimate indifference. The early hours are a weak time, a time of confessions made not so much to your companion as to the murmur of the machines around you. We had been fixing something – I forget what. Something that had taken the whole evening and into the night. It was almost dawn before we finished and as we sat and waited for a few minutes more to make sure everything, was still working, he had asked me casually about my family, and I had told him, letting the words drop one by one into the humming quiet. I talked to the cursor, to the blank eye of the monitor, and Don had said nothing, even when I had finished. He had never mentioned it again. And when I finally turned to see his face the look he gave me then was that same mixture of sadness and pity with which he was looking at me now.

Judy was blundering on. 'What Donald and I have discussed is giving you a few weeks' leave of absence to get yourself together. Provided – and this is university policy, I'm afraid, so it's not negotiable – you get a note from your doctor and some help. GPs are very good these days with depression.'

Depression. That word. 'Two lousy days off, and you're shovelling me into the nuthatch.'

'Manda, you've been awol for longer than that, mentally if not physically. Just look at yourself. Apart from anything else, you've been sat here in the car park for almost an hour. I have been watching you.'

'Get that note to the central office ay-ess-ay-pee, Manda, and you'll find we're very understanding. Trust me. But we need you to work with us.' Judy was closing up her file now. I could see she wanted to get out of the cramped space in the back of the car, but she'd have to wait for Don to get out for that, and he wasn't finished. The car had grown cold while we had been sitting there. My refuge, my sense of security, blown away in the cold wind.

'Manda, I want you back, back the way you were. I need you back, OK? So do this thing for me, please?'

I held his gaze, wanting to believe him. I took a breath. Maybe I'd let things slide a little. Maybe he was right.

'Manda?'

'OK.'

They both shot out of the car like rabbits, as fast as they could. I watched them cover the distance back to Don's office, never once looking back. Swiftly I put the car into reverse, craning my neck round, eager to get away. Judy's mention of the central office had reminded me of something and I needed to get there before she did.

The admissions section was in another part of the campus. News of my new pariah status hadn't travelled this far and as usual my face was my pass into the back office. One of the admin secretaries obligingly booted up her system and gave me access to the student database.

'We've had a couple of problems with the accounts so I'm just verifying some details,' I said vaguely, and she waved me to her chair, probably worried that I was going to say something technical she wouldn't understand. As she wandered back with a cup of coffee, I chose a couple of accounts at random, scribbling notes on a piece of paper, paging through the student mug shots and home addresses. I knew David's official student account – he'd logged enough calls with us in the past couple of weeks that I had it memorized – and casually called that one up too.

Even the sleepy-eyed secretary noticed as I sat up sharply when the details came up on screen. A round-faced red-haired boy stared into the camera, his face stark and pale in the flash. 'Found the problem?' she asked, peering over my shoulder.

'Yes, the, er, image concordance may be out,' I improvised. 'Are these the right details for David Harrison? Doing Computer Science?'

She shrugged. 'They're all just students to me.'

Another secretary leaned over. 'The name's familiar, though. I think he went on long-term sick, last year it was. Leave of absence. I had to take his name off all the entries. I remember that.'

'Do you think that's the problem?' asked the first secretary. 'Is the system broken then?'

'No, I've sorted it now.' I didn't want her calling the help desk to get it fixed. 'I've re-indexed the widgets and unbaffled the registry. It shouldn't happen again.' They both nodded slowly at this nonsense, mouths open.

'Nervous breakdown, he had,' said the second secretary, stirring her coffee. 'No wonder, doing computing like that.'

Another morning, another car park, another set of rain-stained concrete buildings. Why did all healthcare facilities have to look alike, I wondered. This time I managed to get out of my car and as far as the reception. Arranging an appointment had only taken a couple of days, and I was a few minutes early. I was motioned to sit among the plastic chairs and torn magazines and wait until I was called.

I'd brought nothing of my own to read, and month-old *Sunday Times* magazines didn't appeal so I just waited, scanning the signs on the walls, casting a few glances at the other patients. They all seemed to be the sort of people you'd expect to see in a health centre – a mother with a baby, an old woman, two old men seated side by side ignoring each other. Apart from an annual visit to have my blood pressure taken and to get my prescription for the pill, I hadn't troubled our practice much since signing up with them years ago. And now with Gareth gone, I had had even less reason to visit. I couldn't even remember my GP's name when I rang for the appointment, agreed with a shrug when they told me what it was. Signs on the wall told me not to smoke, to ask for help quitting, to attend the diabetes clinic regularly. Older signs, peeling off the wall, told me I'd be barred if I was abusive. One of the old men started coughing, subsiding in a series of dry heaves that set the other one off hacking quietly in turn. The baby cried, in staccato interrupted bursts as its mother tried to soothe it, jiggling it on her knee. She looked tired, depressed if you will. I felt a fraud, healthy, taking up valuable resources.

I stopped reading the signs, stared at the ceiling, waited, reasoning with myself. I knew – from casual conversations, newspaper stories, snippets of information – that depression these days was treatable, easy. The new drugs actually worked. Doctors handed them out like candy.

'My niece went in for a chest infection,' Janet had said once indignantly over the phone to someone who'd only called to get space allocation on their email account increased, 'came away with Prozac. Doctor seemed to think she was making excuses to see him. Anyway, it worked . . .' There was no stigma, any more. People weren't incarcerated, sectioned, shocked, brought back stumbling and slurring and confused for weeks afterwards. People didn't have to drink to numb the pain, or spend their days staring at walls, or weeping, or kill themselves. I folded my hands under my arms to hold them down, to stop myself fidgeting. People walked into the doctor's and walked out again with a piece of paper. They didn't disappear. They weren't dragged off like my mother was. The drugs worked.

Once, Zannah had tried to stop them taking my mother away. I never did. I would be relieved when the crises broke and they came for her, against her will or not. It meant an acknowledgement that things were wrong, that days spent lying in bed, weeping at nothing and at everything, were not normal, that we could stop pretending things would be OK. It was just that Zannah was better at make-believe than I was. My father had come into the sitting room of one of our short-term rented flats one day – towards the tail end of a dreary Easter break – and sat beside me on the broken-backed sofa where I was watching some old film on television. I would have been thirteen then, Zannah just eleven. I didn't acknowledge him, too sunk in my own misery, my disappointment in another ruined holiday.

'I can't cope, Manda,' he said. 'She's got to go back to the clinic. But she can't bear it.'

'She's not exactly happy here.'

'It frightens her,' he said. 'She loses her memory of what happens, and then that makes it worse.'

I'd looked it up since, in idle moments, on the internet. Treatments for depression. Back then they hadn't much option if the old drugs didn't work, which they often didn't; still used the old voodoo of the ECT, still do for that matter.

But only now as the last resort, surely? If the drugs don't work . . .

My father went over to the phone and paused. 'Am I doing the right thing, Manda?' I think at the time I just shrugged. I wanted to tell him to put her away for good, get out while he still could and take me with him. I didn't want to be asked, to take responsibility for anything. On the television, two men danced, happiness in every line of their bodies.

When Zannah came out of the kitchen and saw the discreet van pull up outside our building she ran and bolted the door. She knew the drill as well as I did. When the doorbell rang she shouted at them to go away.

'She's better. I'm making her a cup of tea.'

Outside there was tolerant laughter. My father put his hand on Zannah's shoulder but she batted him away.

'Come on, love, let us in.'

'She's better. She hates you. Go away.'

'Zannah . . .' Zannah fought my father with all her strength, biting and kicking as he pulled her away. She looked to me for assistance but I ignored her. When he reached to unbolt the door she wrenched herself free from his other hand and launched herself at the knees of the first of the men through the door. Behind them, I could see a nurse, boot-faced, arms folded. I turned back to the television. Zannah didn't give up the struggle, not in the tiny hallway, not across the sitting room, not down the corridor where my mother lay. A dreadful keening started up – Zannah and my mother together – interspersed with the low soothing voices of the men. The nurse waited in the sitting room, still unmoved, between me and the television. I had to lean to see around her to keep sight of the screen. My father went and sat back by the phone, his head in his hands. The keening stopped as though it had been switched off. Neither my father nor the nurse moved. Laughter poured out of the television, then swelling orchestral music. The credits would be rolling soon, the Hollywood happy ending. After a moment the nurse went into the bedroom and re-emerged with my mother leaning on her arm while Zannah trailed behind her, all defiance gone. Even so I noticed the orderlies kept a cautious distance as they took leave of my father, told him to ring in a while when my mother would be 'settled'.

'Quite a girl you've got there,' one of them said, smiling, as he left. Zannah threw herself into my father's arms and he held her close, stroking her hair, not looking at them but at her. When I turned to watch them he held an arm out for me, too, but she turned and glared at me, eyes narrowed. I turned back to the neat certainties of the world on screen, and turned up the volume to drown them both out.

I realized, snapping back to the present, that my name had been called, once or twice. I looked around. The receptionist was looking straight at me. 'Ms Brooks?' she asked. I shook my head. 'Manda Brooks?' She waited a moment or two then spoke to one of the others behind the counter. One of them shrugged. She spoke into the phone, nodded, put it down, addressed the waiting room once more. 'Mrs Johnson? Amy Johnson?' As the mother stood up and gathered her baby's things I stood up too and slipped out into the rain, revelling in the feel of the cold fresh air on my face after the fug of the health centre. Sod HR and their sick note, their policies, their job. I knew what depression was, and this wasn't it. That wasn't the problem. My problems were other people.

The story I had told Don was a simple one, a straightforward, everyday tragedy, the truth as far as it went. But I hadn't told all of it, for how could I? I hadn't the words that could take him there, could make him understand. Just the bald facts were enough. My father had arrived unexpectedly, the day she died, to take us out from school, to take us all on a surprise day out. I don't know why he chose that day particularly, that weekend. Maybe, feeling the days lengthening, spreading his shoulders in the new warmth, he had let the bright hopefulness of spring get to him, get under his skin. He was prone to these little bursts of doomed optimism, especially towards the end. Even though anyone could see my mother was locked in the same struggle with drink and depression that she'd always been, he would let some bright spark of a doctor or some few weeks of mild improvement talk him into finding a hope for the future. It had been a long and unrelenting winter that year. Every time he'd settled her somewhere and made plans to return to Dar alone, to get on with his work and his life, she'd relapse in some way, forcing him back to her. The longer he stayed in England, the worse he seemed to look, grey and drawn, as though the cold and damp were eating him away. I was seventeen, locked into the trajectory of A-levels and university applications, my own freedom finally within reach. I looked at him fading away, still caught in her dead grasp, and wondered why he didn't make his own escape, now, while he had time, before she dragged him under. I had made my own plans, only tentatively shared with him, to take a year off, spending it with him in Dar, maybe helping him out with some of the students. It was a dream I clung to in the idle moments between classes, during the long evenings, while trying to get to sleep at night. I thought we could build a real relationship that way, father and daughter, finally making up for lost time.

This day out must have been a last-minute thing, because he didn't phone ahead, didn't warn us, just turned up one Saturday morning while we were all idling in the day room staring out the window with the blank boredom of a term-time weekend. When I saw the car pull up and my father emerge, I thought for a minute that he was on his own. All I saw was him springing out of the car with new energy, smiling, his jacket hooked loosely over his arm. The thought came to me, unbidden, that he was coming to take us away, and the old childhood longing for rescue flooded back undimmed, catching me unawares, like a jab under the ribs. But it was only a moment, and then I saw her, slumped in the passenger seat, and I realized it was just another one of his fantasy days out, us together as a family, pretending to be happy, pretending to be whole. I wished fiercely for a moment that I could refuse to go along with the whole charade, that I could plead pressure of revision, slam the door in his hopeful face and storm up into the solitude of the dorms and be alone. But he was smiling as he approached the door and though I hated him for it, for his delusions, his blindness in the face of reality, I knew I couldn't be the one to break his spell. She would be doing it herself, soon enough.

I sighed and stood up, grabbing Zannah out of the junior common room, hurrying to forestall the gloating announcement of their arrival. People left me well enough alone these days, mostly just pretending I wasn't there, but I'd heard the stifled muttering as someone mentioned my mother, a suppressed laugh and then a silence as eloquent as a dozen taunts. A few years ago I would have risen to it, would have challenged them, but now I no longer cared. Another few months and I'd be out of the school, free to return to Africa and out of their reach forever.

'Come on,' I said, snatching the door open in my father's face. 'Let's get out of here.' I fidgeted with impatience as he went through the formalities of signing us out. Next door in the common room I could hear a muttered comment, a laughing reply, the words muffled by the door but not the sense. My mother had made it out of the car before, had once got as far as the dorm, drunk and rambling. They still remembered that occasion. I pushed my father backwards through the door, away from the sound of stifled laughter.

'Come on,' I repeated through gritted teeth, dragging him back down the path too while Zannah trailed behind us, buried in her headphones, oblivious to everything. We scrambled into the car and I saw the curtain swinging at the window as we drove away.

'A little sea air,' Dad announced. 'Spring has sprung, after all.'

Zannah sat back and blew her fringe sarcastically out of her eyes. 'Marvellous.'

I caught his eyes glancing at mine in the rear-view mirror, pleading for someone to play along with him, but I was in no mood to. My mother remained slumped in her seat. I could see only the back of her head. Zannah was playing her tape again, withdrawn into her own world. My father chattered on, not letting any of us break his light-hearted mood, doing the talking for all of us. It was as though he thought he could make us all happy single-handedly, erase the past, return us to the family we never were.

We started off in Brighton but that was too much, the bustle and crowds bothering my mother, and she clung to Dad's arm and turned her face to his jacket. Peacehaven was better, quieter, but despite the early promise of the day, the sea mist hadn't lifted here. As we walked along the promenade we seemed to be alone in the world, walking on endlessly with no destination ahead of us, the way we had come disappearing into the mist behind us. The cliffs rose steep above us, white against white, fading out gradually with no visible end. There was an eerie sensation of silence. Even the sea's hollow roar against the pebbles seemed muffled by the fog.

My parents walked on ahead together, saying nothing. Zannah lost herself in her Walkman, disassociated herself from us all by trailing as far behind as she dared. I held the gap in the middle thinking my own thoughts, trivial teenage things: wishing my mother just wasn't there, wasn't clinging to my father in that obvious, feeble way, wasn't ruining my life, all our lives.

We walked too far, as though hypnotized by the strange atmosphere, the sea mist luring us on. We stopped at a set of steps and Dad decided to run back and get the car and meet us in the car park at the top of the cliff.

'Manda, you wait with your mother.' I felt the huge unfairness that I had to be the one to do this, while Zannah got to go smugly with my Dad. She only wanted to claim the front seat, hog the tape deck and inflict her music on us all. My mother slumped theatrically onto a nearby bench. It was only as I joined her that I realized she'd been drinking.

I didn't need this, any of it: the recriminations and the crying, the pleading and cajoling that it would now take to get her up the steps, Dad's silent disapproval at our – my – slowness, the ruined weekend. The tide was high, sucking at the stones as each wave withdrew, throwing its scummy harvest of polystyrene and plastic bottles onto the shore. My mother let two tears slide down through the foundation on her face.

It was the detail of the make-up that did it for me. I had always liked to watch the careful ritual of her morning make-up, its transformative power over her mood. Make-up meant a good day; one when if she cried she did it carefully, head tipped back to keep her mascara from running, dabbing at the corners of her eyes with a handkerchief. She must have sat down that morning believing it would work, that she could keep control. I saw for a second the woman who had sat beside me at her dressing table and painted herself into perfection, smiling at me in the mirror, blowing me a scarlet kiss. I weakened. Instead of telling her to get up and climb up the steps I seated myself alongside her on the bench and allowed her to clutch at my hand, which she stroked as she talked.

She was drunk and she was rambling, but she made herself clear enough. I thought I'd heard it all, her misery, I thought I'd learned to tune it out, but this was different. She sat there and held and stroked my hand in a gentle parody of affection and told me she'd never loved me. Told me he'd never loved me either, had resented me from the moment he'd found out I was not a boy, this baby that had trapped him into a loveless marriage. Told me how she saw him watching, waiting, wishing she were dead so that he could return to Africa and forget we ever existed, any of us.

'You'll not see him for dust,' she said. 'The minute I'm gone.' And I remembered the blank days of waiting in Tanzania, waiting for him to return. 'He'll go back to live with that whore of his,' she said. 'And then he will be happy.' And I saw him in my mind's eye, grey against the grey sky, longing for freedom, choking on his guilt, and knew she was right.

The promenade at Peacehaven is long but it is not long enough. You can walk for miles alongside the sucking, restless sea and never walk the poison out of your head. My mother's voice was always soft and hesitant, and to hear her, against the sea, you have to lean forward close to those painted lips. You have to strain to hear her even in that dead muffled air, because her words drop quietly against the stones. You have to gather each slurred syllable and pick it apart, catching at the sense. You have to listen hard to make it out. And then, eventually, you have to walk away. Because listening will drive you mad.

In that strange atmosphere that day it seemed I walked on for miles alone below the cliffs, the fog receding on before me, closing up behind me. I know I had an aching weariness in my legs as I finally returned. I stood at the base of the cliff stairs and felt a terrible sense of something wrong, and then I was running up them, my heart pounding as though it might pound out of my chest altogether. I remember looking up to see the mist thinning and the faint blue of the sky like a promise above me. And I remember no sound, no sound at all, as though I had been struck deaf. I climbed up the stairs, faster and faster, endlessly upwards, and saw the sky darken briefly above me, and then clear and the spring sun finally break through.

And as she fell, I thought maybe her words could fall with her, tumbling through the air, dropping away from me as I climbed and I wouldn't have to hear them echoing through my head. That it was my fault, all my fault, everything was. That I should never have been born.

When Dad returned with Zannah and the car he found the excited little cluster of people at the top of the cliff and something terrible below, broken on the hard surface of the promenade. When the police led him gently away to the car he looked wildly round for me and found me at the top of the steps, still gasping at the effort of the climb.

Fixing me with a sudden glare he pointed his finger and cried out that it was me.

I shook off the memory, trying to focus, trying to get myself back to the present. I had walked out of the health centre, and out of my job, on Wednesday. Only yesterday. I had gone back to the house and took my seat once more at the kitchen window, watching the birds. Chaffinches and goldfinches and greenfinches. Blackbirds and robins. Sparrows and dunnocks. You knew where you were with birds. You knew what they were. As they flew in, I checked the time, made a note, counted the numbers, watched them go about their lives and felt a measure of calm restored to me. This was what I needed, not drugs. The birds worked out their pecking orders at the feeders. Great tits before blue tits, blue tits before coal tits. Everything giving way to the bullying aggression of the wood pigeons, landing on perches meant for birds a tenth their size. The blackbird seeing off his rival, over and over, playing out the dominance game. I watched it until the light faded and the show was over and then I went back to the sofa and slept once more, the television soothing me to sleep.

The television. That made me stop and think. The television had been off when I woke up, that much I remembered, because I had had to switch it on. I went back into the sitting room and switched it off now, cocking my head to listen. There was a sound in the house, a familiar sound, something I hadn't noticed before because it was so familiar. The computer's almost silent hum. Upstairs in the spare bedroom the screen was lit up, the screensaver on, just the default setting, the Windows logo bouncing endlessly around its notional space. A shake of the mouse woke it up. The operating system was restored, everything back in place, my backup CDs scattered around my desk. And a note, on the screen, in a window of its own.

'Good morning, Manda. You look so sweet asleep, I couldn't bear to wake you. Goodbye, and thanks for everything. X'

As soon as I went to print it, it disappeared with a pop and an electronic blast of laughter that faded into silence. Shaking, I backed away from the machine, unwilling to touch it further. I fled downstairs for the kettle, seeking comfort in the rhythms of the morning, needing to settle my pounding heart. Outside the garden seemed different but it took a moment to place what was wrong. The bird feeders were gone, and it was deserted; every bird had flown.

CUCKOO

Cuculus canorus, family 'Cuculidae'

I roamed the house for the rest of the morning, restless yet trapped, unable to face going out, not sure of what to do next. There seemed to be nothing else to do but wait for something to happen, someone to come. I jumped at every sound and each time the phone rang I froze, waiting for the answering machine to kick in, waiting to hear who it was. Don rang first, asking how I was. Then Zannah. Then Tom, apologizing for leaving so abruptly after dropping me off, asking me hesitantly if I'd call him. During each call I stopped and waited as I listened, straining after every word, then went back to my pacing. Zannah tried again. I stood in the doorway of the spare room, listening to her voice without really hearing it, watching the endless cycling movement of the screensaver on the restored computer, wondering what lurked beneath. I knew I should go and look at it, should try and find out what had been done to it, but the thought of touching it filled me with dread. In the end, I just pulled out the computer's plug at the wall and silenced it with a tiny pop.

The phone rang again. My own voice mocked me with its cheeriness. I snatched up the phone to silence it. Zannah again. As soon as she heard me answer it she launched into a tirade.

'Where the hell have you been? I've been calling here, calling your work, calling your mobile. You don't even answer your email.'

'I've been here. Home.' I had to clear my throat to speak. It had been a while, I realized, since I had talked to anyone. All the unsaid words buzzed in my head. I shook it to clear it, trying to concentrate on what Zannah was saying to me.

'. . . and even your work don't seem to know what's going on,' she concluded. There had been more but I must have tuned it out for I had formed no memory of it. 'What's wrong?'

'Nothing,' I said. 'Well . . .' Was there something wrong? Other people seemed to think so. Zannah's voice was going off again, rising and falling, then pausing, waiting for an answer. 'Look, it's not what you think, it's not me, I'm fine. It's . . .'

I started to tell her. I tried to lay it out, what had been happening. It was hard to get it straight, into a coherent order, keeping all the threads of the story separate and clear. I'd thought too much about it, these last few days, confined to the house alone, waiting for David to return. There was too much to say. And as I spoke I could hear the words I was saying as though they were coming from somebody else and I faltered into silence. It sounded thin and unconvincing, improbable even to me. Bird feeders that appeared and disappeared. A computer that got hacked into and then restored. A student who wasn't a student. A bird that might have been killed by a person or by a cat. Even as I tried to marshal the facts into order they shifted and rearranged themselves, became inherently implausible, evaporated into smoke.

'He was spying on you through your computer?' Zannah asked sharply. 'Look, Manda, I think I should come round. Don't go anywhere.'

'No, don't,' I said, but it was too late. I was left with the dial tone and then silence. She had rung off.

Resuming my pacing helped clear my brain a little. I couldn't let Zannah find me here, not now, not yet, not until I had more concrete evidence, something that would show her I wasn't imagining things, wasn't losing my grip on reality. I knew how she'd take charge, sweeping all before her. I knew I was in no state to resist her. I set aside the heavy chair that had been barricading the front door and stepped out cautiously, looking up and down the street. No sign of Zannah yet, of course. Then I went back in and out through the back door, making sure I'd locked it firmly behind me. I couldn't think in the house, not properly. I needed some way to clear my head, to get it all straight, and then I would be able to persuade her.

I was halfway to the gravel pit before I noticed the change in the weather. It had been warm when I stepped outside at first, unseasonably so for spring, almost oppressive. But I could see now that it was gathering for a storm. Behind the rooftops the sky was purpled dark with cloud but the roofs themselves were gilded by the fragile slanting light of the sun. The wind was picking up, swirling a few loose scraps of litter around the streets. I turned down the track that led to the gravel pit and picked up my pace, reaching for the shelter of the trees. The afternoon light had gone now, replaced by the onrushing sweep of cloud.

The first drops of rain fell fat and hard about me as I sprinted for the hedge-line, head down against the wind. The sky had turned black and it was dark as dusk. I crouched down to wait it out, as I remembered doing as a child caught out in an African storm. I pulled up my collar and turned my back to the wind, curling in on myself, bowing my head to the fury, hugging my knees to my chest, making myself as small a target as possible. The sharp smell of rain on dry earth caught at the back of my throat and overwhelmed me with the memories it summoned up. Then the rain swept in with tropical intensity, followed by a battering onslaught of hail, ripping through the leaves of the trees around me. Branches danced and beat the air in fury, debris whipped past, and I found myself hurtled back by the whirled frenzy of the storm, back into the past. I perceived only dimly the thrashing hedgerow around me, the white froth of flowers and the muted greens of an English spring. Instead, I was back in Dar, watching the rivulets of red mud that ran through the streets and everywhere, the bursting intensity of new life after the dry. And I was thrown back to the edge of the open pit of my father's grave, for we buried him in the middle of just such a storm.

It was so real that it felt like more than a memory. I was there, really there, still sleepless and crumpled from the hastily arranged flight, still jet-lagged and sleep-deprived.

Zannah was there with me too, clutching my hand, and Mrs Iqbal aloof in her grief, solid in her sari, the three of us soaked through to the skin but unwilling to come in from the rain, watching the spades of the gravediggers as they battled to fill the grave against the storm. Zannah had grabbed me as the coffin was lowered. 'You're not walking away from this one,' she hissed, but there was no need, for whatever it was I had walked away from then was being buried in the red earth. My father was at rest at last, at home at last, where he belonged. The service had been drowned out by the drum of rain on the tin-roofed church. Only the singing could cut through, a great choir of voices, raising a banner of harmony against the thundering rush of the rain. Who were they mourning, these people, I wondered, who was this man they had thronged to bury? As we left the funeral hand after hand reached out to us, face after face greeted us, claimed us. Bwana Brooks's daughters.

Zannah had arranged, somehow, for a goat to be roasted in the garden for all the mourners and the rain lifted and the steaming heat of the day resumed. Mrs Iqbal sat in the sitting room of the house and fanned herself with the order of service, lifting her still-heavy, still-black plait off her neck to catch the breeze in a gesture so reminiscent of my mother that I had to turn away. I couldn't face the crowds outside so I drifted upstairs and wandered through the empty rooms. I tried to phone home once more to tell Gareth what had happened but there was no answer but my own voice on the machine. I felt his absence as an ache. He had been too busy to come, and that in itself said everything. Too busy and too distant these days, wrapped up in his work, his own world. I left a brief message down the crackling monsoon lines and stared out of the window at Zannah laughing in the garden with a trail of children behind her, all dressed up in their Sunday best.

On my last evening I sat out on the veranda, watching as the rain came and went. Zannah was busy indoors, making arrangements, contacting old friends. Her voice changed as she talked on the phone, regaining the accent of her childhood. The night shrieked with life around me, the air damp and still and warm. I was getting bitten to death by mosquitoes but I couldn't bear to move, to disturb the weight of memories that had settled around me. This is the last time I'll sit here, I thought to myself. The last time I'll hear these noises, smell the rich smell of the African monsoon. The thought summoned no answering pang. Among the half-remembered night noises I could make out the call of the coucal, mourning for its family. *I have no mother, I have no father, I'm all on my own, own, own.* You and me both, buddy, I thought.

I wasn't even sure if Gareth would meet me at the airport on my return, but he was there and he greeted me with a fierce tenderness, hugging me so hard I was crushed against his chest. He held my face in his hands and stared at me until I looked away.

'I've missed you,' was all he said.

'Me too,' I said, but I was tired and feeling grubby and soiled from the flight, itchy with insect bites, wanting only to get home and bathe and sleep. When I finally sat down on our bed and let the tiredness and the strange loneliness of the past few days overwhelm me, Gareth came and held me while I cried. I felt battered from a fortnight of demands in Africa – the clutching outstretched hands of the children in the marketplace, the curious stares and avid sympathy and Zannah, always Zannah, trying to tug some response from me, some acknowledgement of grief. Gareth's solid arms around me felt like just another demand, something I couldn't fulfil. He was too close, too insistent, kissing my neck, a lover not a comforter, asking, needing. I withdrew and curled up in my own arms, realizing as I turned away what a habitual gesture that had become. He quietly stood up and walked out of the room, shutting the door behind him. I woke to an empty house and stood at the window watching the grey street and longed to take that moment back, but it was too late, too late for us now. You can never go back.

It only lasted that brief moment, while the storm passed over and roared itself out through the trees. Then the illusion was gone and I was back to myself again, back in the familiar surroundings of the gravel pit, beginning to shiver a little as the wind blew through my wet clothes. But the memory had unsettled me, left me shaken by the intensity of the emotion, rocked by it. I crouched for a moment more, eyes tight closed, as though that might bring it back to me. And then as I straightened up and pulled back further under the tree to shelter from the slackening remnants of the rain, I saw Gareth standing there by the water, only a few yards away, as though I had conjured him up.

I stood for a moment, just watching him, waiting for

him to vanish, to morph back into someone else, a stranger, but he didn't. His back was turned, but it was Gareth's back, indisputably. Yet still I didn't move to approach him. I didn't like coincidences, not any more. I thought about turning back, using the shelter of the hedge-line to get away, but it was too late to escape. He was already turning, his shoulders hunched as he brought up the binoculars, and I saw them glint once in the renewed sun as he trained them right on me.

And then he was suddenly waving and approaching me, pulling off his jacket and throwing it over my shoulders so I was surrounded by his familiar smell and the warmth from his body, there too fast for me to react, to do anything but stand there, caught in the onslaught

'You're soaked,' he said, without preamble, as though the past weeks – months, years – of estrangement had never happened. 'Look at you. Look at the state of you.'

And the way he looked at me as he spoke reminded me of the intensity of his gaze when we had first met, the way his eyes had caught mine, they way they had rested on my face, unwilling to leave. His hand reached up and touched my cheek, just lightly, just a brush with fingers that burned against my chilled skin. 'You're frozen.'

'Caught unawares,' I said. His hands caught up mine and enclosed them, chafing them to get them warm. How many times had he done this? They seemed to fit exactly, familiar as an old glove, and when his arms pulled me into a hug and I buried my face in his shoulder, that fitted too, like coming home.

I pulled away sharply, breaking the spell, trying to recover my equilibrium. This was all wrong.

'I thought I'd find you here,' he said. 'You're a hard woman to reach these days.'

'Look, if it's about the house,' I said, and the illusion of resumed intimacy between us suddenly evaporated. Of course, he was just worried about the house, getting rid of it, getting rid of me, getting on with his new life. His jacket felt awkward on me now, heavy and harsh against my wet skin, and I struggled out of it. The rain was passing anyway, the sun shining through the last remnants of the cloud, bringing up a smoke of vapour from the wet grass. Everything around us sparkled, drops of water shivering in the breeze.

'Yeah, the house . . .' he said, but he didn't pursue it, turning instead to look at the water. 'Grebes still there?'

'Oh yes,' I said. 'Still hanging in there.' We set off without a word, as though we had met by arrangement, had planned to do this, to walk together round the edges of the lake. We were close, side by side, but not touching. I had his jacket still, over my arm, he had his hands thrust into his pockets, his head down, watching our feet as they trod the rain-softened path. 'I was thinking the best thing is just to sell it. Put it on the market soon. Then we can split the proceeds, if that's all right by you.'

'Yeah, fine.' He seemed to realize that more was required of him, shook himself a little. 'Yes, good idea, selling in the spring. Better price. But I didn't really come about the house.'

'No?'

We walked on some more in silence again. There had been so many silences between us, so many different kinds, that I had become an expert in them. This was a companionable one. I waited for him to tell me more, letting him take his own time.

'I didn't want you to hear it from anyone else,' he said finally, stopping and looking at me.

'You're getting married,' I said, jumping immediately to the worst news I could think of, to get it over with.

'No,' he said, 'although, well, that will come too, I suppose. No, it's Ruth. She's pregnant.'

I searched for the words I was supposed to say, but I was struck dumb, wrenched by the news as though by a physical force. He was still looking at me but he was abstracted, lost in his own thoughts, speaking slowly as though dragging the words out from some depth. He didn't seem to notice that I had said nothing.

'We're – she's – very pleased. Excited.' We resumed walking for a while. 'I also came down here to think. About things.'

'It's a good place for it,' I managed to say. He nodded, and we fell silent again, walking onwards. Glancing sidelong at him, I could see that he was smiling a little to himself as he went. I had never wanted children, never wanted to inflict myself, my genes, on an innocent baby. It had never occurred to me to ask what Gareth had wanted, and we had never discussed it. Watching him now, I could see that he would be the sort of father who becomes besotted, especially with a daughter – taking her with him on trips, letting her trot along behind him already carrying her own pair of binoculars. I could see them together – Gareth and a tiny female Gareth, with his dark blond hair and dark-ringed blue eyes, bossing him about with a toss of the head. I turned my head away and looked out over the water until the urge to cry had gone.

Halfway round the lake our thoughts were interrupted by a faint call, the buoyant double note of the cuckoo. I don't know which of us heard it first, but we both stopped and turned to look at each other simultaneously, unsure of whether to believe our ears. Then we heard it again, plaintive in its cry, just audible over the sound of the traffic.

'In the trees,' Gareth said. 'There, low down.' I had no binoculars with me but he had his, as ever, ready to hand, and he passed them to me. The bird was perched low in the branches, framed in the green of the spring leaves, his whole chest bobbing with the effort of his call. As we watched all the other birds around us began to set up a racket of alarm, unrelenting, driving him off from his post. When he left, the cries died down into a steady and resentful chucking as the birds settled back to their nests. Gareth and I moved on after him, following the direction he took. We could hear him call again, heard a renewed army rise up to disturb his courtship – the many different mobbing calls of the woods and fields: crows and jays, warblers and thrushes, all united against him. Over and over again he perched, called, and then he was forced on, ever onwards. Silently, we followed his restless, hounded progress, never once hearing the bubbling answering call of the female. We watched him until he gave up, stopped calling, and flew straight off and out, over the motorway, disappearing without a sound.

They would wreak havoc of course, the cuckoo and his mate, if they were left to breed in peace. The birds that drove him onwards were fuelled by an atavistic dread of him and his kind, protecting their own broods, guarding their nests. The cuckoo chick is a creature of pure murderous instinct, levering any other eggs and chicks it finds out of the nest the moment it hatches, driving its adoptive parents ragged with demands for food, even after it has grown to twice their size. I knew all this but still as I watched the lonely cuckoo fly off I felt a pang of pity for him, hounded wherever he went, unable to rest anywhere, condemned to be alone.

I handed Gareth's binoculars back to him, apologizing for hogging them. His fingers brushed mine as he took them and I jumped, jolted by the shock I felt at his touch. I crossed my arms and shivered, trying to mask the movement, and he offered me his jacket again, but I couldn't take it. It would be too much to bear now, the instant sensation of nearness to him that wearing it had given me. Instead we started back, and as we trudged along the path I couldn't resist asking him what he'd come to this spot to think about.

Gareth didn't answer at first. He stopped, and caught my hand to stop me too. Our fingers laced together automatically through force of habit. I met his eyes, his blue eyes, so unchanged, so utterly unchanged.

'Whether I'd made a mistake. Before it's too late.'

I caught my breath. I had dreamed of this happening, had longed for it, exact in all its details, even down to the way his fingers felt, the way his face inclined towards me. He looked at me and I looked at him. It would have been so easy just to succumb. I allowed myself a brief second to dream, and then I shook my head, pulling away, dragging my fingers clear of his. You can't go back. You can never go back. I felt my anger rise at him for even suggesting it, for tantalizing me with the thought.

'It's already too late.' I remembered the little girl I'd conjured up in my head.

'Hey, hey, Dunnock,' he said, and he tried to grab my shoulder as I twisted away. 'Don't say you don't miss me.'

'Don't call me that,' I said, and I couldn't control the rising flush of blood to my cheeks, a hundred unwilling memories summoned up by the words.

He considered my face for a moment, as though he had sensed my hesitation, and then he shrugged, smiled a little rueful smile, and seemed to square his shoulders, as though steeling himself for a battle ahead.

'You're right,' he said. 'It's too late.'

He walked on and I let out a breath I didn't even know I was holding and followed after him. We resumed our walk around the lake, pausing for a moment here and there to look at a bird, to follow the activities of the grebes as they went about their lives.

'Your sister was right about you, you know,' he said as we both stared out at the lake. 'You don't give out second chances. One mistake and you walk away.'

'Zannah?' I asked, furious at the thought of being discussed like that. 'When did you talk to her about me?'

'She didn't tell you?' He smiled a rueful smile. 'I rang her up round Christmas time. To see if she thought you'd have me back. She told me where to get off.'

I had tracked Ruth down once, back when Gareth still thought I didn't know about her. I had only her email address to go on, and her telephone number. But I knew where she worked, and the type of car that she drove. It was simple enough to watch her company car park as people emerged from the office, narrowing down the possibilities. I sat in my car, daring to use the binoculars only sparingly until I was sure I had her. She was blonde, of course, flashily dressed, a pointed little face with widely spaced eyes, her mobile phone clutched to her ear. I wished I could lip read, and then as she giggled and blushed, was glad that I couldn't. I called Gareth's mobile and went straight to voicemail. As she ended the call, I tried Gareth again and this time I got through.

'I know who you've just spoken to,' I said as he answered, and I wondered if it was guilt I could hear in his voice, or just indifference. 'I'm watching her now.' I ended the call and sat running the engine, letting it idle in neutral, watching her juggle her phone and her bag and a folder, looking for her keys. She was barely a hundred yards away. Whatever resolve I'd had, whatever I'd planned to do, ebbed away. I drove off in silence, before she had noticed I was there.

Zannah was right, of course; she always was. Our relationship was dead, had broken beyond repair long before Christmas, long before he left. And I'd known it from the moment I'd seen her, laughing in the sunlight, as though she belonged to him. It had just taken me until now to work it out.

'Are you going to be OK?' Gareth asked as we reached the road where he'd parked his car. 'You don't, frankly, look OK.'

I paused, toying with telling him everything, what had gone on these last few weeks in his absence. But he was caught in the slanting afternoon light, lit up by it as though it shone for him alone, his face tinged with the warmth of the sun. This was the way I always thought of him, a creature bright as day. I didn't belong in his world, not now, not the way I felt, not ever. The gap between us was as wide as it had ever been. I had been a fool to think it could ever be bridged.

He swung his keys restlessly in his hands and I could see he was anxious to be off now, his mind already turning homewards.

'I'm fine,' I said, feeling anyway that it was almost true. Simply talking, having someone there, thinking about practical things, had been a relief. I'd been so bound up in my fears, I realized, I'd let them feed off each other, strengthening as they grew. For the first time in weeks I began to feel there might be a way out of this, that I would be able to rebuild a life for myself. He paused for a moment and I waited for him to go, wondering what I would do when he'd gone. Then, decisively, he strode forward and gathered me up, hugging me hard with an old and easy familiarity, shoving something into my hand.

'Take this,' he said. 'Take it and go, escape, get out of here, have a break. I mean it.' He smiled and then was serious for a moment, his gaze boring into me. 'But do me a favour, Dunnock. Promise me this. Keep away from Tom.'

He was gone before I could react. I looked down at the keys he had thrust into my hand, puzzled at first and then remembering. The van.

The lockup smelt of damp and dead leaves and oil. The garage door was stiff and clanked open with a groan. I had to brace myself and stretch to lift it high enough, shoving it over my head. Inside the van sat disconsolate on its sagging suspension, canted off gently to the left with a rakish air. It didn't look like the subject of anyone's dream. It looked a wreck, hopelessly unroadworthy, fit only for the scrap heap. But the tax disk was valid, I noticed, quite recently renewed, and the tyres were pumped up. And when I turned the key in the ignition it started after a couple of tries and the engine ran sweet and true. I wondered when Gareth had last been down here, how often he came and sat in the fraying front seat, dreaming of freedom.

The back was still half-empty, a wilderness of torn and sagging upholstery, barely fit to be called a camper van at all. I climbed in and sat on a piece of loose foam and looked around in the dim light. It had been Gareth's dream, really, not mine, to escape in the van and make our lives on the road for a while. Something we were going to do, someday, when we had the time, when our schedules allowed it, when we had the money. It was his van, too. He had bought it; he had made it roadworthy. He had even started mapping out a route once, a tour round all the high and wild and lonely places of Britain, the places where the birds are. The route intrigued me, caught my interest in the way the van hadn't, and for a month or two we had seriously thought about it and how we could make it happen. But we had already grown to be strangers to each other by then, and even a month alone on the road together would have driven us mad and we knew it. We had let our lives roll on and overtake us. Gareth found another means to escape. But the van had sat on, waiting, ready, and now it was mine.

I was soon snapped back to reality. Dusk was beginning to fall as I walked towards the house and I stopped as I approached the street before I turned the corner, checking first for familiar cars. There was no sign of one that I recognized, but there was something about the house that made me pause and approach with more caution. I had left the curtains open and the house unlit, and the windows were still dark and empty at the front. But there had been a brief flash of movement, a faint light appearing and disappearing, as though someone had opened and closed a door into a lighted room. I froze, watching, the van keys clutched in the palm of my hand, wondering if I'd imagined it. But the faint light appeared again, brightening, and the hall light came on, and then the one on the stairs. Not a burglar, or else a very confident one. I shivered. Without my coat, I was also without my mobile, my car keys, even my wallet. The lights went off again, and the house went back to darkness.

I think I must have stood there for a while, simply waiting for something to happen. I knew I couldn't go back into the house again, back into what might be an ambush. The house sat and stared back at me, keeping its secrets, no longer a refuge, repellent in its bland familiarity, exuding an air of expectant menace. There were no further signs of movement. Whoever was in there was waiting and patient. I walked back down the street and sat on a wall for a while to think. Then I turned and walked back to the lockup.

This time the van started easily, first try, its lights blazing on with barely a flicker. The fuel gauge needle slid up slowly to a quarter tank – enough to get me to Tom's. I said a silent apology to Gareth as I backed it out of the garage, slammed the creaking door shut and pulled away. I couldn't run to him. I couldn't trust Zannah, not now, couldn't trust her to believe I wasn't suffering delusions. I didn't have anywhere else to go.

It was still not quite dark as I turned off the road and into the forest where Tom lived, but the trees soon saw to that, closing over my head as I drove, cutting off the last light from the sky. My passage lit up each tree, one after the other, so they seemed to jump out at me in sudden brightness, but beyond them there was nothing to see, nothing but the swift passing shadows cast by the beam of the headlights. The road twisted more than I remembered and seemed endless in the darkness, but the cottage appeared just as the van itself was threatening to give out, the engine jumping and juddering on some obstruction. It coughed and died with a hundred yards to go and I killed the lights, getting out to check that there was room for others to pass, and then set off on foot. My eyes searched the gloom, barely able now to make out the surface of the track, or the deeper blackness where the ditch beside it lay. Tom's gate was just a guessed shape in the darkness, and I had to open it by touch, clattering the latch before I found it. Once in the small garden, the kitchen spilled the same cheerful yellow light I remembered from before through wide-open curtains. But Tom wasn't there. The kitchen stood spare and empty, the rest of the house was in darkness. I knocked but got no answer. All around me there was nothing but trees. I stood on his doorstep and let my eyes grow used to the darkness that seemed now absolute. The moon was yet to rise. The forest was hushed and stilled, the night birds not yet up, the rest settling down to roost. I was alone.

I settled down to wait. The step had been in the sun and the warmth seeped in through my thin clothes. The light from the kitchen window spilled out over the garden and would light up any intruder. I felt I had come to rest at last. For days, for weeks, I had been hounded, driven ever onwards as the cuckoo was, never able to settle, harried by fear. But I was safe here, surrounded by the trees, cut off from the world. Nobody knew I was here and nobody could find me. Tom would be back soon. All I had to do was wait.

I woke with him leaning over me, shaking my shoulder, calling my name.

'I've been out looking for you. Your sister rang. She's worried.'

'I know.'

'You came here,' he said.

'I was frightened.'

He bent down so his face was level with mine. It was still dark, but his eyes caught the light a little and I could see the strong bones of his face, outlined by the rising moon. He was smiling, unable to conceal his happiness. He reached a hand up and touched my face as though to verify that I was real.

'You're safe now,' he said. The van keys were hard and sharp against my palm, still clenched in my hand.

PART THREE

SWIFTS

Apus apus, family 'Apodidae'

The first night I slept in the van, I woke at dawn and walked out to catch the first light of the day. The hide was a chill refuge as I sat on the hard bench and watched the mist rise from mirror-calm water. The sky had a pearly sheen of pink that tinged the vapour as it rose. All around me the woods were loud with the challenges and counter-challenges of the summer warblers. It was too early for traffic to be heard, too early for the dog walkers and the sailors and fishermen that used the waters of this reserve. I revelled in the knowledge that I was the only person there, awake and alert in all my senses. Seeing and unseen, crouched in the dark cavern of the hide watching the world wake up. This was how I had hoped it would be.

I sat as long as I could, until the sun was fully up and I had grown numb with cold. A brisk walk around the lake restored my circulation and I returned to the van glad in the knowledge that there was food there and tea; no need to face the drive home or the fruitless hunt for an open cafe. Everything was tucked into its appointed corner, neatly stowed, in the place that Tom had made for it. I took out the gas canister and set up the ring, filled the kettle from the large water container and ate my breakfast as

I waited for the tea to brew. Above me swifts hawked the air for insects, chasing and screaming, faster than thought. I sat on my camping stool among the white frothing flowers of the cow parsley and felt I was the monarch of all I surveyed. It had taken me longer than I'd wanted to get away and it was May, almost summer now. The spring migration was over, and I was playing catch up, chasing the birds north. But none of that mattered to me now. I was on the road, and I was free.

I had Tom to thank for it, this getaway, this transformation. He had taken me in that night, calmed me down, explained that Zannah had let herself into the house to try and find out where I might have got to. He put me up in his spare room without complaint and let me stay there, treating my fears with a gentle scepticism that never quite broke through into words. I slept that night in the narrow spare bed and woke to a green light filtering through the trees, the forest loud with birds. Tom was up already, looking at the van. He had unblocked its fuel line and changed the filters, and when I ventured out to find him, he was looking at the interior with an assessing eye.

He said, 'Last night you were terrified. But yet you want to live alone in this thing, and take it halfway round the country.'

'I need to get away from here. From him.' Easy to be brave now, deep in these enclosing woods, hidden away from the world.

'You can stay here.' We were standing, facing each other. I looked into his face, but he betrayed no emotion. A breeze stirred the trees and stilled the birdsong for a moment so that there was no sound but that of a million leaves, whispering against each other, the sound building and then passing until the woods fell quiet. So easy to stay. So easy to feel safe here. Tom was watching me, waiting for an answer. 'No strings attached.'

I shook my head, closing my ears to the whispering entreaties of the leaves. 'I can't, really. Not now. Not yet. Let me get away and clear my head. Let me think, Tom. After that, who knows. I may even come back.'

I smiled, and my smile was a weak affair, knowing my words made no sense. Tom smiled back, the same flat insincere smile that I had given him.

'Who knows indeed,' he said. And then, as though he had come to a decision, a little jolt passed through him, galvanizing him back to life, and his smile became a real one. 'Well, then, in that case, there's lots to be done.'

First, I had to sell the house. I found an estate agent and set to work clearing it out, carting out my possessions box by box, taking them down to the garden and burning them there, as though that could cleanse the house of its memories. Inch by inch I stripped it down back to the carpets and the bare boards. Hard work brought exhaustion and exhaustion brought sleep, but neither managed to still the fears I felt, for even as I slept I dreamed of being chased, of being watched. I knew David was out there, lurking, biding his time, watching me. In the garden I caught myself constantly checking, looking over my shoulder. Out on the streets I thought sometimes I saw him – rounding a corner and hurrying away before I could look again, a face at a window, a figure in the distance or just something glimpsed and then gone, no more than a flash of movement in my peripheral vision. He had stopped the direct harassment, at least, or there was nothing I could really pin down. He had become more cunning now, perhaps, or else he was frightened.

Tom humoured me and stayed around while he could, helping me carry things out, rescuing books and other oddments from my cleansing fury. The last things to go were the contents of the attic. We spent a long hot Sunday working together in the stuffy air under the roof, shifting boxes. It was getting dark as Tom handed me down the last box, the one crammed into the furthest recesses of the eaves. I blew away the dust as I took it down to the bottom of the garden and started putting the contents onto the fire. Tom followed me down.

'You can't burn that, Manda!'

'Not much use to me now.' The *Field Guide to East African Mammals* curled in the flames. Page after page of plates caught with a blue flicker from the coloured ink, and some rose burning in the breeze, swirling in chaotic spirals upwards on the heated air.

'You'll set fire to half of Berkshire.'

'Not much chance of that.' I raked up the remains of the fire into a white-hot centre and emptied the last contents of the box into the middle. The letters were bound with bands and didn't fly loose as they burned. Instead, they curled inwards on themselves, each layer giving way reluctantly, my father's handwriting darkening first before the thin onion-skin paper caught and crackled.

'What's in those?' Tom asked as I poked at them to make sure the last remnants were destroyed.

'I don't know,' I shrugged. 'I never read them.'

It's hard to convey to someone who wasn't sent away to school as a child the emotional kick of the letter home, of the letter from home. Sunday mornings were letter-writing time at school. Zannah wrote yards, pouring her heart out, her head bent over the paper as her hand flowed endlessly on. Mine were a less fluent affair. I would write the date, and the greeting on the top of the block of airmail paper, and then stop, waiting for the next line. It was my father I was writing to, always, in my mind. And it was he who wrote back mostly, his neat hand filling one or two bare pages of flimsy onion-skin paper. His letters seemed as painfully stilted, as hesitant, as my own, the long hard pauses between the sentences as apparent on the page. As I sat, pen in hand, watching the other girls scribble away, or staring down at my own few inadequate sentences, stretched out to fill the paper, I could imagine him doing the same thing, sitting at the desk in his study, his tea cooling beside him. I wrote little because there seemed to me to be little to say, little that would interest him in the narrow world of the school. And he may have felt the same thing: that after he'd told me of Juma's news, and what Mattie was doing, and how the weather had been, that there was not much left. My mother's news, or non-news, filled the next paragraph, dutifully set out, in more and more detail as I got older and more able to understand. And then the longest pause as the ink dried visibly on the paper while he searched for the next phrase.

I didn't care. Just getting the letter was enough. We'd get a letter each, Zannah and I, and I'd squirrel mine away as soon as it arrived, not wanting to read it among the bustle and rush of a dining-hall breakfast, saving the moment. A letter from home needed peace and quiet, a sunny spot, if possible, somewhere I wouldn't be disturbed. The paper smelled of home. The words took me back there, just for a moment, bridging the gap, holding us briefly together for the minute it took to read it through, read it and reread it, until the words were sucked dry of all meaning.

After the funeral, the letters still came, but I would no longer read them. I would have burned the old letters, eight years of them, bundled in a shoe box and crumbling with age, had Zannah not stopped me. The new ones piled up unopened. They followed me from school to university and onwards, through every move. I don't know why he kept on writing them, what he thought he could say, who he even thought he was writing them to. Outwardly they were unchanged – the same stamps, the same envelopes, the same neat backwards-sloping hand, but yet they were utterly different. I kept them only because I couldn't throw them away.

'Why don't you just read them?' Gareth asked, but I couldn't explain. Just to put my thumb under the flap of the envelope and ease out that paper so evocative of the past was too much, too painful to contemplate. I boxed them up in the attic and did my best to forget they had ever arrived. This last clear-out seemed to be my chance to obliterate them for good.

It was Zannah who brought them. It had started the summer after my A-levels, when she had tracked me down to the flat I'd found to fill the gap before university. I came in from my temping job and found her sitting on the doorstep, drenched by the rain. Zannah was nothing if not manipulative. I let her in reluctantly, hunted down a towel, made tea when her teeth started to chatter. A few months later she turned up in my room at university while I was out. I found her there gossiping away easily with Gareth while they both waited for my return.

'You never said you had a sister,' he complained later. I took the letter from Zannah and put it aside. Gareth had already made her tea and she sat and chattered brightly while I waited for her to go.

Throughout university the visits settled into some kind of a ritual. Zannah always started off by handing me the letter, which I would set to one side. Then she would sit and stay until politeness compelled the offer of a cup of tea. No amount of moves – from halls to student digs to rented flats – could shake her of her determination to track me down. She never told me how she did it, and I never asked. Every move would give me a few weeks or months of respite and then she'd be there, just waiting, the letter in her hand, as though this was the most normal thing in the world. After a while it seemed easier just to give her my forwarding address each time we moved. She seemed to need the fiction that we were a normal family so much more than I did.

It took them less than ten minutes to burn. I threw the box in after them for good measure, and leaned back on the rake and watched the flames falter and die in the rain. Afterwards, Tom and I walked through the house together. Even now it was empty, I couldn't shake off the feeling of dread I got walking from room to room. Such an ordinary house, modern, suburban, identical to the ones on either side of it, but the walls seemed to close in on me. I shut the front door for the last time and hoped I could lock away the feeling forever.

For the rest of the month of April we worked side by side in the cramped confines of the van, fitting it out. Tom was meticulous, did most of the design and planning, while I handed him tools, took measurements, cut wood to order, held things in place while they dried. We built up a rhythm of silent communication as slowly the shambles of plywood and torn foam was replaced with the neat interior of an ocean-going yacht for one. Straps held anything loose in place, and everything else could be folded or tucked away or stowed in any number of ingenious ways. Tom came home from his work in the forest every lunchtime and evening and went straight out to inspect what I'd been doing and correct it.

As the days wore on I began to wonder if Tom were weaving a spell with this van, hemming me in with a coat of wet varnish here, a problem with the paintwork there, finishing and refinishing jobs, refining what was already perfect. It was as though he knew that with each day that passed I felt a greater reluctance to leave the haven of the forest and venture out into the world. It took an effort of will to leave it at all, even for a few hours. Driving out on the simplest errand – an appointment with the solicitor, dropping keys off at the estate agent – filled me with dread. The minute I turned onto the open road and the forest fell away behind me, I felt exposed and vulnerable. In town it was worse. There were too many people around, too many places for someone to hide and watch unobserved. I hurried past mirrored-glass windows feeling the creeping sensation of unseen eyes, watching, waiting. I rushed through my business and fled back to the refuge of the car, counting the moments until I could turn off the road and back into the shelter of the trees, feeling the tension lift from my shoulders, knowing that I had got back safely, and alone. The cottage was my refuge now. The van beside it left me with a vague sense of unease, the reminder that sometime I would have to summon the courage to leave forever.

Once in the cottage, though, I was restless. Tom and I spent the long evenings together in the kitchen after the light had faded and we could no longer work on the van. I couldn't settle to anything. Tom was a brooding, watchful presence. We could work for hours together, at ease with each other in the cramped space of the van, but as soon as we were released into the kitchen, I felt his eyes on me again, felt the growing strain between us. His head turned as I passed and re-passed his usual spot in the chair by the fireplace, his eyes never straying from me. The clock ticked down the hours until it was decently possible to go to bed. We cooked and ate, and occasionally talked about unrelated subjects, a few words exchanged before we lapsed back into silence and that quiet watchful gaze of his sought me out once more.

Every night, after I had gone to bed, I lay there still awake and listening. Every night I heard him come up the stairs and pause outside my door, as though waiting for something, some signal, some invitation. I wondered if he knew I was awake as he stood there, separated from me by no more than a few thin planks of wood, secured by a flimsy latch. I wondered what he was thinking as he stood there in silence. And I wondered what I would do if he ever knocked, or if I ever saw in the dimness of the darkened room the latch lift and the thin crack of light grow wider as the door swung open. I didn't know. He never tried. And in the morning, I never mentioned it.

My world was narrowing, funnelling down, circumscribed by the forest, the van, Tom, Zannah. If Tom still saw Jenny and Alan and Will, he never mentioned it and they seemed remote to me now, part of someone else's life, people from the distant past. Zannah rang, or showed up briefly at the weekends, picking her way along the track in narrow shoes, peering into the forest with suspicion. When my phone burst into life with a text message, I was startled and fumbled for it, surprised it was even on. I was working with Tom, sanding a cupboard door, the air heady with varnish and sawdust. The message said, 'Oi, I warned you.

Not Tom.' His number was still in my address book, unchanged. Gareth. I was annoyed with myself for the start of pleasure I got when I saw his name, and with him for sending it, knowing or guessing what the effect would be.

'It's not what it seems. And how did you know?'

'Little bird told me.' Despite myself, I laughed and shoved the phone back into my pocket, not bothering to respond. Tom looked up curiously.

'Zannah,' I said casually, not sure why I felt the need to lie about it. Tom nodded and returned to his work, but I couldn't dispel the little glow of pleasure or shame the exchange had brought and for the rest of the day I worked with a new will, remembering I had to get away, that I couldn't bury myself here forever.

The next day he texted again while Tom was at work, picking up the conversation where we had left off. I felt a guilty rush of pleasure at the sight of the message, knowing I shouldn't be encouraging him, unable to quite let go.

'So why Tom then?'

'He's fixing the van.'

'You're really going?'

I looked up from the phone and gazed at the sky. I was alone, except for the swifts which had arrived that morning, announcing the last phase of the spring migration. Swifts are the last of the common migrants to arrive in this country after their long journey from their winter feeding grounds in Africa. They filled the air with their shrill screaming cries, their speed incredible as they chased their prey, feeding frantically in the late-spring warmth.

'Yep.' I answered.

'Better hurry. Swifts are here already,' Gareth responded after a pause. I imagined him sitting as I was somewhere in the sunshine, looking up at the birds, smiling to himself as he thumbed in his message. He loved texting, would go back and forth for hours, long after the point where simply picking up the phone and having a conversation would have been cheaper. 'Like passing notes in class,' he'd said and the secrecy appealed to him. I wondered where he was, whether he could even see the same birds I was seeing as they spiralled high up into the sky, almost disappearing, no more than specks against the blue. I wondered also who was with him. I shook that thought away.

'I know.'

'Got them on your list yet?'

I didn't respond immediately. My list was gone, sunk into the bottom of the gravel pit lake on a CD-Rom, along with everything else on the computer. My notebooks had gone up in flame. I would have to start from scratch.

'My list needs a little work,' I admitted.

I looked up again at the swifts, listened to the many sounds of the forest birds. How long since I had been out watching them? Too long, I realized. The phone added a warble of its own. Gareth again.

'Then what are you waiting for?'

That night I was more restless than ever. The kitchen couldn't contain my pacing. I roamed through the whole ground floor while Tom, abandoning his usual spot, hovered in the doorway, still watching. The solicitor had rung.

The house was all but sold, the papers ready to be signed. Her voice had been blandly reassuring, matter of fact, something from another world.

'Just pop in and we can get everything sorted tomorrow,' she said. 'Then we'll transfer your share of the proceeds into your nominated account.' The sum she was talking about seemed ridiculous, even after the mortgage had been cleared. Months of freedom. Years if I were frugal. There was nothing keeping me here, nothing at all. In daylight, leaving seemed possible, sensible even. At night, I wasn't so sure.

Tom finally broke his silence as I stood once more in the kitchen, peering out through the uncurtained window at the glimpsed shape of the van in the dark.

'*Zugenruhe*,' he said.

'I beg your pardon?'

'*Zugenruhe*. Migratory restlessness, it means. In caged birds. Even those reared in captivity for generations. When spring comes, when autumn comes, they start to get restless. Hopping round the cage. The migratory instinct is built in.'

'I know how they feel, then,' I said lightly, forcing myself to sit down at the kitchen table and unroll one of the maps, the one we'd planned my journey on with Tom's usual meticulous care. But even as I did so, I knew that caged birds don't always fly the coop. Even with an open door, even with the great wide beckoning skies in front of them, they don't escape. They come to prefer the gilded cage. They choose safety over freedom.

*

That night I lay awake after Tom had passed and paused and moved on and my mind was with the swifts, asleep on their great swept-back wings, high in the sky above me. We had sat on the steps of the cottage and watched them climb, seeking the lift of the day's thermals, spiralling upwards to gain the height they needed to sleep in safety on the wing. Tighter and tighter they turned, dwindling upwards into the deep dusk blue. These were the birds that never came to rest except to breed, single-mindedly built for flight and flight alone, pared down, stripped to the essentials.

I remembered we had found one once, Gareth and I, grounded in the long grass, its wings useless to it on the alien surface, its feet and legs too small to launch it back into the air where it belonged.

Gareth was reluctant to interfere. 'It's probably injured or weak, or it wouldn't have fallen,' he said as I hovered over it.

'Fine,' I said. 'You wring its neck and put it out of its misery then.'

But I knew he wouldn't have the heart to do that, not to a swift. The bird lay quiet while we discussed its fate, its feathers gleaming a dull charcoal. He picked it up and held it firmly while he looked at it, checking it was OK. It struggled strongly in his hands, no longer calm, both wings working equally. It was fully fledged, an adult, with long powerful wings reaching far back beyond its tail. It made no sound beyond the light scratching of its feet against Gareth's skin. Extending his hands in front of him, he held the bird aloft and loosened his grip so it sat for a moment poised on his palms, just lightly cupped there, suddenly still. Then he swung his arms up further and opened his hands as he dropped them away, launching the swift in a scramble of wings. At first I thought it would fall, drop like a stone to the ground, but it didn't. The great wings unfolded and it began to glide, skimming the grass until the wings beat out a rapid rhythm that lifted it up and away. I tried to follow its path, our one swift among the multitude, but with one twisting manoeuvre it had gone, merged with the flock, indistinguishable from the rest.

The next morning, at breakfast, I told Tom the sale was going through.

'I'm going in to the lawyers today. And then that's it. There's nothing to keep me here.' The airiness in my voice sounded false even to me.

'Nothing?' he asked.

'Tom, I can't stay here forever.'

'Manda, can't you see?'

'See what?' We sat among the breakfast dishes, each with our matching mug and plate, the meal finished. Tom put his tea down and reached for my hand. Blindly I put my own mug down and let our fingers touch.

'I love you, Manda. Can't you see that? I want you to stay forever.'

I couldn't speak. The words sat there between us, like our clumsily joined hands. I looked down at my plate, avoiding his eyes.

'I've always loved you.'

'Have you?' I tried a jokey smile. It didn't work. My

hand felt dead, numb, slightly clammy. I fought the urge to pull it away.

'Ever since I first saw you. Only Gareth got there first.'

'Tom . . .' I didn't know what to say. He disentangled his fingers, patted my unresponsive hand. It still felt numb to me.

'It's all right. I know you don't feel the same way. But as long as you're here I thought I'd have some hope. I thought you might, I don't know, feel safe with me. Come around to it. Stay.'

He waited. I couldn't answer. So easy to stay here, I thought. So easy just to sink down and stay, a traveller falling asleep in the snow. I almost opened my mouth to say that I'd wait, for a little while, just a few weeks. The words rang in my head. But something stopped me from saying them. My hand now looked like someone else's, dead on the kitchen table. I brought it back into my lap. He shrugged.

'Oh well,' he said.

He looked so sad as he stood up and cleared away the dishes. I could feel the remembered touch of his hand as a phantom on my own. His words ought to have touched me, I knew, ought to have triggered something, some answering emotion of my own. I didn't know why I could feel nothing. I didn't know what I should feel. And so I sat on, unmoved and unmoving, while Tom finished tidying and left, and I was alone again. I fingered the phone, hoping for a call from someone, a message from Gareth, something to distract me, to break this strange blank mood I had fallen into, but it remained mute and I knew there were no answers there.

I went outside and looked at the silent van while the swifts screamed indifferently above my head. I sat in the back on the narrow bunk and touched all the polished surfaces, examining it minutely. It was ready, and it was perfect. The door of my cage was open on its hinges. I knew then that I had to go. Tom would trap me here, if I let him. It was time to get away.

I took the van into town, trying it on for size, getting used to the way it handled. For once it was the forest that felt oppressive and close, no longer a place of safety. The trees crowded in on the track and as I burst out of the gloom into the ordinary daylight of the road I felt a weight lift, my senses ease. Swifts, swallows and martins zipped around me, soaring high for invisible insects, stooping low for water and mud for their nests. Even in the town centre they I could see them, high in the gaps between the buildings. The sharp twittering chatter of the swallows filled the air. At the solicitor's desk I set my signature down in the spaces indicated, page after page, my name next to Gareth's, joined together for the last time. The house was gone, shed from me like a load. I was free.

I dropped off the last set of house keys at the agent's and walked back to where I'd parked, jingling the van keys as I went. On impulse, I popped into a stationers and chose a stack of hardbound notebooks. They weren't the proper field notebooks I'd been using before, but they would do, and the blank ruled pages filled me with a little rush of anticipation. I could start from scratch. Each bird in it would be fresh and new and mine. I saw how it could, after all, be made to work. Settling in the van's front seat felt like coming home and even with its awkward steering and sluggish engine, I felt more in control than I had done for weeks. My heart rose with the swifts and I lost all sense of foreboding among the spring-green woods.

The cottage looked neat and trim and cheerful, welcoming now that I'd resolved myself to leave it. I whistled as I gathered up my stack of books and papers and a bag of provisions for the van. I didn't notice the crow until I went to push open the gate and its heavy bulk flapped and banged against it, head swinging down in a familiar slack gape. It was suspended by its feet, wings hanging down, flies already gathering about its eyes, long dead. Its feathers had lost their sheen and hung black and stark, rusty with blood. For a moment I must have stood there, lips still foolishly pursed, arrested in mid whistle, unable to move. My hands uncurled of their own accord, dropping my bag. Then I backed away, unable to turn my eyes from the sight of the bird which moved still, softly, as the gate settled. If I turned I knew I would run and not stop running. Instead I retreated, fumbling for the safety of the van, and sat there staring at the hanging crow in silence.

I don't know how much time passed while I sat there. It might only have been minutes. I sat in an almost trance-like state, watching the crow swing and settle, until my phone dug me out of it. Gareth. A message.

'Lawyer called. House gone. Now what?'

I clutched the handset to me as I got out of the van and braved the gate, inching past the dead bird, gritting my teeth to force myself past it without flinching. Once in the house I stuffed my few clothes into my pack along with my binoculars and scope, rolled up my sleeping bag and tied it shut. Our breakfast dishes still sat where I'd left them by the sink. I thought about leaving a note, but I could think of nothing to say. I squeezed myself back out through the gate and into the van, backing and turning to get myself onto the track again. My heart was hammering with the effort. Only once I had reached the gate did I feel I could thumb in a response, once I was sure it was true.

'I'm on the road.'

That night I slept with only the thin roof of the van between me and the turning stars. Hour after hour through the night I opened my eyes to the unfamiliar darkness of the van and realized where I was, then settled back into my dreams. Every time I shut my eyes I saw spiralling flecks rising endlessly upwards, not swifts, this time, but ash. I saw my father's letters burning one by one and for the first time I wondered what he'd written in them, month after month, year after year until he died. The only words I'd glimpsed of them had been the salutation, letter after letter, endlessly repeated. My dear Manda, My dearest Manda, My dearest daughter. Too late to read them now. I was freed of them now, free from the reach of their reproach. I never had to know now what he had felt, what he had meant, whether I bore the burden of his forgiveness.

*

The next morning, when I had returned from the hide and prepared my solitary breakfast, I felt the pleasure of being alone and undisturbed, beholden to nobody, my where-abouts unknown. My phone sat on the front seat, glowing with a recent message, burring to remind me of a missed call. Gareth and Tom and Zannah, each of them in their own way demanding to know where I was. Let them wait, all of them. I needed none of them. I packed away my things carefully, strapping everything down, making them ready for the road. Then before I could set off I did two more things. I opened the virgin pages of the first notebook and listed the birds, meticulously, in the order I had seen them, ending with the swifts. And then I switched off the phone and buried it, deep in the bottom of the bag.

I settled in the driver's seat, my birding gear beside me loose and ready to hand. The engine started with a slight shudder and I could hear faintly the domesticated rattle of the dishes behind me. I glanced at the map and turned the nose of the van north. I was on my way.

PART FOUR

RED KITE

Milvus milvus, family 'Accipitridae'

I sat on the rock with my back to the rough stone wall and looked out towards the sea. Theoretically I was checking out the raft of eiders that floated just beyond the crashing breakers. But really I was just taking in the endless restless energy of the North Sea as it worked against the ragged edges of the shore, unpicking Britain's fraying coast. The day was fine, with only a light breeze, but some unspent fury from a still-remembered storm drove the sea onwards against the rocks. The eiders bobbed, buoyant as toys, rising and falling with each wave. In among them there could be other birds, something new perhaps, ducking through the surf. In a minute I would look for them, spend the time, make the effort to identify them. In a minute. For now I was content with the company of the sea.

The day before I had crossed the invisible border and I was in Scotland. That felt like an achievement, although nothing really had changed. Something like the same remembered restlessness that drove the sea had propelled me up this far, but now it was beginning to ebb. I was beginning to feel I had nowhere left to run.

*

That first fine springing morning, escaping with the swifts, I thought I had got away. For a week I pottered east, stopping off at every reserve and forest I could find, following up every pager alert for rarities, making up for lost time. The days began to merge together as the birds mounted up, each day distinguished only by the new list in my notebook, dozens of memories tucked away behind the scrawled names. A nuthatch, slaty-blue against the rough bark of a tall pine. The slow and careful moments distinguishing, definitively, between a marsh and a willow tit. A long frustrating day spent chasing hawfinches that always seemed to have just flown until I tracked them down in the bushes around the car park, their feathers bright against the fading light of the day. The further I got from the familiar roads and closed-in views of my home, the freer I felt, the stifling memory of the last few weeks dropping away with the miles. Day after day the skies opened out around me until finally I found myself cresting a low rise and turning along a banked road that dominated the flat drained landscape of East Anglia with the rising sun above me and the fenlands spread out below, black and rich and flat, stretching to merge imperceptibly with the water.

It was another beautiful calm morning with the early mist still burning off, colours brightening with every minute. I pulled over and stopped, got out, stretching my back, and listened. There was no sound save the birds. No other cars, no planes, no trains rattling busily along, just a cacophony of birdsong reasserting itself now that the alien note of my engine had gone. I leaned against the cooling bonnet of the van, absorbing its warmth, and closed my eyes to bring the sound closer. Larks and wrens and chaffinches, robins and thrushes, the scratchy repetitions of the warblers, all competing yet distinct. I drank them in. And then I felt, despite myself, a sharp bubble of regret, physically present as though lodged in my chest, that I had no one to share it with, this moment of pure joy. It caught me unawares, ambushing me, and I opened my eyes to the lonely road, still empty to the horizon, and climbed back in, searching for my phone, long abandoned at the bottom of my bag. It peeped into reluctant life and I turned it off again and put it on to charge, postponing the moment of actually using it, getting back onto the road.

Once in a campsite, another day's birding under my belt, and my phone now fully charged and waiting, I switched it on. My thumb paused over the keypad, waiting for a decision. Not Tom, too complicated, too many difficult explanations to make. Not Gareth, either, although I hovered for a moment, allowing myself to dream. Only family remained. I pulled up Zannah's number and reluctantly reconnected myself to the thread of the world. I didn't know it then but I was to have just two more days of freedom before the persecution returned, dropping out of nowhere like a sparrowhawk tipping its wing to spill the air and power down on its prey.

It happened in Norfolk on a late afternoon when the flat lands and raised banks of the fens had lured me into walking too far, too long. It was a grey afternoon, the sky hanging heavy above me, with nothing but a narrow layer of clear air between the earth and the cloud. I was looking for the upraised vee of a harrier's wings soaring over the dark flat soil of the land. Distances were hard to judge but it seemed as though I could see for miles and miles in all directions. As I followed the curve of the bank, landmarks – the windmill which marked the entrance to the campsite, the low rise of a road bridge over a drain, a bank of poplars – rearranged themselves relative to each other, never seeming to be any nearer or any further away, but always shifting in a slow and stately dance of perspective.

With the grey weather, the evening had come on imperceptibly and it was now dusk. Only the water and the sky held any real light. The land was dark, the bushes and trees darker, pools of blackness. The last time I had seen another person was more than half an hour before, a canoeist who had paused in the still water for a brief moment and watched me as I scanned the river, then paddled away. His passage was marked by the calls and splashing runs of scattering water birds, and as the fuss died away I began to notice the silence and how alone I was in the landscape.

I walked more quickly, keen to get back to the warmth and light of my little van, suddenly eager for the sights and sounds of humanity in the sprawling shanty town of the caravan park. But there was no quick route back. I could still just make out the tall silhouette of the windmill across the reed beds but the way was barred by ditches and marshes and long gleaming cuts of water that glinted in the dark. I had taken a wrong turn somewhere, I realized, stopping and trying to make sense of the map in the half light, and I had a long walk ahead of me. As I resumed I heard behind me a scurry of activity, birds propelling themselves out of the reeds with raucous alarm calls. I turned and looked back but saw nothing; when I resumed, so too did the trail of disturbances. I was too high on the bank to be causing them – these were the tell-tales of a predator down below. A fox, I thought to myself. A fox or a stoat, on the prowl for chicks or eggs. A partridge whirred up with heart-stopping suddenness and I turned and glimpsed or thought I glimpsed a figure slipping behind a tree, felt rather than seen in the thickening gloom. Not a fox, then, or a stoat. A human predator.

Panic took me. I didn't stop to think. I ran, guided by the last shimmer of light from the sky in the water beside me. I didn't stop running until I reached a road with a farmhouse sheltering behind a thick hedge. I drew myself into its black shadows and waited, making myself invisible. I could hear nothing any more, no running feet, no birds, no calls. My legs trembled with the effort, my heart finally thudding back to a steadier pace. I waited some more. Whoever it had been was gone, or else very patient. The run had made me sweat and as the moisture dried I began to feel chilled, unable to stand there much longer. I was forced onwards, back out into the open, reasoning with myself, jumpy with fear. The walk seemed endless. The campsite glowed on the horizon, drawing me towards it. The van was parked on its very edge, a humped and humble shape beside the bigger caravans and mobile homes. I could see it long before I got there, outlined by the halo of the lights, looking somehow wrong. It was odd, cockeyed, slightly slumped. As I approached it I could see why: three flat tyres, the fourth still hissing.

'Call the police, I would,' said a voice out of the darkness, husky with cigarettes. 'Sorry, love, give you a fright?' I turned and saw a woman lit up suddenly by the warm flare of a match, her face there and gone, replaced by a small orange glow. She was sitting on her own caravan steps and as my eyes adjusted I could make her out better: cropped blonde hair, short skirt and vest top, flip-flops.

'Kids,' I said, and it sounded unconvincing to my own ears, but she shrugged and said nothing more. I watched her smoke and considered her advice, knowing I wouldn't take it. I had had enough of the police after the death of my mother, after my father's wild accusation. I had had enough of their questions, their professional scepticism, soft questions and hard eyes, probing, always probing, taking nothing at face value. My father had withdrawn his words almost immediately, but I had been led away, a firm hand gripping my elbow. The key had turned in the lock in the cell with a click that seemed final, a sound I still heard in my dreams. They went over my story, time after time, and all the time they were watching, my eyes, my face, my hands. I wondered what they saw. Perhaps through my story, my half-truths, my partial tale. Perhaps right into my guilty heart.

It was only a few hours before I was freed, but enough to know the way their minds worked. Enough to know I would never call on them for help, not if I could avoid it. My name would lie in their files somewhere, their suspicions still there, I knew it. Calling the police was not an option for me.

The woman finished her cigarette and stood to go in, taking one last look at the van and at me, her face unreadable in the dark.

'Some kids,' she said with scepticism, and then closed her caravan door behind her.

From that night on, the van seemed to become the focus of some malevolent fury – flat tyres, scratches, siphoned-out petrol – a steady drip of harassment, demoralizing and constantly there. My nights were besieged. I lay awake for as long as I could, listening, the heavy weight of my torch in one hand for comfort, poised for a confrontation that never came. I slept to dream of things prowling, man or wolf, surrounding the van. I became grey with tiredness, my eyes gritty with the need to sleep, a danger to myself and others on the road. Night after night as the waking hours ticked by, I half persuaded myself to give up. But each morning, as the birdsong filled my ears, I found a fresh resolve to make it through another day. As long as I was vigilant I would be all right. As long as I kept my wits about me. As long as I never admitted I was scared.

And so I kept up the front. People picked up the pieces, put my van back together for me, looked at me as I stood there, contemplating the latest manifestation of David's spite, wondering if they should be concerned.

'You all right, love?' they asked, uniformly. 'You OK?'

A question expecting the answer yes. I could see the

relief in their eyes when I nodded, laughed it off, dismissed their half-hearted suggestions that I call the police.

'Yeah, no, it's great, fine, everything I was hoping for,' I said unconvincingly to Zannah on her nightly call and she seemed content to believe me. 'I'm in King's Lynn – the Peak District – the Lakes – Yorkshire – Northumberland.' She pressed me for details, routes, but I was growing cagey about my exact whereabouts. I didn't trust the phone any more. I didn't trust those half-friendly conversations – over a flat tyre, in the hides, pleasantries exchanged in the campsite bar or chip shop – about routes, mileages. And I didn't trust myself either, not to talk to Tom, to hear any genuine concern. I let his calls go unanswered, deleted his text messages unread. There would be time enough for that later. For now I let the birds draw me on, the prospect of another sighting, another tick, the list mounting up towards some target I hadn't yet set, that would free me from this endless journey.

And so I had reached Scotland. And even though there would be nothing new there for me, I found myself drawn to the high buffeting winds and sheer cliffs of St Abb's Head. There were guillemots there, and razorbills, fulmars, kittiwakes, gannets – the birds of the open sea, touching down to nest on the inaccessible crags. The cliffs were alive with them, with their racket. For a while I sat on the grass and just watched the birds in the colonies go about their lives, indifferent to my gaze. Something about their busy preoccupation left me with an ache of loneliness. Behind me, dog walkers and hikers and other birders passed on the path, all in their bright clothes, cheerful in the early summer air. I was as lonely and alien among them as I was among the birds. I would pass through their lives unnoticed.

I stood up and stared over the cliff with the steady force of the wind pressing against me. The grass sloped gently down towards the drop and there was nothing between me and the cliff edge and the sea roaring hungrily beyond. The cliffs dropped several hundred feet down into an inlet of the sea, and the air was filled with birds. It would be a quick end, I found myself thinking. And a sure one. There wouldn't be time to be frightened as you fell, and if the rocks didn't get you, the tumbling maw of the sea quickly would. No time for second thoughts. Nobody called a leap from a cliff a cry for help. I held the gaze of the sea as it tried to hypnotize me forward, that endlessly restless, sucking, retreating, roaring mass of water. A quick end, and a sure one. No horrible drugged aftermath of stomach pumping and hospital. Just the final rush of fresh air and oblivion. I didn't know where the thought had come from but once it was in my head I couldn't shake it out. A quick end. A quick end. And a sure one.

Perhaps I should have just fallen then, gone to join the screaming fulmars as they plummeted through the air. Perhaps it would have been for the best. The birds would not have noticed as I fell. I would have been no more than a darkening of the sky above them, a rush of air. Instead, I gathered my shaking wits and stepped back. A woman was standing on the path, a Labrador on a lead beside her, watching with concern.

'You OK?' she asked, touching my elbow, her eyes meeting mine.

I smiled weakly. 'I'm fine,' I said.

'Those cliff edges, they can crumble,' she said. 'Easy to slip on that grass too.'

She kept her voice light but her gaze still searched mine, looking for clues.

'I know that,' I said. 'Moment of madness.'

It was a feeble joke but she granted it a smile. 'If you're not all right . . .' she said, and left the offer open.

'I'm fine,' I said firmly, stepping back onto the path, and bending down to greet her dog, covering the moment's weakness by burying my face in thick yellow fur and the warm rough smell of it. And I was fine, too. Suddenly I was fine. The moment had passed and left me trembling, but OK. The woman walked away, looking back occasionally, acknowledging my wave as I turned away from those seductive cliffs and back towards the shelter of the trees. I was fine. And I wondered about my mother, about the moment when she had poised herself to leap to her death, what she had felt, what she had seen, how close it had been to what I'd just experienced, how close I had come to following her. Was that really all it took, all it would have taken to stop her, a few words of kindness at the right time from a stranger? Did words really have that power?

I looked back at my saviour, her and her dog, both of them ordinary, unassuming, going about their lives. And I wondered what she would have done had she known, if she would have stretched out even a finger to save me.

And so I had come to rest in this unremarkable car park, down away from the cliff edges further along the coast, washed up. I no longer knew where I was going. I no longer cared what I was running away from. The van, for once, had escaped attack, but that no longer seemed to be the problem. I felt I had reached some sort of a turning point, perhaps my journey's end. The problem was that now I didn't know where to go next.

I let the birds decide. Eagles, in fact, golden eagles. Two text messages were waiting for me on the phone. Eagles showing nicely in the mountains around Aviemore. And Tom.

I was treating him badly, I knew, and the guilt made me impatient, as though it were somehow his fault. But loneliness can do funny things to you. I no longer felt as though Tom's patience was a dead weight pulling me back towards him, wanting to tie me down. That tug now felt like something I wanted. And the thought of eagles made me think warmly of Tom, the way he loved raptors, would watch them for hours, his face lifted to their soaring heights. I sat on the sea wall and read through his message, asking me if I was OK, asking me to call him. I looked at the restless sea now calming into evening. I thought about the way an eagle rose, big as a barn door yet seemingly effortless, feeling the rising thermals, undisputed master of the sky. That was a bird to end a trip on. That would be something for the list. And that might free me from my quest, my journey, allow me to return to Tom, waiting so patiently for me to come home. I dialled the number. I waited for him to answer, heard his voice, quick and eager, 'Manda?'

What was it I felt for him, I wondered. Not love, not the love that was written about in songs or books, anyway. Not what I'd felt for Gareth, that immediate need to have him, that feeling of completion. Tom used to intimidate me with his precision, his stern judgement. I had once thought him cold, disdainful, unattractive.

'Manda?' he said again, less certainly this time. 'Are you there?'

I felt sorry for him, a little. I felt grateful towards him. I realized that I had grown to need him, a bit, needed to have him around, waiting. Needed to be needed.

He said nothing, but I could hear him breathing. He tried again. 'Hello?'

I found I dreamed about him. Disturbing dreams that left me restless. I caught myself thinking about him when I awoke, when I saw a good bird, thinking about sharing it with him.

I wasn't sure it was enough. He hadn't hung up yet, I realized. I clicked the call off.

'Sorry,' I said, talking to the sea. 'I'm going to need more time.'

I rang Zannah instead, told her I was going up to Aviemore, would stay there for a while.

'When are you coming home?' she asked, as she always did. *When I work out where home is.* I didn't reply.

*

On the road up to the highlands I stopped at a lay-by and watched a single red kite, its forked tail twisting as it mastered the cross winds. It was no eagle, of course, but this was a bird that, more than any other, I associated with Tom; his bird, his special favourite. And they were the first birds I'd ever 'got' without Gareth, on a trip organized by the university club, back when we were students. Alan had made the plans and borrowed the minibus but Gareth had been ill, flu or something, and when he'd feebly insisted I go anyway, without him, I surprised him by agreeing. By the time we climbed out of the minibus in the car park at Aston Rowant I was ready to see a kite up every tree, jumpy with the desire to be the first one to spot it. I could feel my palms sweating and Gareth's borrowed binoculars were heavy around my neck and slipping in my hands where I gripped them. It was the year when the offspring of the first Spanish reintroduced birds had bred in their own right, the year the population had become established and thus, crucially, tickable, so for many of us this would be a first, a lifer. Not for Tom, of course, who at fifteen had hitched down to Wales to see the last holdout of the British population. Even Alan was deferring to him as we made our way along the edge of the escarpment and paused at a likely spot, scanning the skies. We stood high above the dramatic cut of the M40 and below us the motorway roared and glittered in the sunshine. Beyond the road lay rough grassland, dotted with bushes, sloping back up to a skyline of trees. Ahead of us the patchwork scenery of fields and hedgerows and clustered farmhouses was laid out at our feet, diminishing into the distance. The air was gin clear and the sky washed with a few faint smears of cirrus, but otherwise crystalline blue.

It was Tom, of course, who gave the first shout of recognition, pointing first to the moving shadow of a bird that was projected onto the hillside opposite, and only then upwards to the gliding speck that had cast it.

'That's it,' cried Alan. 'That must be it.'

But Tom was more cautious. 'Wait, wait,' he said, still watching, still pointing with his hand following the movement as the bird soared, was lost for a second, then reappeared above the trees. It caught the sun, glowed briefly russet, then dropped back in among the trees.

'Red, red tail,' Alan said, more excited now than ever. 'That's it, that's definitely it.' But Tom was still cautious, waiting, watching, for the bird to reappear.

'Wait for it, wait for it,' he was saying under his breath and I allowed myself to be impressed by his honesty, requiring of himself the same standards or proof that he imposed on others. I watched and waited too, tracking the cast shadow until the bird rose once more above the trees, higher, nearer, quartering back over the rough grass until it seemed almost within touching distance. It banked over the motorway and hung suspended against the green of the distant fields, then turned and swooped on something in the grass, settling with a shuffle of the wings, a last flick of its ever-mobile tail.

'That's it,' Tom sighed at last, binoculars still held up in readiness for the bird's reappearance. 'That's it.' And we turned to each other and he grinned with pure pleasure, for we had seen it all – not just the sighting, the diagnostic forked tail, not just the tick, but the bird in all its glory. And I was grinning too, unable to help myself, because the bird had been everything I wanted; beautiful and rare, and framed against the hazy background of the English countryside like a jewel in a velvet case.

They are commonplace now, the Chiltern red kites, a reintroduction success story. And anyway, kites are not what they seem. All that twisting mastery of the air is just show, for they are garbage birds, scavengers. Outside the villages in Africa the black kites spiral like ash above a bonfire, swooping to pick up the scraps and leavings, marking each settlement long before the houses have been seen. In Europe the red kites live on roadkill; we have long since driven them out of our cities, replacing them with the scuffling feral pigeons. Once they were hounded almost to extinction. We don't like scavengers, however useful a function they perform. We don't like the reminder that all flesh is grass. And we suspect them of being impatient for our end.

Once in Aviemore, I found a busy campsite and chose a pitch right next to an elderly couple seated in deckchairs outside their neat white caravan, hoping they'd be around most of the time, watching, a deterrent to David. They looked a little askance at me as I arrived, the woman granting my nodded greeting a sour pursed smile which was quickly withdrawn; her husband merely staring, tracking my progress with his eyes. I didn't care. They'd watch the van all the more closely if they thought I was up to no good. In truth, the van looked terrible, its paintwork scratched and scarred from scrubbings, the ghost of scrawled obscenities still visible here and there. One mirror hung at a defeated angle, one window wouldn't properly shut now and had to be taped up. The interior was no better; six weeks on the road had seen to that. Tom's meticulous handiwork had been undone by my own carelessness, stuff thrown hugger-mugger into the back rather than being put away, my cool box a foul sewer of melted ice and stray scraps of food. I spent the first day cleaning it all out, repairing what damage I could, bringing the van back to a faint echo of what it had been. As the machine in the laundrette whirred and mumbled through a backpack worth of dirty clothes, I found an internet cafe, followed up on the golden eagle sightings. It would be a trek, I realized, as I bought a Landranger map from a nearby walking store, but worth the effort. Golden eagles were something I had always missed out on in the past. What a way to end the trip – not in defeat, but triumph.

And for the first time since I'd left Tom's cottage, I could actually picture myself returning, going back to pick up the pieces of my life, beginning to make some sense of it all. I had got this far, after all. I had not been frightened off. In a way, I had won.

When I got back to the van the couple seemed not to have moved. Now both of them ignored me, or tried to, their heads none the less following my movements. I packed and folded away clean clothes, scrubbed and refilled the cool box, made myself a cup of tea. The summer solstice was approaching, the longest day, and the light seemed reluctant to leave, the evening barely darkening as I sat on my step and watched the comings and goings of the campsite. It felt good to be still, no longer on the move.

For three days I hunted eagles through the long hours of daylight without success. I saw other birds, of course, and I filled my eyes and ears with the sights and sounds of the empty hills, often spending whole days alone except for the sheep and the hares and the birds, no other living soul present. Each night I checked for sightings and got fresh leads, then fell into an exhausted sleep born of fresh air and exercise. The couple seemed never to move from their post beside their caravan, side by side, silent, endlessly staring. I spoke to nobody, not them, not Zannah, content with the cycle of my own thoughts.

Then one evening, two days before the solstice, I was jerked back into the harsh reality of my life. The endless fade of dusk was barely beginning. I had walked into the town, leaving the van under the couple's unblinking stare, and made my usual check at the internet cafe for the latest bird sightings in the area. I scribbled down a map reference, and was looking around for a supermarket to stock up on food, when I spotted a familiar beaked profile, just at the end of the street, ducking into a shop doorway as though to avoid me. David.

Intellectually, of course, I had known he was likely to be about, following me. But I was surprised at the way the fear returned in a sickening rush, physically nauseating. I stood on the pavement, tourists bustling around me, unable to move, eyes pinned to the door where he had disappeared, willing myself to confront him. Sweat started from me – I could feel it beading my lip, prickling under my clothes. The sour taste of terror filled my mouth. I couldn't go near him. The thought of it made me sway and weaken. I hadn't the courage to face him down. He had me in his power, the mere sight of him enough to reduce me back to the wreck I'd been, huddled on the step to Tom's house, waiting for him to come home.

People were looking at me curiously now. I forced myself to move, to walk away, my whole back rigid with terror. Once out of sight of the street where he'd been I sat down weakly and took a few deep breaths, reasoning with myself. Of course he was here, he had to have been following me. Having seen him, I was better off than if he had remained hidden. But I thought of those lonely places I had been and shuddered. Had he been there then, hiding somehow, watching me? This was it, I knew now. I could not go on. I would pack up and go right now, drive down as fast as I could, be back at Tom's within a couple of days.

I walked back to the campsite, fighting to keep my pace normal, not to break into a run and not to look behind me. I was relieved to see the van still parked in its spot, unblemished, whole. Once more I reasoned with myself. Seeing David hadn't changed anything, not really. Two or three days without attacks meant nothing. I'd done little to shake him off. So I would be overreacting if I rushed away now, with the night drawing in, weary to my bones. Better to sleep and leave in the morning. Better to go on my own terms. I thought about ringing Tom, properly this time, preparing him for my arrival. But then I decided against it.

I didn't trust the phone these days. I knew they could be bugged, easily intercepted. I deliberately kept my preparations for leaving minimal and discreet, glaring at the elderly couple as I moved around the van. I was finding their surveillance disturbing now. In the morning I would go, early, before anyone was up. I would slip away.

How I slept that night, I will never know. The fear must have finally exhausted me. Worn down, I simply closed my eyes and slept, undreaming, until seven, later than I'd planned. The camp was slowly waking around me as I made my final preparations, closed up the back of the van and settled at the driver's seat, ready to go. The beep of my phone startled me and I had to rummage around to find it, slipped under the seat, glowing with a message.

Get out of the van.

I looked at it stupidly for a moment. The number of the sender was blocked. It beeped again.

Get out of the van.

A minute must have passed. Around me people were getting up, exchanging brief pleasantries, running water, boiling kettles. A dog barked. A child cried, then laughed. Music played somewhere. Another beep.

Get out of the van now.

Before I did, some instinct had made me grab my pack, my precious Leicas, map and notebook, but everything else I owned was in there, neatly packed away. For one more minute the van just sat there, gleaming a little in the morning sunshine. And then it was gone, replaced by a ball of flame, the whoofing sound reaching me before the sight of it did, so that it seemed a magical transformation, untouched by reality. Children scattered, people turning to watch as I stood rooted and open mouthed and watched my world burn. The bones and structure of the van showed starkly through the billowing flame and smoke.

There was one final message on my phone, coming through even as I stood and watched, thinking about calling the fire brigade. Two letters – NN – and then a string of six digits. A map reference. And a familiar one.

Fury replaced fear instantly. In the distance, sirens were sounding. Someone else had called the fire brigade. I heard a timid noise behind me. It was the old couple from the next door caravan, who had emerged in their night clothes and were staring at me in horror.

I rounded on them. 'Who did you tell? Why have you been spying on me?'

The man shook his head, bewildered, pushing his wife behind him as I approached. She cowered behind him, her face slack with fear.

'Did you see who did this?' I asked, shouted. 'Did you see? Did you send me those messages?'

He hadn't put his teeth in, I saw. His face was shrunken, suddenly ancient. His wife whimpered and he clutched at her hand. I waved the phone at them. 'Did you?' They backed away, still staring at me, and then stumbled back into the safety of their caravan. The phone still glowed in my hand, a smug reminder. I threw it into the flames.

I didn't wait for the arrival of the police and the fire brigade and all the rest of officialdom. The fire was already subsiding as the petrol in the tank burned out and with the dying of the flames the extent of the damage was clear. The bare framework had survived but the paint was blistered right off, the tyres gone, everything in the interior a mass of still burning wood and fabric. It was destroyed. People were gathering around it at a safe distance, drawn by the rising column of smoke, their eyes catching the reflection of the dancing flames. Quietly I threaded myself through the flow of people, slipping behind their watching backs. The sirens were coming, I could hear them, could see in the distance the red bulk of the fire engines and preceding them, speeding in, the blue strobing lights of the police. I had to get away before they found me, before I got caught up in their questions. I turned my face away and down, and hurried towards the train station.

The taint of smoke was still on my face when I boarded the train, the map reference still burned onto my mind's eye. I had recognized it immediately because it was one I had written down myself that morning. It was still in my note-book – one of the golden eagle sightings I'd seen on the internet. David must have been behind those too, luring me onwards into ever lonelier locations. This was the loneliest of all. A train would get me part of the way there, but the rest would be on foot, a long walk according to the map, fifteen miles of walking deep into the high hills, far from the reach of roads. The spot pinpointed on the map showed no particular place or summit, just a shoulder of mountain, pressing out beside a steep cliff into a corrie, a ruined hut, no track or path or road within miles. I sat with the map spread open on my knee and watched the countryside rattle past, listening to the voices flowing indifferently around me.

As I got off the train and shouldered my pack I felt no sense of hesitation, the fear all burned away, replaced by a kind of blank determination. There was but a brief walk along the road and then onto a path that led out into the mountains. The morning was just getting going, the sun already high and warming the air. Above me black birds circled like dust, their calls croaking and deep. Rooks, I thought at first, squinting up at them, but then my eyes adjusted to their scale against the looming mountain. Great black birds with a wedge-shaped tail and a huge wingspan, much bigger than a rook or crow. Ravens.

I squared myself to the path and began the long walk in.

RAVENS REVISITED

He was ready for me, waiting, totally unsurprised. He must have had hours, I realized, to observe my approach, watching me toil steadily towards him from the moment I stepped off the path in the valley and began the long climb upwards. By then I was no longer thinking about what I was climbing towards, or why I was doing it. I had set my teeth for the last burst of effort and faced the final slope and he chose his moment well. The light had been fickle and changing all day as the wind set the clouds racing, their shadows playing across the whole emptiness of the valley. As the sun appeared from behind a cloud, he stepped out from the loose crown of rocks where he had been hiding so his shadow reached out towards me, cast black across the bright radiance of the heather. I was forced to look straight into the sunlight, squinting, unable to make him out. It was as though he had appeared out of nowhere.

'David,' I said, and that was all I could say before he grabbed my arm, looking hastily over his shoulder, scanning the bare expanses of the mountain.

'Are you alone?' he asked, and I knew then the stupidity of what I had done, the futility of coming out here to confront him. 'Does anyone know you are here?'

Maybe I should have bluffed it out then, told him I'd talked to the police, threatened him with exposure. Anything better than the craven shake of my head as I struggled to free my arm from his grip, my struggles getting fiercer as he drew his face closer to mine and hissed at me how stupid I'd been, how foolish, how little I saw, how little I understood. And his words only served to echo my own thoughts, my own recriminations.

'Don't you see what danger you're in?' he asked, as though to taunt me. 'Have you really no idea?' And then his other hand grasped me too, so that I was pinned by him, both arms trapped by my sides. The pack on my back left me feeling destabilized, pulling me off balance as I struggled to free myself to no avail. Then I felt the weight of my fury descend and after that there were no more words. The speech I'd prepared in my head about leaving me alone and letting me get on with my life evaporated in the need, the fierce animal need I felt to be free of him, free of his grip. It was a grim and silent struggle, him against me, twisting around on the rough grass and loose scree up there in the shelter of the rocks. Terror lent strength to my arms and one last explosive burst of effort pulled me free of his grasp, free and falling backwards onto the turf.

Him against me. That's what I thought it was when I fell sprawling and saw how we had moved in our struggle, right to the edge of a steep drop. The ground was sloping away from me, loose stones and grit as much as grass, the drop gathering momentum towards the final plunge down to the waiting rocks below. We were poised right over it and he was stronger than me, bigger and fitter and not encumbered by a pack, at home on this ground. Him against me. Acting in self-defence. Those were the words I comforted myself with afterwards, through the long dark hours of the night. I was frightened and it was fear as much as fury that had me scrabbling for a stable footing, trying to get upright, bracing myself as he loomed over me, grabbing at me once more. It was fear, not fury, that made me shake him off even as I realized he was off balance now, that he was saying something, words I didn't listen to, didn't want to hear. They changed into a gasping plea for help as he lost his footing on the uncertain turf. I let him turn towards the sloping drop, his feet scrabbling on the loose scree, his words dying as his grabbing hold grew desperate. He was grabbing for his life, trying to stop the acceleration of his fall. It was because I was frightened that I shook him off, even as his grip failed on my arm and he slipped, tumbling and twisting, pulled inexorably towards the drop, even as my last wrenching kick for freedom sent him to his death.

It's easy to say that it all happened so fast, that what really happened was confused and unclear. But it wasn't fast, not really, not that last bit as his hand lost its grip on my arm and he slipped, twisting and grabbing at the loose rocks and grass. Although I tried not to, I heard his last words, his last despairing gasp as he reached out towards me, his hand coming out even as his body slipped away, retreating, inevitable as the tide. And I caught the last look in his eyes as he realized he was falling and that there was nothing that would stop him. His mouth opened and he asked me to help him, and I couldn't, it was too late, there was nothing

I could do but watch. Watch him as he fell. It happened in the stretch of a reaching hand, not quite reaching far enough. Him or me, I had thought, it was him or me, and nobody could blame me for acting in self-defence.

And yet even so, the words echoed still and wouldn't be chased out, however far and furiously I walked, trying to drive them away. 'Help me,' he had said as he reached out. 'Help me,' as he had slipped, had fallen. Help me. And I hadn't.

After the long hard night spent in the bothy, I spent the next day crossing the hills, walking like one possessed. The ravens were a constant, brooding presence. I kept my eyes down, avoiding the sight of them, and walked all the faster, spurred on by the need to get away. The landscape was empty, scoured clean, valley after valley, hill after hill with just sheep and moorland, seemingly untouched by man. I stumbled on blindly for hours and the thought was there that it might in the end be better if I just died out here in the hills, but in the end I found I could not quite shake off my own sense of self-preservation. I came to a path and I took it, conscious of the day drawing on, of the need to find shelter. Other walkers appeared, bright dots of colour strung out along the path, and then, further along, I caught the glint from the windscreens of cars parked in a lay-by below.

By the time I reached it, I didn't need to feign tiredness to cadge a lift back to the nearest town. There there were rows of anonymous bed and breakfasts, ready to take me in. I had cash, plenty of cash, taken out in readiness for the journey down south. I found the cheapest place I could and crashed in my single room, bone tired, and slept the last dreamless sleep I would have for weeks.

I meant to move on, but somehow I didn't. I was weary of moving. I feared being found, hunted down, and was still haunted by the sensation of being watched, but hiding seemed better than flight for I had nowhere else I could flee to. I had no idea when someone would report David missing, or when I myself would be missed, when his body would be found, when we would be linked in some way or another. I husbanded my cash carefully, not wanting to take out any money from my account and give away my location. At some point I would run out of cash, and then I would have to decide what to do. But for the first few days I simply kept my head down and waited.

I spent my days out walking, not in the hills but around the few streets of the town, pacing its bounds. There were enough tourists there to render me inconspicuous for a while, just another holidaymaker on a walking holiday. The town was a strange little pocket of neat pebbledashed houses and clipped lawns set down among the brooding hills. I passed the tiny stone-built police station every day as I walked and I kept my eyes down, my head averted. I sat in the miniature park with its immaculate grass and bright flower beds and tried to think, trying to get my story straight. Above me, high and distant, I saw or thought I saw the ravens, riding the air, watching, waiting for something to feast on, their presence a grim remembrance of death. Not just David's, but my mother's.

'Did she fall?' the police had asked me, over and over, but the answer to me seemed self-evident. Of course she fell, everything falls, in the end, after all, the same acceleration, ten metres per second per second, towards the waiting earth. Accident or suicide or murder, it all ends the same way. It's how it starts that's important.

Zannah asked me the same question too, years back, before we called a truce, weary of picking over the same ground. She had taken me on some ill-thought pilgrimage to find the spot where it had all happened, as though the answers might be lying there, broken on the promenade. Did she fall? she asked, and I knew then, too, what the question really meant: did she fall or was she pushed? Did she fall or did she jump?

I said I didn't know, and that was the truth. I could tell her only what I saw, the darkening of the air, and in the strange atmosphere of the sea mist that was all that there had been to see: a thickening shadow passing over me, like the darkening of the sky in an eclipse. A sight that I could never properly put into words. A sight that I had never managed to shake from my mind's eye.

But Zannah heard only something simpler, a fact.

'So you didn't . . .' she hesitated and changed tack in mid sentence. 'You weren't at the top of the cliff then? Dad was wrong?'

'Did you ever believe that I had . . .' I couldn't say the words either, as though that might break the enormity of the accusation, make it seem likely, make it real. Her eyes met mine and her silence said more than she ever could.

She broke her gaze and turned and hugged her knees. We were sat on the sea wall where we thought my mother had gone over. Even that had been hard enough to establish with any certainty. I remembered the scene with such clarity – the houses neatly spaced, the clipped green hedges hallucinatory in the thinning mist, the road so suburban in its ordinariness, but ending abruptly in open air and nothingness – yet now I could recognize none of it. Hedges had grown, houses had changed. The retirement home I remembered had gone completely, replaced by crammed-in houses canted at awkward angles to catch their glimpse of the sea. Only the car park and the steps were as we remembered them, and even then there was no real rush of recognition, just a sense that this must be it, after eliminating everywhere else.

We had gone back on a day of bright breezy sunshine, clouds scudding over the sea and casting shifting shadows on its surface. In my memory the place had had an eerie silence, even the sea muffled, but now it was loud with the waves and with birds, the sounds of voices carried up in bursts from the promenade below. But Zannah remembered it differently. She had no memory of the silence.

'I heard her scream,' she said, kicking her heels against the wall and talking to her fingernails.

'You were with Dad, though,' I said. 'In the car.'

She shook her head. 'I decided to wait for him at the top. But I didn't see her. Not here in the car park. She must have jumped from somewhere else, over there, further west.'

'It was right by those steps.' The steps I'd been climbing,

racing to get to her, trying to undo the thing, the terrible thing that I'd done. She had to have jumped from them or near by them, had to have. Because she went right over me, passing like a dark shadow in the air. And fell in silence past my outstretched hand. Too far, just too far, to reach.

Zannah shook her had again and then we sat, replaying our respective memories. The truth seemed stretched somewhere between them, unreachable.

'You didn't see her?' I asked again.

'Only the scream,' she said. 'That's what I remember.'

After a pause I said, 'You thought I'd pushed her,' and I kept it flat, uninflected, not a question, but a statement.

She dropped her head and cradled it in her arms, resting them on her knees, balling herself up tight against the memories. 'I didn't know what to think.'

'Is that what you thought Dad meant, when he blamed me?'

She looked up now, frowning. 'Isn't it? What else could he have meant?'

And I said nothing further, for there was nothing more I could say. We drove back to her flat then in silence but I felt her gaze returning to my face over and over, dark with suspicion, not quite dispelled. She opened her mouth when I dropped her off, as though to get in the last word, but then she thought better of it and merely waved. We never returned to the subject again.

The room in the B&B had a mirror over the sink, flyblown and faded with age. My face in it seemed remote, receding. Long sleepless nights had hollowed out my eyes. More and more I saw my mother's features looking back at me, as though she were taking me over. I thought I caught too in my face her look of desperation, the one I had glimpsed sometimes at her worst times, as though there were another person looking out through her eyes, pleading for release.

At night I had stopped trying to sleep. I sat at the open window and my thoughts flew further back, into my childhood, before all our troubles began. Africa seemed more real to me then than the neat rows of houses, silvery in the moonlight. My mother's voice floated through the night, caressing, addressing the unknown darling, whispering down the phone. I listened to her lies. Juma had been told off the next morning, harangued like a sullen child by my father for using the phone. He didn't defend himself, but stood with his eyes down, saying nothing, absenting himself in all but the physical sense. I stood in the doorway listening, saying nothing either. She sat there too and listened, the picture of ease. A long drink clinked in her hand, ice cubes cracking cold against the gin. I could hear the faint fizz from the tonic. Occasionally her eyes would drift over my face as though in challenge, daring me to tell the truth.

I didn't buy papers, avoided the radio and the television that blared in the B&B's lounge, but the news filtered through all the same. The body had been found, had been brought down from the mountain, what there was left of it. The ravens had come down lower now as though following the body, drifting in circles over the town, and their calls were constant in my ears, guttural, croaking, low and harsh. I turned my eyes from them, the thought of their claws and their tearing beaks, what they had feasted on. The feeling of being watched, of being pursued, intensified. I avoided the police station now, kept to the park and the back streets, biding my time, still lost in the past.

My father had turned to me for confirmation, once Juma had gone back to the kitchen. He crouched down to my level and his voice was soft and kind, his eyes levelled on mine. I basked in his attention.

'Did Juma use the phone, Manda, while we were out?'

So many things I can see now I could have said. From the kitchen came banging pots, plates clattered down on the counter, no singing, no bantering with the garden boy.

'You won't get into any trouble.'

But it wasn't that that caused me to hesitate, mind racing, choosing an answer. I felt the stillness of her attention, for all she lounged in such a casual pose. I felt his eyes catch mine.

'I need you to tell the truth.'

I chose the answer that might make him smile, make him love me, make me his favourite girl.

'It was her,' I said.

My face blew through the streets, crumpled on newsprint, lifted on a summer breeze that tore through the town. It was caught on the legs of the bench where I sat in the park, watching the ravens, waiting for them to land. It was a terrible picture, one from my staff pass, badly pixellated. David's photo was better, relaxed, gently smiling, unrecognizable as the person I'd known. 'Great promise,' the paper said about him. 'Troubled history,' it said about me. The police wanted me to help with their enquiries. I smoothed out the crumpled sheet and folded it, wanting to hide my face away. On the other side they had interviewed his sister and her face, her hawkish profile so like his, caught my eye. I looked a long time at the photograph, read through her words over and over, trying to make sense of what she had said.

'A gentle soul,' she had called him. A Don Quixote, chivalrous, a knight errant, protector of the women he thought he loved. 'They were just crushes really,' she said. 'I suppose some girls found it a bit annoying, but he was harmless. I never thought it would end in tragedy.'

This time I left the town, taking the track up through the forests, out to the hillsides as far as I dared. I turned her words over as I climbed. The ravens flew up, guarding their kingdom, casting huge fleeting shadows over the slopes, blocking out the sun. Their voices sent me back. It was they who were watching me, tracking my every move. I felt their eyes on me, assessing me. I was running out of money, out of time. People were eyeing me too in the town, curious, suspicious, no longer a passing stranger. I waited till dark to slip through its streets and back to my room. I averted my eyes from the shadowy face in the mirror. The ravens were perched round my bed. From time to time I could hear them, shifting a little, clearing their throats with a soft murmur, otherwise patient and still. Voices came and went in the street outside. Then it was just the voices in my head. A gentle soul. A knight errant. A brother. A son. The newspaper picture floated before my eyes, the smile suddenly contorting with fear as he slipped away from my grasp, tumbling and turning in the fall from the cliff, transforming himself into a great black bird that flew off, laughing. But it wasn't David in the dream, not any more, but Tom, Tom's face, Tom's mocking laugh. I woke up and sat up, gasping for breath in the empty room, still swept up in the emotion of the departing dream and unable to shake it off. Not fear, after all, not sudden blinding panic, but anger; a burning sense of rage.

There was sunlight filtering into the room, the early sunlight of the Scottish summer. The ravens had gone, the face in my mirror my own. I got up and dressed and walked through the quiet Sunday streets. Even the police station was closed, its door firmly bolted. I stood on the steps and knew I couldn't face it alone. I walked down to the phone box and picked up the heavy receiver, fumbling for coins in my pocket. The digits came up unbidden under my fingers. Zannah's voice was unchanged but wary, answering a call from someone she didn't know, an unfamiliar number.

'It's me,' I said. 'I think you'd better come and get me.'

I knew from the moment the words left my mouth that I'd given my father the wrong answer. I saw something shift in his face as he slipped through the gap between suspecting and knowing, even though I was too young to understand then what that might mean. He jerked his head backwards as he heard my words and she moved sharply behind him, sitting up straight and letting out a sharp hiss of denial.

'She called someone darling,' I added, in for a penny, knowing that I was sunk now anyway, unsure of what I had done wrong. It was no more than the truth, after all. No more than what he had asked for. 'And then she lied.'

I held my breath, waiting for the coming explosion, but he had forgotten my presence and had turned to her instead. He said nothing. He stood up slowly and carefully, moving like an old man. She tipped up her chin in defiance. The ice cubes in her glass rattled and rang like tiny bells and she took a long drink, draining her glass, never moving her eyes from his. I longed for someone to speak, even to shout, to break the tension of their silence, but he never opened his lips. He just stood and watched her finish her drink and then turned on his heel and was gone in the click of a closing door. She put down her glass on the table, missing the coaster, and gave me the full force of her glare.

'Satisfied?'

They are clever birds, ravens. They have the ready opportunistic intelligence of the scavenger. They are generalists, like humans. Long lived, for birds, and long memoried. The Scots call them corbies, but it wasn't just his name that put me in mind of them with Inspector Corby. And nor was it his bright dark eyes, and the way he cocked his head as he put a question to me, waiting for the answers that never came. It was his constant, restless intelligence, revolving the facts, always ready to find another picture, another arrangement that fit.

The lawyer, too, had something corvid about him, with his black glossy head. A magpie, maybe, or a thieving jackdaw. He sat beside me, alert to pounce on the slightest slip in correct procedure. I might as well not have been there for all the part I was playing in their proceedings. Ravens are the only birds that will turn their heads to follow another creature's gaze; awake to the existence of other animals' desires. Yet if these two had followed mine, they would have seen that up through the high window of the interview room there could be glimpsed a square of blue sky, and in it, today, the screaming flight of the swifts.

The inspector talked. I listened. We had established that routine already in our two days together. Then, afterwards, the lawyer talked and Zannah listened, while I just watched the way his face moved, the rubbery precision with which he closed his mouth over the words, like the closing of a fridge door. I grasped at a few phrases as they passed through the air between us and turned them carefully in my mind while the rest of the words flowed on and Zannah nodded and took notes. 'Manslaughter' was one of them. 'Self-defence' was another. 'Not proven' seemed to be a particular favourite of his, pronounced with a peculiar Scottish relish.

I wasn't under arrest, not yet, not formally. Zannah had come up straight away, with the lawyer, rounded up from some Edinburgh contact of hers, and we had walked into the tiny police station together. From there we had gone to Aviemore, greeted by a knot of photographers pressing against the car window. We fled from the aggressive glare of the flashes with our heads down. I had wondered sometimes how a bird felt at a big twitch; now I had some idea. Hunted.

'Prejudice,' the lawyer said, examining the papers the next day, my dazed face gazing out of the front pages. 'Innocent until proven guilty,' he had added, looking over the top of his glasses at me, for that was back when he was still bothering to address me.

Inspector Corby had started the first day briskly enough with his questions. But even the police find that hard to keep up when they are met not with answers, nor even with a refusal to answer, but with someone who is gazing up through their high windows at the convocation of swifts. The lawyer was struggling too, with an absence of information beyond what I'd told Zannah in my first outpouring of relief, over the phone. So by now, the second day, the questions had sidled round, had stopped being mere requests for information, become more in the nature of speeches.

'My client is the victim of harassment,' the lawyer tried now. 'First by this disturbed – this deeply disturbed – young man. And now by the police.'

Inspector Corby picked up a file, a fat file full of loose bits of paper, and let it drop six inches to the table, throwing up a dance of dust that filled the shaft of light from the high window.

'Do you know what a stalking case looks like, a harassment case?' he said to the lawyer, to me, to the mute blonde policewoman who sat beside him, her face gravely turned towards mine. 'It looks like this. Page after page of calls, of complaints, of infringements and restraining orders and witness statements and anonymous letters. Thick. Huge.

The desk sergeant will roll his eyes at the mention of it. And you know, we've talked to Thames Valley Police about this, about this young man and about Miss Brooks, and they have nothing. Nothing.'

He paused. It was hot outside, muggy and oppressive. The swifts were spiralling lower, following the insects which rode the falling air pressure of a storm front. If I leaned and twisted my head I could see the edges of the clouds building, ramparts of them bruise-dark against the mountains. Rain coming.

'Nothing. And so we tried nationally, looking for evidence of this alleged' – he laid a heavy emphasis on the word – 'stalking. And this time, Miss Brooks's name did crop up. Once. It's an unusual shortening of Amanda, Manda, and so it stood out. Years ago. More than a decade. West Sussex have been getting their files onto the computers, it seems. One Manda Brooks, age seventeen, accused by her father – the accusation later withdrawn – of pushing her mother over a cliff.'

He let the word hang in the air. I turned my eyes to him for a moment. He laid down first one, then a second sheet of paper, squaring them carefully on top of each other, then looked straight at me.

'It seems you're a dangerous person to be around.'

We took a break after that, after the lawyer had protested strongly at the accusations. He went off and huddled with Zannah in the corridor. I could see their faces through the reinforced window glass, his dark head bent towards her as she made some point, stabbing with her finger. I sat on in the empty interview room and watched my cooling tea. The policewoman had brought it, hovering sympathetically for a moment, then leaving as silently as she had come.

As we started again the policeman tried another tack.

'You know,' he said, as we sat down again, resuming our accustomed positions. 'The police these days, we're not monsters. Whenever we see a case of a man dying at a woman's hand, we have to ask ourselves: who is the predator, here, who is the prey? The courts are lenient now with women who kill, much more lenient than they used to be. A full and frank admission of the circumstances, a plea of self-defence, we would be lucky to get you even for manslaughter. Leaving the scene of an accident, failure to report a death – you might only be looking at a suspended sentence. But without an admission now, without a sob story – well, the courts don't like that at all. It looks,' and he paused here, as if to choose his words, 'well, it looks a little cold blooded.'

We sat in silence. The walls were too thick, the windows too tightly sealed for me to hear the screaming of the swifts. I closed my eyes and tried to conjure up the sound, but failed. When I opened them again, I found that the policeman seemed to be waiting for me, waiting for my full attention to continue.

'And there's another thing the courts don't like, that juries especially don't like,' the policeman went on meditatively, ruminatively, as though in conversation. 'Up there on the mountain it's your word against – well, against nothing. So they'll be looking for corroboration, evidence that you have told the truth when that truth can be checked.

Like this harassment. Starting in . . .' he made an elaborate show of checking his notes. 'Starting in around January. And continuing more or less without letup until June.' He paused, as though for confirmation. Out of the corner of my eye I could see the hesitant nod of the lawyer. That is what I had told Zannah, after all. What she had told him.

'And yet, this man, this young man, this disturbed – yes – and unfortunate young man had suffered what we lay people would call a nervous breakdown towards the end of March. A breakdown so bad that his GP had recommended he be hospitalized for treatment, for his own safety, which he duly was. He remained there, under more or less close supervision, until the beginning of June.'

'More or less, you say,' cut in the lawyer, leaning forward.

'More or less. More as in a locked ward. Less as in his presence being noted, checked, accounted for by one person or another three or four times a day. Making it difficult for him to get from Berkshire up to' – and again, the elaborate show of checking his notes – 'Norfolk, I believe, and Derbyshire, and points north, and back without his absence being noted.'

Silence from the policeman, his point made. Silence from the lawyer. Silence from me, for I had nothing to say, nothing to add beyond what I thought I knew. Silence. Silence. Silence.

That evening Zannah continued my interrogation. She sat on the bed I was trying to lie on and talked at me.

'Why won't you talk to them, Manda?'

I didn't know. I couldn't say. I'd come here fully intending to tell them everything, to make a clean breast of it, to offer my wrists up to the handcuffs and be led away, but it hadn't been quite like that. I had found myself caught between the pair of them, lawyer and policeman, like scavenging birds. They tore at the shreds of the story, the few fragments they had of it, pulling it now this way, now that. A cold-blooded killer who torched her own van to cover her tracks, destroyed her own phone to prevent its tell-tale signals from tracking her down like a radio tag. Or an innocent victim, firebombed out of her only home, who had fled unaware that her tormentor had already killed himself. I recognized neither story, and worse, the one I knew, the one I thought I knew was true, had just been blown apart, shattered by the fact of David's incarceration. I shut my eyes to concentrate on what I had, what I remembered, to try and keep some fragile grip on what had really happened, marshalling the facts. But they shifted like shapes in the mist, receding before me. I didn't know any more if what I remembered was true.

'Don't go to sleep on me,' Zannah said.

'I'm not asleep,' I said with my eyes still closed. It was the first thing I'd said all day.

'Whatever happened up there, Manda, I'll support you. But I need to know the truth. The whole truth. And your silence is frightening me.' I opened my eyes to look at her. Her eyes were my eyes, my father's eyes. Blue shards of summer sky. Thunder rumbled somewhere over the hills and the swifts shrieked and flew lower. When I closed my eyes once more and let her words wash over me I could still see them, bright specks of light against the dark, dancing before me.

The next morning the climate had changed. The storm the swifts had forecast had broken in the night and now the mountains were gone, buried under the lowering cloud. A steady fall of drizzle chilled the air and slicked the roads with rain. The climate seemed to have changed at the police station too. We reported to the front desk as usual but instead of being ushered into the interview room as had been the routine, we waited out in the lobby. After a few minutes Inspector Corby emerged, wiping his palms down the side of his trousers as he greeted us almost cheerily.

'No further questions,' he said. 'We are no longer pursuing this line of enquiry.' New evidence had come to light, apparently. The lawyer, wrong-footed, wanted to protest anyway, but the inspector shook his head and waved him away. Zannah went out to make a statement to the few remaining reporters, the lawyer at her side. When they had gone, the inspector pulled a plastic bag out of his jacket pocket and held it up to show its contents.

'Not yours, I suppose?'

It was a mobile phone, a Nokia, the entry-level one, the kind everyone had. I shook my head. The inspector looked through the lobby window at the rain sliding down the glass and spoke almost as though to himself.

'We thought you'd sent that text to yourself, as a decoy. But the world and his wife saw you in Aviemore, watching your van go up in flames. The phone companies have just come back with the records. A different mast relayed that message. It was sent from half way up Ben Alder.'

'David,' I said.

'Could be,' he said. 'But then the phone ended up in a bin in Kingussie two days later.' He looked out of the window, still meditatively swinging the little bag with the phone in it. 'I don't believe in ghosts, not ghosts with mobile phones. There was someone else up there on that mountain, someone who must have known you.'

Then he turned and looked at me and said, as though it were a casual remark, 'Of course there's more than one way to send someone over the edge of a cliff.' And his eyes were bright with the penetrating intelligence of the raven, seeking truth, as though he could see right through me, right into the layers of lies I'd built up over the years, right past them into the core, into the heart of it. As though he saw back through into the chasm of the past, through the blanketing fog and the haze of memory to the seventeen-year-old walking along that promenade, away from the hateful spite of her drunken mother. Walking away, and then stopping and turning back. And seeing the shrunken figure of her mother getting unsteadily to her feet, her brave red lipstick a smear across the wreckage of her face. Saw me stop and watch her as she made her way to the first steps that led up the face of the cliff, hundreds of feet above the promenade. And staying there, still watching, as my mother turned to look at me, to give me an imploring wave, asking her daughter to stop her from doing what she was about to do. And seeing me not move, not go and lay a restraining hand on her arm as she clutched the handrail. Seeing me stand instead and fill my lungs, fill them with sea air and hate and shout it out so loud that the birds themselves were startled. 'Go on, then, and kill yourself; see if I care.'

They were only words, after all, only air and noise hardly louder than the panicked cries of the gulls, and just as meaningless. And even then, it wasn't too late, wasn't too late as my mother made her way slowly, painfully slowly up those steps. I was young enough, fit enough to stop her, any time, as she climbed up and up and disappeared into the mist. Instead I stood and watched her go in silence, raised not a hand to save her. And waited there alone until my nerve broke and I pounded up the steps, hoping it wasn't too late, too late for me to stop her, pounding upwards until I thought my heart would burst; until the sky darkened briefly like an eclipse, darkened with her passing. I heard nothing as she fell.

And then I looked at him again and saw that the intelligence I'd seen was just a trick of the light, a passing glimmer, and he was just an ordinary man with dark hair and dark eyes, his mind on his next cigarette, and he had known no more about it than my father, distraught and not knowing what he said, had done. I fought back the urge to confess, nodded non-committally as he went on.

'I was thinking suicide pact you know, initially, you and the young lad, but now we've got this third character on the scene, I'm not so sure. I'm beginning to wonder if you were set up.'

And like the last fragment of a kaleidoscope pattern slipping into place, I saw it suddenly come clear and true, the image I'd been seeking these last couple of days, the truth of it.

We went back by train, two trains, seven hours to cover a month's journey. Zannah handled everything – the tickets, the packing, the conversation. She sat opposite me, travelling backwards, speaking of the past, speaking of her dreams. I watched her faint reflection in the window as I listened. In the tunnels she sprang into sharper relief, her eyes meeting mine, acknowledging that I was paying her attention, that I was listening to her at last.

'Listen, Manda, now this is over, I should let you know. I'm going back to Tanzania. They've offered me a job out there, in Dad's college. Teaching business administration. Why don't you come too? They're crying out for people with IT, and there's nothing keeping you here.' She talked of her plans and smiled secretly to herself at the thought of it, of her escape. I watched her head lift and her shoulders relax, and the busy animation of her hands as she talked. She was restless in her seat, poised to be off.

'As soon as I made the decision, I felt I was whole again,' she said. 'Coming home, that's how I think of it. As though these past twenty years have just been one huge mistake.'

'*Zugenruhe*,' I said suddenly, my eyes on her reflection still.

'Zugen who?' she asked, smiling, but I didn't answer. I was remembering Tom's watchful gaze on me in the kitchen as I battered against his four walls in my eagerness to get away. There was something she wasn't telling me, I could see that, some extra secret that she was fizzing with. Something that made her happy, that made her curve her arms around her body and hug herself as she gazed out over the wide expanse of the North Sea. Scotland gave way to England as the shadows lengthened and the flatlands stretched out around the train. Clumps of cooling towers advanced and retreated in their slow dance across the landscape. The train rocked and screeched until it slowed to crawl through the brick canyons of London and into the smoky darkness of King's Cross. Zannah kept her silence as we travelled west to her flat, although at times I caught her opening her mouth as though to break it, then thinking better of it. It was only as we collapsed onto the sofa, in among half-packed boxes and all the paraphernalia of departure, that she finally broke down and told me.

'There's something else,' she said. 'I'm not going alone.'

'I thought there was something you weren't telling me,' I said, and I was unworried, unafraid, oblivious of the coming blow.

'I hesitated because I thought it might be a bit of a sore point,' she said.

'Anyone I know?'

'Yeah,' and she looked down at her hands before looking up, peering up through her hair almost coyly. And even as she spoke my heart sank and then gave one convulsive leap of fear. 'It's Tom.'

When I awoke, the air was frantic with sirens, the disregarded background wail of London. They filled me with an undercurrent of unease as I slowly realized where I was, remembered what had happened. Something was nagging at me, insistent, urgent, a sense of danger. Words, my father's words. 'Look after her, Manda,' and Zannah's hand so trustingly placed in mine, as though I might after all be able to protect her.

The conversation we'd had the night before came back to me. I hadn't known how to get through to Zannah. All I had at the time was a seething mass of suspicions, circumstantial, no proof, the evidence gone. Handwriting in a notebook, David's words re-remembered in a different context, an unfounded sense of unease. How could I put it into words, the feeling of something slipping into place, a pattern coming true, suddenly, after being muddled and unfocused? What I had said had come out wrong and she had turned it on its head, accusing me of jealousy.

'You can't bear to see him happy with someone else, that's all,' she said. 'You can't bear to see *me* happy.'

Tom had called her after I'd left that day in the van, wondering if she knew where I'd gone. She hadn't then, but the minute I got back in touch, she'd told him. That was when the trouble started. And everything I'd told her since – where I was going, where I had been, the problems with the van – it had all been faithfully relayed to him. He'd always been better on the phone than he had been in person, I remembered that now. He came across as more relaxed, cooler, less intense. They'd talked nightly, week after week, always on his mobile because he said his landline wasn't working. Gradually they'd talked less and less about me, and started to talk about other things, other subjects, Tom's own worries, Zannah's hopes and fears. And then, at the time when I disappeared again, Tom had gone silent for a few days before showing up at Zannah's flat looking dishevelled and drawn, with three days' growth of beard. He'd eaten half a loaf's worth of toast and then slept on her sofa for almost twenty-four hours. At what point he'd transferred into her bed, and how, she wouldn't tell me.

'What's this?' she shouted finally. 'Christ, Manda, get your thrills somewhere else. You didn't want him but now you've changed your mind? Or now you just want him hanging on around you, keeping stringing him along? Can't you not begrudge me one little piece of happiness in my life, something that's mine?'

'He's using you, Zannah,' I shouted back. 'Can't you see that? Using you to get at me.'

'It's not all about you, Manda.'

'Jesus Christ, Zannah,' I said. 'I was trying to hide.'

'Yes, but not from Tom,' she wailed. 'Not from Tom.'

The police had told us David had gone up to Scotland 'with a friend', a trip to recuperate, an ideal convalescence. Fresh air and exercise, a little birdwatching, beautiful scenery, what could be more helpful to a fragile young man who'd had a difficult time of it? But they had never mentioned the name of the friend. Someone who'd suggested the trip, had arranged it, had chosen Aviemore as the destination. Someone who had done all the damage to the van, who had hounded me up the length of the country. Someone who had camped up there in the bothy, awaiting my arrival in that lonely spot.

'If it wasn't David, it could have been anyone,' she objected. 'Gareth, even. He warned you off Tom, didn't he?' But Gareth's handwriting was an untidy sprawl, his notebooks a mess of crossings out. The notebook I'd found in the bothy had the neat precision of one of Tom's.

'It was Tom's handwriting, I should have recognized it at the time,' I insisted. 'It must have been Tom who was up there with David.'

'So you say,' she said. 'But it's all just what you say, isn't it? Maybe there was nobody else up there at all. Maybe there was no damage to the van, no notebook. Maybe you made it all up.'

There was nothing more we could say about it after that. She apologized, backed off, and I was exhausted enough to be persuaded that we should sleep, that we could discuss it again in the morning. I had forgotten her cunning at getting her own way, her persistent refusal to give up, until I had woken to the dawning realization that the flat was empty, that she had gone to Tom, walking as confidingly as a child into a danger she couldn't understand.

I wasted time even then, ringing her phone and getting no answer, ringing Tom's phone and getting through to his voicemail. I even walked round the confines of the flat, opening doors, hoping against all expectation that she would appear, somehow, among the wilderness of boxes. But the rooms were all empty. Zannah was gone.

Once outside her flat the unaccustomed bustle of rush-hour London hit me. I was hurrying now, struggling through crowds, dodging and weaving through the indifferent mass of people. The tube was no better, nightmarishly lit, a press of backs and elbows and shoulders swaying as it screeched through the dark, stopping and starting, waiting endlessly in tunnels. The passengers around me seemed dazed, comatose, uncaring whether the train moved or not, staring at nothing. How could they be so calm? I scrambled through the doors at Paddington and forced my way up to the concourse, trying to get my bearings. Train after train delivered endless waves of people, all unspeaking, moving with the relentless fixed purpose of automatons. Every face was a blank, unseeing, a multitude intent on their journey. I pinballed between them until I found a train that would take me out west, back to the place I'd called home. Only as London gave up its grip and the fields spread out around the tracks could I begin to relax, begin to plan what I would do next.

The taxi driver was reluctant to drop me off at the gate to the forest.

'Here?' he said. I could see his point. There was nothing but trees, even the gate well hidden behind the summer growth of weeds.

'Here,' I insisted. 'It's OK, I'm meeting friends.' He gave me one of his cards and I could see him peering at me in his mirrors as he prepared to drive off. I squared off my shoulders as I opened the gate, feigning a confidence I didn't feel.

I wondered how I could ever have thought of this spot as a haven, a place of refuge. The leaves were dark now, and thick, and the air beneath them as cool and as still as deep water. Tom's cottage was shut up against the bright sunlight of the clearing, and the trees seemed to have closed in around it. No Land Rover, but Zannah's car was there, parked at an angle as though hurriedly abandoned. The cottage door was locked, the windows closed tight, curtains shut. Uselessly I called and waited, listening. There was no response.

No response, but there was a sound. I stood, tuning my ears in to the faint drone, barely audible against the noise of the forest. I could faintly hear the traffic from the road, rising and falling as the cars passed by. I could hear the birds, busy with their own dramas, as indifferent as the London crowds. I could hear the sound of leaves being touched by a slight breeze that came and went in a moment. And, borne in on that breeze, I could hear more clearly the rise and fall of a chainsaw, biting through wood.

There was nothing else to do but to walk towards it, drawn further and further into the woods, my unease deepening with every step. I found myself walking along an old neglected track, almost completely overgrown. Here and there I saw a broken branch, or a deep rut where the Land Rover had forced its way through, tearing at the overhanging vegetation. I paused every so often to get my bearings and each time the sound of the road had receded a little more, my sense of isolation grown. Then I hurried on, hastening towards the sound, stumbling on my way. The trees were thicker here, tangled with undergrowth, the ground heavy with dead leaves. Fallen trunks and branches were rotting slowly into the ground, new growth springing up in the gaps they'd left, consuming them, covering them over.

I was being drawn by the sound towards a clearing that shone lighter through the shadows of the trees. As I approached, I glimpsed the dark gleam of water, saw the lush green of a reed bed, and I recognized the spot. We'd come here once before, Tom and Gareth and I, back when the track was better, still easily negotiable. There were old brick pits here, long abandoned and half filled with water. We'd picnicked and watched the dragonflies dance in the shafts of sunlight, and the kingfishers flash by on the wing. I wondered now what Tom must have been thinking as he sat there watching us, Gareth and me, laughing and happy. Out of the blue, I had run to him, driven by fear. And then, when I must have seemed almost within his grasp at last, I had gone again, disappeared, tipping him over the edge.

As I took the last few steps towards the clearing, the sound of the chainsaw stopped at last. The forest noises filled the silence, reasserting themselves. There was a moment of stillness and calm. I could see through the trees Zannah and Tom, facing each other across the clearing, frozen there as though in a tableau. Tom had put the chainsaw down, but he held in his hand a sharp and shining bill-hook, its blade honed to razor thinness. I'd seen him wield it once, flaying a young sapling in a fit of impatience, splitting the tree from tip to stem like slicing through butter. His head was averted from her, looking upwards, and I could see his profile was a stony mask. I knew that look, that locked-down expression of total indifference, closing off all human contact, cold with rage. He was watching the tree that still stood between them defiant of gravity, a flay of bark around its base, its trunk cut through. It was an old oak, once magnificent, grown half leafless and gaunt, stag-headed, its branches home to a colony of rooks. I felt the sense of a stalemate between them, even as I stepped out into the open ground. Then the last rooks flew upwards from the surrounding trees as though they knew something was about to happen, their cries filling the air. Zannah's eyes met mine and they were wide with fear, fear and something else, an acknowledgement that I was right, that I had been right all along. She screamed and as she screamed the tree fell, slowly at first, pushing its way through the surrounding branches, then accelerating towards the ground.

It should have missed them both. Tom knew how to drop a tree precisely, reading the weight and the lean, angling the cut so it fell where he wanted. But I saw him move towards her while she was distracted, the wicked blade held upwards in his hand, and I thought only to save her. I sprinted towards him, forgetting the tree, catching the small of his back so he staggered a step or two forward. And Zannah, instead of moving back to safety, ran in towards us just as it fell with an explosion of shattered wood, crashing into the hard dry ground. And under it lay Tom and Zannah, caught up in its tangled branches. I stopped in my tracks. All I could see at first was blood and all I could hear were the birds' cries, as they circled in the suddenly opened air. Zannah lay motionless, but the blood was Tom's, not hers, fountaining out, sparkling in the sun. His arms had flown up to protect himself and the tree had driven the blade of the bill-hook hard into his arm, severing the artery, draining him of life. By the time Zannah had come round from her brief stunning and scrambled unhurt from under the branch that had pinned her, he was dead.

Zannah backed away from me, white under the drying blood.

'You've killed him,' she whispered, but I knew better. I'd seen him start towards her, I'd seen the murderous intent. I had had no option, I knew. Look after her, my father said. Look after her, when so often it had been her looking after me. At last I had fulfilled my promise to him.

'I saved your life,' I said. 'He was going to kill you.' She remained silent, shaking her head in confusion, kneeling down beside his fallen body. Together we pulled him out from under the wreckage of the tree, knowing it was too late even as we did so. He lay inert and silent, his helmet knocked awry, arm twisted and gashed horribly open, still slick with all the blood.

'I just wanted him to tell me the truth,' she said.

'You shouldn't have come here,' I said, but she dropped her head and wouldn't answer, wouldn't meet my eye. I wanted to give her some comfort, but I was afraid she'd shake me off, afraid she'd flinch away from me again in terror if I did. Finally I reached out and tentatively touched her shoulder with my fingertip. She didn't move.

'I needed to know what had really happened,' she whispered again finally, and then she just sat and looked down at him for a long time in silence as if waiting for an answer. 'You know, I really thought he loved me.' The tears washed pale clean streaks down her face. I had nothing to say in reply. She buried her face in her arms and sobbed while I stood uselessly by, my hand still resting on her shaking shoulder, watching her cry.

When the storm had passed and she was calm again, I pulled her up, unresisting, and led her back down the track to Tom's cottage. The key was hanging where it always was, under the window sill beside the kitchen door. I washed her down as best I could, removing her blood-caked shirt and giving her mine, scrubbing the evidence clean from her skin while she sat silent and compliant with everything I did. I needed to erase all traces of her from the scene. I needed to let her get away.

'When was your flight?' I asked.

'Tomorrow,' she whispered. 'I was going to change it, but I was too busy.'

'Take it,' I said, and she looked at me, the uncertain look of a child being given permission to do something it had barely dared even hope to do. 'Take it, go.'

'And you?' she asked.

'I'll be all right,' I said, with all the breeziness I could muster. 'You just need to go home.'

When she had gone, I found I could wait no longer in the dank chill of the cottage. It was warmer outside, even in the deep shade of the forest. I walked back through the trees to where Tom's body lay. Nothing had changed except that his blood had dried and darkened, blending in with the dark rich leaf mould of the forest floor. Zannah's shirt was stiff with it, rank with the charnel-house smell and uncomfortable to wear. Tom lay pale and still where we'd left him, almost peaceful, almost as though he were asleep on his back among the branches of the felled tree. His face as he lay there was the face of my dead father, gaunt and still on the hospital pillow.

I was almost too late to see my father before he died. He had slipped into a coma before I arrived. The staff there had made him comfortable; that was all that they could do. They'd found the cancer too late and besides they had nothing, none of the skills or drugs a British hospital could muster. He had refused to go back, preferring to die with the sound of the birds and the insects around him, the air of Africa the last air he breathed. Zannah took me straight to the hospital from the airport, and I was still dressed in my travelling clothes and stiff and crumpled from the flight. Despite the heat I felt chilled, as though I'd trapped some of the damp air of England and brought it there with me, deep in my bones.

I sat in the little private room where he lay, and waited there while Zannah went off to snatch some sleep. Such a basic room, for a hospital, with breezeblock walls that were open to the elements, white painted and clean. I could hear everything going on around us, the calls of children playing, the passing back and forth of jokes and comments from the doctors and nurses, distant traffic. I felt remote from them all. The room was a still point of silence, shaded and cool. My father lay in the bed, wasted and thin, hardly disturbing the covers except for the rise and fall of each slow rasping breath. I sat, barely moving myself, too late for words, too late for anything. Just him and me in the fading light of the afternoon, together at last.

Unconsciousness had smoothed out the lines of age and illness. It had lent him an air of calm and detachment: the grave, still demeanour of the judge. I had not come for forgiveness, I realized as I sat there beside him. I had come to be judged, to be held in the balance, and be told it was all right, my exile over, restored to my rightful place beside him. But I had been too stubborn to forgive him first, to submit to his judgement, and had come too late, for he did not regain consciousness. Instead, at some point between one breath and the next, he just stopped and was stilled and breathed no more.

As the light faded, and the evening insects started up their noise, a nurse came in, singing softly to herself, a hymn I recognized but couldn't name. She smiled when she saw me, but didn't speak, turned to the body on the bed and started to lay it out. Gently and carefully she washed the wasted limbs, with as much care as if he had been alive. She crossed his hands upon his chest, never once breaking off her song, an act as much of worship as of work. Finally, she pressed shut his eyelids over his eyes, cutting off his gaze. He looked dead now, all sense of presence gone, only the shell remaining. The insects seemed to chime in with her singing, a background chorus. She stepped back and looked at the figure on the bed, then at me, and, smiling once more, stepped out of the door and was gone, leaving me to my vigil.

I sat on beside him through the dark of the night,

knowing that I was alone, knowing that I had come in vain. I kept my vigil for him anyway, for there was nothing else I could do. He had loved Africa, he had chosen this end, he had carried on without me. All I had ever been able to do for him was set him free.

Zannah had wanted the truth, but there could be no truth now, no final reckoning. I turned back to Tom, and the resemblance I had thought I'd seen had vanished; his face once more was the face of the boy I'd first met, all the defences gone, absurdly young under the protective helmet. I knelt and touched the cooling white skin at his throat, where the tan didn't reach. His freckles stood out stark against the pallor of his face. Only the eyes, half opened but drained of life, looked really dead. I closed them the way the nurse had done, crossed his arms across his chest. They say the hearing is the last to go, and the woods had been full of birdsong all day. I wondered if he had heard them, if they had been the last sound he heard on this earth. Perhaps even then he would have been naming them, nailing them down, accurate to the last.

The afternoon passed, and the evening, dusk falling with the blackbird still singing his irresolute song, a handful of wandering phrases, over and over. Then with the darkness came silence, and the slow passage of the night. No owls called, no insects here, just the murmur of the leaves, soft rustlings in the undergrowth. Perhaps I slept a little as I waited in the chill for the dawn. In the morning, as the birds erupted into song around me, I would ring the police, once Zannah's plane had safely gone. No need to mention her name. I'd have some explaining to do, but I was used to that. They wouldn't question my guilt, not with my past. I would be submitted to judgement at last. For after all, if I wasn't guilty of this, I was surely guilty of something. I was a dangerous person to be around.

Visit **www.panmacmillan.com** to read more about all our books and to buy them. You will also find features, author interviews and news of any author events, and you can sign up for e-newsletters so that you're always first to hear about our new releases.